HEAVEN OR SPELL

FATE WEAVER
BOOK SEVEN

REGINA WELLING

ERIN LYNN

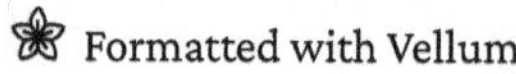 Formatted with Vellum

CONTENTS

Prologue   1
Chapter 1   7
Chapter 2   20
Chapter 3   27
Chapter 4   39
Chapter 5   50
Chapter 6   54
Chapter 7   70
Chapter 8   74
Chapter 9   82
Chapter 10   84
Chapter 11   95
Chapter 12   108
Chapter 13   117
Chapter 14   120
Chapter 15   129
Chapter 16   136
Chapter 17   145
Chapter 18   149
Chapter 19   164
Chapter 20   171
Chapter 21   178
Chapter 22   186
Chapter 23   193
Chapter 24   203
Chapter 25   209
Chapter 26   222
Chapter 27   232
Chapter 28   237
Chapter 29   248

Chapter 30	257
Chapter 31	268
Chapter 32	283
Chapter 33	295
Epilogue	302
Other Books	309

HEAVEN OR SPELL

PROLOGUE

Night wind sang in discordant harmony across wings of ebony leather, the sound echoing the darkness of Diana Diamond's thoughts as her feet touched down on the tiles of her penthouse terrace.

Be thou the most perfect version of thyself.

Coming from the Balmorrigan she'd raised to do her bidding, the curse had been simple but effective, which only added more fuel to Diana's rage. She stalked the space between the sliding doors and the terrace railing, threw her head back, and wailed in fury, the sound pressing viciously against the inside of her skull.

Lexi Balefire had ruined everything.

Everything.

Hooked talons scrabbled against the frame of the sliding doors. The glass reflected pure evil in an ugly, bird-like form. Seeing herself, Diana screamed until her throat went raw, the pitch of her cry rising until the glass bowed inward, webbed, and burst in a glittering rain.

One greasy feather fluttered loose, caught on the

wind, spun twice, and sailed over the balcony railing as Diana walked over broken glass, slunk inside to stand facing the empty space between two paintings on her bedroom wall.

A space that stayed empty even after she knocked over a lamp while trying to complete a complicated gesture with her left wing. Her blood pressure hit red-line levels when the portal to her secret room failed to appear, but she held off on another sonic scream. Breaking the invisible mirror probably wouldn't be the wisest thing to do, and she had at least that much control of herself.

Drat Athena and her inferior glamour charms. The box said the spell would render her earthly belongings invisible to others, not to their owner.

All Diana wanted was to get to the place she'd built with blood, sweat, and magic—the place where she could be her truest self. Only in her secret lair, among the trophies of her successes, might she find the strength to slough off the Balmorrigan's curse and take back her true form.

Unless he'd been right, and she was destined to remain in this foul condition forever.

She tried again to make the portal appear but only managed to clear everything off the top of the dresser. Her frustrated cry sounded like the garbled squawk of an annoyed, evil chicken, which, when you looked closely, was what Diana had become. It was probably a good thing no one was around to point out the resemblance.

Despite what she'd thought was a foolproof plan to rid herself of Lexi Balefire once and for all, Diana hadn't had a good day, and it didn't look like it would be getting better anytime soon.

She waved her arms again and again, but her newly-sprouted wings couldn't manage the proper gesture to complete the incantation. The resulting tantrum ended with bed linens shredded by talons bloody from the trip over broken glass, the dresser overturned, drawers emptied out, contents flung into corners, and the heel of a designer shoe jammed into the wall next to where the portal should have appeared.

Chest heaving, Diana paused to consider her options.

Being locked out of her sacred space would have been enough to make her wring her hands in despair—if she was the hand-wringing type and if she actually had hands. Neither of those being the case, she cast about for a solution to the problem, and that was when she noticed the bloody sheets.

Of course; blood carried power.

Diana lifted a clawed foot, wobbled a little to keep her balance, and, as gently as she could in her present state, pressed the appendage against the wall.

When the expected failed to occur, she stifled another shriek of fury and realized her wounds had sealed over. Rage-filled, Diana purposefully returned to the wrecked patio doors and ground her feet into the shattered glass.

Dark red prints marked her path back to the bedroom,

where she planted herself firmly and swiped bloody power across the empty space. The mirror portal appeared. Diana crowed in triumph. Literally.

Tentatively, she stuck the tip of a wing through the portal, crowed again when she saw the feathers melt and morph into human fingertips.

Victory. The blood of mighty goddesses ran in her veins, gave her power such as had not been seen in this lowly place. Nothing in the mortal world of pain and fear could touch her, she thought. Nothing.

She gathered herself to step through the portal. Caught up in the sensation of her body changing, Diana made it halfway through the opening before heat and light slammed into her back, whipped away the remaining feathers, pulled her deck of cards from her, and tossed her through the doorway as if she weighed nothing.

Red, gold, and seething, lightning webbed the sunlit sky over the town of Port Harbor, crackling as it descended like fury. Precisely-aimed heat burned the moisture out of the air, leaving an ozone-scented smear as the bolt sought the life it had been charged to take.

Once, then twice, it struck with laser precision and a thunder of power.

Once, then twice, it failed to take that life before retreating to fruitlessly quest elsewhere.

Some fortunate sod captured the whole thing on video

when the top floor of a ritzy apartment building in the newly-renovated industrial sector simply disappeared as if wiped away by the finger of an angry god. The news outlets paid him a small fortune for the footage.

There was no video to profit from when a second strike took out a downtown office building, leaving not so much as a scratch on the church next door. A choking cloud of brick dust and heat hovered over those two sections of the city as people screamed and ran for cover.

The office building, the newscaster reported, had been empty, the former tenant having vacated mere days before. When pressed, an officer on the scene at the Harrington Arms apartment building shook his head and said no, no human remains had yet been found.

"She was home." Wearing the pale face and wide eyes of one who had survived a cataclysmic event, the middle-aged woman who'd lived in the apartment below insisted, "I know she was because I heard her stomping around on those hardwood floors right before it happened."

"The search for conclusive proof of death continues as authorities try to make sense of this senseless event," the reporter said at the end of the segment.

Inside her sanctuary, Diana Diamond paced like a wild thing, screaming and ranting as she watched her mirror to the outer world go dark. Lank hair hung over a face gone feral. It might have interested her to know she'd succeeded in ridding herself of a portion of her humanity.

Whether that success was a step toward gaining access to Olympus was a question Diana would have to consider when not ridden by the fury of being thwarted and hunted.

But not until Lexi Balefire got what she deserved.

CHAPTER

ONE

"Hold this, and mind you don't drop it," Aunt Mag thrust a potion vial into my hand. I barely had time to close my fingers over it before she let go. "Unless you fancy letting chaos loose on the whole town."

"Should you be carrying this around if it's that powerful?" I held up the vial, observed the snot-green swirl of viscous goo inside. "What does is it do, anyway?"

"That would be your basic fateorum veritas potion," Sylvana, my mother, answered instead. "And don't let her scare you. In that form, it's inert."

"Which," Mag grumbled, "you would already know if you spent more time in the proper study of your craft."

Lamenting on my lack of craft knowledge was a theme Aunt Mag shared with my familiar—one Salem harped on daily, so I didn't need to hear it now. Or ever, for that matter.

The dome Sylvana cast to hide our activities from prying eyes also blocked out the city's lights around us, but Aunt Mag's witch-dark light spell turned night into day.

The three of us prowled around the ruins of Diana's apartment, searching for evidence of her death. The police hadn't found any—not a tooth, not a hair, not a shard of bone—but we had a few tricks up our sleeves. Or, to be more accurate, in Aunt Mag's fanny pack.

That's right, I said fanny pack. A woman of many times, Aunt Mag preferred her home decor from the Victorian era but dressed like a throwback from the early seventies except for the fanny pack, which, in hot pink with chartreuse trim, was all eighties. Worse, I'd caught my mother eying the thing with envy. But then, she'd been a teenager in the eighties, got accidentally imprisoned in the nineties—recently released—and her fashion sense still hadn't caught up with the years in between.

"What does the fateorum veritas potion do?" I thought I'd figured it out from the name, but since making assumptions had come back to bite my backside before, it was better to ask.

"Compels truth." All her attention focused on the mini cauldron she'd pulled out of her pack, Mag held out her hand for the potion, snapping her fingers when it didn't land in her palm fast enough.

"This next part is tricky." Sylvana grabbed my arm, pulled me into position next to her. "Unzip your jacket, and help me block the wind." She did the same, and I followed suit.

"Ready?" Her fluffy hair blowing in the breeze, Mag uncorked the vial, spit into the container, and when a tiny cloud of seething green emerged, used her breath to send it into the cauldron. Before another cloud popped out, she slammed the stopper back in and tucked the potion away.

"Phew. Close call," she said.

Confused, I caught my mother's eye, shot up a questioning brow. Sylvana returned the look, and it occurred to me for about the hundredth time how very much alike we looked. Dressed, as we both were, in head-to-toe black, we could be taken for twins.

"How so?" My mother ventured to ask.

"Lost track of my thoughts for a second there. If you're going to use fateorum veritas, you must maintain a tight focus on your intentions. Let a puff of that potion loose without the proper direction, and you'll have everyone in a five-mile radius speaking nothing but the truth."

"What would be so bad about that?" I asked. Seemed to me, a little more truth in the world might be a good thing.

Mag leveled me with a look that belied her fake, chirping tones. "Oh honey, do these jeans make my butt look big?"

She lowered her voice and answered her own question. "Only if by big, you mean like two pigs fighting under a blanket, and by the way, your mother is the most annoying woman on the planet. You should give her back that pot roast recipe because it tastes like boiled shoes."

"Oh, really?" Mag's imitation voice dropped to a

vicious snarl. "Well, your brother is better in bed than you are."

Sylvana snorted. "Like it or not, the world runs on little white lies."

"Okay, I get it. Can we move on, please?" I was more interested in finding out what happened to Diana Diamond than learning a lesson in human nature. "What do we do next?"

Aunt Mag is a consummate show-off, and for good reason. In her tragically foreshortened youth, she'd hunted and neutralized rogue magic while perfecting her own. Aunt Mag might look like your slightly eccentric grandmother, but she was a magical badass.

Eyes still locked on mine, she waggled one finger toward the cauldron. With a screech of metal on metal, the thing twisted itself into something resembling a gas can with shoulder straps and a spray nozzle. When the dust finally settled from the transformation, she turned her pointed gaze on my mother, who went over and picked up the thing.

"Lexi, help me with the straps." We got the apparatus settled, and Mag leaned in to adjust the sprayer setting. To tell the truth, it felt a little anti-climactic to watch my mother using what was basically a very large spray bottle to spread a fine mist of potion over the whole area.

Especially since nothing seemed to happen.

"Is that it? I can't see anything."

"Don't be a damn fool," Aunt Mag snapped. "You

don't get pumpkins until you plant the seeds." The spraying finished, she moved forward to intercept Sylvana, helped her remove the tank, and said something so low I couldn't make out what it was.

"No, I won't do it. You know I've sworn off that kind of thing. You can't ask me to—"

Mag cut her off. "And you know we can't locate a dark soul without using a bit of the black. Now, we only need a trace, and it's not a blood spell. You're younger than I am, so you can make the effort."

"Never thought I'd see the day when the Mudwitch couldn't throw down a spot of black magic if she needed to." My mother and her aunt had never been close. Mag thought Sylvana was a spoiled brat, and Sylvana thought Mag was a cranky old bat.

Both of them were right, but since I didn't want to spend the next week sporting a tail or a butt pimple—or both—I kept my mouth shut on the subject.

"I'll do it," I offered. I didn't know much about the darker side of the craft, but I was just as powerful a witch as either one of them and younger to boot. It stood to reason I was the better choice, but apparently, there was one thing both my mother and Aunt Mag could agree on.

"No!" They chorused in unison. Then Sylvana capitulated, "You just better keep my mother away from the house for a few days, or she'll smell black magic on me, and I'll never hear the end of it." She was right; if Gran got so much as a whiff, there would be hell to pay.

"Done." The air shook a little with the force of Mag's vow.

After casting her aunt another annoyed look, Sylvana raised her hands and spoke a few words in a language I'd never heard before. Alternating between guttural and sibilant, her tone made the hairs on the back of my neck stand up.

When the hollow echo of Sylvana's chant fell to silence, Mag doused the witch-dark light. Very little was left of Diana's penthouse but scattered brick dust and the slagged remains of her kitchen appliances. Whatever I'd expected to find when we decided to investigate, it hadn't resembled a surgical strike that contained the damage so precisely to one area.

"Well, this has been a colossal waste of time," was my opinion.

"Hush now," Mag ordered in a tone that meant business. She might look like a frail octogenarian, and I might be able to outrun her in a footrace, but her magic packed a punch, and she could take me down with it from a distance. I hushed.

In the inky dark, tiny pinpricks of firefly-green light appeared. Only a few at first, then a few more. As much as I wanted proof of Diana's death, the idea we'd been walking around on bits of her body kind of creeped me out. I wondered if there was a spell that would let me pick both feet up off the ground at once.

After waiting a few moments for the magic to fully

take hold, Mag fired up the witch-dark spell again, only this time at just enough strength for dim twilight to rise under the dome. Through the lessening darkness, I made out her shadowy shapes as she arrowed toward the largest spark.

"What are you waiting for?" Mag tossed back over one shoulder. "Get over here."

I stubbed my toe on a jagged chunk of something metal. Maybe part of the oven or the refrigerator. It was hard to tell by the shape. Pinwheeling my arms, I caught my balance at about the same time I heard the sound of another boot meeting a solid object followed by a thump and a string of language that turned the air blue.

"Are you okay?" I went to help my mother up as Aunt Mag bumped up the light by a degree or two. Not enough to see the look on her face, but enough to avoid further mishap.

Sylvana waved me away and scrambled to her feet. "I'm fine." She brushed herself off, dislodging several of the glittering motes. Toe throbbing, I limped with her to join my aunt and stare down at the shard of light wedged into the gap between two floorboards.

"What do you think it is?"

Mag declined to answer but performed probably one of the top five pieces of magic I'd ever seen. Don't tell her I said so, though. She already has enough ego for any three witches combined.

"Revivify!"

A green miasma rose from each spark at the whispered command, whirled and funneled before coalescing into a single shape. Where I'd hoped to see Diana's form—even just a basic outline would have been proof of her death—the image resolved into a square the size of a deck of cards.

My name is Lexi Balefire. One woman in each generation of my family has had the honor to be the keeper of our namesake: the mighty flame that gives all witches their magic and power. Even the Balefire hadn't been able to destroy one of Diana's tarot cards, so whatever blew her penthouse off the map had carried some mega juju.

As I opened my mouth to say as much, the particles of light blew apart, falling back to their previous resting place and fading as they went. Mere seconds passed before Mag's witch-dark light flared back to life, and the three of us blinked until our eyes adjusted.

"Well, that was illuminating," Sylvana might have been joking, but her face was serious. "Or not. What do you think?" She deferred to Mag for answers, which was one of the bigger surprises of the day.

The biggest came when Aunt Mag handed me her cane, knelt, spun her fanny pack to the back, then pitched forward onto her belly to closely observe the crack in the floor where we'd seen the largest spark of light.

"Tweezers," she kept her eye to the spot and held out a hand.

I exchanged a look with my mother, who shrugged.

"I, uh, didn't bring my purse. I didn't think this was that type of outing," I admitted.

"There's a pair in my pack."

This time, the look my mother and I shared clearly said, "*not it.*"

"For Hecate's sake, Lexi. I'm not keeping a rogue eaflock in there, just open the pack and get me some flipping tweezers." When she put it like that, I didn't dare disobey, so I tentatively leaned down and unzipped the zipper.

Whatever magic that might have let her actually store an eaflock in there—and I didn't doubt she could if she wanted to—also must have come with some pretty good security in place. When I opened the pack, it held nothing more than the requested tweezers, which I gingerly retrieved. No matter what spell she used on the thing, the pink bag rested a little too close to Aunt Mag's backside for my comfort.

"About time," she said when I slapped the tweezers in her questing hand and held the bottle down for her, keeping the cork stopper at the ready. "Now, get out of my light."

I stepped sideways and ignored my mother's attempt to suppress a snort. The tweezers hovered, then went in for the retrieval. "Got it." The *it* made a ting sound against the bottom of the glass, and I shot the stopper home to seal it in.

"Help me up." Because I'd done my part by securing

the specimen, Sylvana had the honor of hoisting Aunt Mag to her feet. While the two indulged in a minor scuffle over brushing the dust off the front of Mag's skirt, I took a closer look at her find.

The former property of mythical goddess sisters, Diana's deck of tarot cards had come to her as something of a family legacy. One she'd perverted and used in an attempt to destroy every shred of her own humanity. Diana reckoned she belonged in Olympus and the only thing holding her back from ascending to that lofty realm was her pesky human soul.

I'd have wished her Godspeed and reminded her not to let the screen door hit her on the way out if that's all there was to it. But soul or no soul, the best way for Diana to get into Olympus without an express invitation involved opening a hole in the barrier between worlds.

Not the barrier between our world and Olympus, mind you, but the one between all worlds.

To put not too fine a point on it, the enchanted barrier enforces a complex set of immigration laws to keep demons, the Fae, and all manner of other magical creatures from roaming the earth—or worse, from pitching battles to gain control of it. Of us, really.

Diana cared nothing for the status quo. She'd proved that by using her cards to turn love to hate, which pushed into the duty laid on me by the other roots of my family tree. My father's name is Cupid—you know him, the one with cute little wings and the bow and arrow—and as his daughter, every love match I make balances some of the evil to which our world is prone.

Yeah, that's me. Lexi Balefire, matchmaking witch, keeper of the flame, and, if I had my way about it, avenger of the evil hag who used one of her cards on my boyfriend, and then another one to kill a dear friend. Diana Diamond had a lot to answer for, and somewhere in my deepest heart, I hoped she wasn't dead, so I could make her pay. I'm not proud of that; it's just the honest truth.

"If she was here, she has to be dead, right?" Both sides of my heritage come with the gift of strong intuition. Right then, mine screamed like a group of teenagers on a roller coaster ride. I wanted to believe Diana was gone but wanting isn't always enough.

"Throw those fire and air faeries together; they could cook up a halfway decent showing in the lightning department." Aunt Mag sounded almost envious. "But this wasn't your everyday, garden variety whiz-bang."

"You're saying you're one hundred percent certain she's dead?"

Aunt Mag shrugged. "More or less."

"It had better be more and not less." Sylvana's voice rose with indignation. "I'll have to pay for that *bit of the black*, as you called it, so you'd better be damn sure I didn't do it for nothing. You're not the one out here racking up the karmic debt, you know."

Mag wagged a gnarled finger in front of my mother's nose, but Sylvana didn't back down. "You got karmic debt;

blame it on that rogue you chose to crawl between the sheets with. God of love, my ass. Look at the mess he left behind. If he'd put paid to Diana when he had the chance, we wouldn't be wasting time out here when I could be home watching Jeopardy. What a wuss."

I did not know Aunt Mag had that word in her vocabulary. She wasn't entirely wrong, either, but my mother would never concede the point. Dear old dad had attempted to thwart Diana's plans, and he'd even imprisoned her for a time. Had he been capable of killing her, I assumed he'd have done so, and Mag knew it. She just enjoyed poking at my mother every chance she got.

True to form, Sylvan's face went beet red. "Don't you say a word about him, do you hear?"

Angry magic charged the air, sent prickles of power like tiny spiders crawling across my skin. I stepped between them.

"I think we're done here." I swiveled my head to give each fury-spitting witch a pointed look. If I didn't diffuse the situation, we could be looking at the witch equivalent of a faerie fight. "Unless there was another spell you wanted to try."

Aunt Mag shrugged and turned away to survey the decimated rooftop a final time. "If Diana Diamond was here when this happened, she's dust. Nothing could have survived a blast strong enough to take out those cards. I'm going home."

"Have a nice night," I said to the empty space where she'd been standing.

"The great Margaret Balefire has spoken."

I couldn't help responding to Sylvana's dry sarcasm with a quirked smile. "All heed the great Margaret Balefire."

The moment of levity passed. "*If* she was here," I said. "That's the crux, isn't it? I was hoping to find definitive proof."

Since there was none to be had, I followed Sylvana down the fire escape stairs, which dumped us out on the side of the building below Diana's former balcony. When she stopped short in front of me, I slammed into her back.

"What are you doing?"

"Look." She pointed toward an inky dark feather fluttering in the bushes. "There's your proof."

Too big to have come from any of the local bird species, the feather had to have come from Diana, which meant she'd come back to her place sometime between when the Balmorrigan cursed her and the lightning strike.

Aunt Mag was right. Diana was dead.

If only I could convince my gut it was true.

CHAPTER

TWO

S IX MONTHS LATER

"Flix! Get in here and fix this blasted thing," I hollered after banging on my keyboard a few times and clicking all the mouse buttons until the cursor began to spin like one of those pinwheels they give children at the circus.

Witches don't have a natural abhorrence for electronics, and I doubt gods do either, but I certainly hated the contraption my business partner had forced me to use. While I could admit that the slim little notebook computer came in handy at times, I tended to get frustrated when it didn't respond as quickly as I'd like.

I suppose I'd gotten somewhat used to being able to manifest my intentions with a flick of a finger or a blink of an eye, and Flix was constantly telling me I needed to have more patience when it came to technology. It's a good thing he's my best friend in addition to my business partner. Otherwise, I might have throttled him. Didn't he know the worst thing you could tell a woman was to calm down?

"I can only do one thing at a time, Lexi. I'll get to it as

soon as humanly possible. For now, stop pressing buttons and restart," came Flix's reply.

I shot him a dirty look over my shoulder even though he was on the other side of the wall and prepared a snappy comeback pointing out the irony of the phrase "humanly possible." Unfortunately, I didn't have a chance to deliver it before the door to my office opened and my friend and former client, Mona, walked in.

Well, *walked* isn't the best word. Mona more waddled than anything, her swollen belly making the action a chore.

Quickly, I rose and rearranged the chairs in front of my desk so she could have a seat, and when she finally plopped down with a sigh, I couldn't help but grin.

"I'm not laughing *at* you, I swear. You look wonderful, actually, if a bit miserable," I said, giving her a hug as best I could.

"At the rate it's growing, this baby will weigh at least fifteen pounds by the time it comes out. And have you seen the size of Mark's head? If our kid inherits that noggin, it's just going to have to stay in there. That's all there is to it." Mona's voice conveyed humor with a tinge of genuine concern.

"I think every mother feels that way, especially with the first baby," I replied, not wanting to think too hard on the subject.

"First baby? More like *only* baby. I'm not sure I can go through this again," Mona replied. "Though, to be fair, I'm also told every mother also says that when they're pregnant. I've been promised I'll change my tune once the little bugger arrives, but we'll see. I think it might be better if we knew what we were having, but Mark's heart was set on doing it the "old-fashioned way," and I didn't have it in me to disappoint him. As long as the baby's healthy, I couldn't care less about gender."

Having no frame of reference for that particular topic, I offered Mona a bottle of water and sat down next to her. "What brings you here today?" I asked. "I would have come to your place if you'd called me."

"No, I'm in the middle of a shift at Crumb. Big wedding cake circa the 1980s. You should see this thing. It's going to have those hideous plastic staircases with posed replicas of the bridesmaids and groomsmen—each one painted to resemble its human counterpart. Gives me the heebie-jeebies."

Mona shivered and then looked momentarily bewildered as though she'd completely lost her train of thought. "Anyway, I think I know what it feels like to be a hairdresser asked to do a perm. You know it's going to be horribly unattractive, but it's not your decision. Mark wants me to take it easy, but I can't sit still. Wait, what did you ask me? Oh, right, why I'm here."

Mona rolled her eyes and grinned, bringing a smile to my face. Under normal circumstances, she was a bit scatterbrained, and it seemed pregnancy had only exacerbated the trait.

"I've got a friend who needs your help to find her soul mate," Mona finally declared.

It wasn't the first or even the second time since I'd paired Mona with her husband, Mark, that the woman had come back with the same request. First, it was her widowed mother who had needed my help, and then she'd tried to get me to mate my own boyfriend, Kin, during the time when he'd been spelled not to remember me.

That was a whole scenario, and Mona couldn't have known the implications of her request, but the echo of her words made me wince.

"Seriously, Lexi, she really needs help. She's with this total jerk—I mean, this guy hits every cliché in the book. He's a musician and not the kind Kin is. He's in it for the women, I just know it; the kind of guy who makes you certain you know the meaning of the word 'slimy.' He's got no real job, though I gather there's a trust fund situation going on there. No way does he want to settle down, but he's got Nadia tied all up in knots. There has to be someone better. I just know it, and I want you to use that magic mojo of yours to find him."

Mona didn't know a thing about my actual mojo, and I had every intention of keeping it that way, though she'd referred to what I do as magic enough times I'd begun to wonder if she had some sort of inkling.

"I'm incredibly busy, Mona," I started, spinning the diamond on my ring finger around absentmindedly.

I received a pointed, narrow-eyed look in response. My relatively recent experience with another pregnant woman —Serena Snodgrass, my former enemy and now, the mother of my nephew—combined with my knowledge of Mona's persistence told me I'd better shut my mouth and agree.

Mama bears were scary.

"But I suppose I could take on one more client. Only for you, and on the condition that you only ask me to babysit once a month."

"Done," Mona replied with a wide grin. "Although, you might as well get used to handling babies. You and Kin will have little ones of your own before long, I suspect."

The notion sent a shiver up my spine. I do love babies, just for the smell of them alone, and Kin's babies couldn't be anything less than adorable. Plus, he was solid father material, but I could barely keep a house plant alive without Terra's earth mother influence.

A child was a whole other ballpark I wasn't quite ready to swing a bat in yet. Then again, I'd grown up with three faerie godmothers and zero traditional parents, so my reluctance had a solid basis in lack of experience.

I could babysit with the best of them, though, because at the end of the day, the little bundles of joy went back to their mommies, who could undo any damage I might have done.

"We'll see about that," was all I said, ignoring the

small smile that refused to leave Mona's lips when she watched the color rise to my cheeks. "Tell me more about Nadia."

Mona blew her bangs out of her face and shifted in her chair. "She's twenty-eight, and she's in luxury real estate —a real go-getter type. Got her Realtor's license the day she turned eighteen and has been climbing the ladder ever since." Mona ticked off Nadia's attributes one fingertip at a time. "Now, she has bus bench ads all over town. You've probably seen her. She's the pretty blond in the bubblegum-pink suit. She met Dean—that's the guy, Dean James, and he claims it's his given name although I have my doubts—when he was looking for a beach house."

Mona's retelling of it was somewhat roundabout, but I was getting the gist of the situation.

"They went out while she found him exactly what he wanted, but after she agreed to shave three percent off her commission and the deal closed, he dumped her, saying things were getting too *involved and complicated.*" Mona made air quotes and rolled her eyes.

"Which, of course, is a slimeball's way of getting out of a relationship with a woman he didn't really deserve in the first place. He walked away without a backward glance, and she's been chasing him ever since. He's making her look a fool, and I know she'll be mortified when she snaps out of it. I was hoping that someone new might help move things along, get her back to her old self again."

Nadia's situation reminded me—a little too on the nose—of the relationship between my mother and father. The scene—one I'd had to go back in time to witness, but that's another story altogether—of Cupid walking away from Sylvana and me after being shot in the butt with one of his own arrows played through my head for the hundredth time. The butt part was amusing, but the rest carried dreadful implications for my whole family.

The two of us, much like poor Nadia, had been too *involved and complicated* for him to deal with. At least, that's how it felt to me.

Suddenly, I was vehemently against Mona's friend ending up like Sylvana, pining away for a man who couldn't care less about her happiness.

"I'll do it," I said with conviction. "Nobody deserves to be treated like they're dispensable."

We discussed the details, set up a time for me to surreptitiously meet Nadia Hale, and then I helped Mona heave herself up off her chair.

"Take it easy," I implored before she waddled back out the door, leaving me lost in thought.

CHAPTER

THREE

Once Mona left, I locked the door, pulled the shades, and lifted the glamour that covered the office formerly known as FootSwept Matchmaking. No, my business wasn't wholly defunct, but I was far from a full-time matchmaker these days.

The closet that, pre-Diana, had been full of designer clothes and shoes—tools I used to help forsaken women feel beautiful and find their courage again—had been completely transformed for the second time in the span of six months.

This time, it wasn't because I'd subjugated my witch side while wallowing in heartbreak and wanted my surroundings to match my cold, unconcerned exterior. This time it was just about getting my mother off my back and trying to construct some semblance of a life for myself.

Flix sat in his old chrome barber's chair, but the scissors he used to wield were nowhere to be seen. Now, he swiveled around in front of a complicated dashboard of computer equipment.

Screens lined the walls, showing security footage from around the world. Because I'd made a promise to help find him, the search for Cupid was well underway. For all our effort—I was certain Flix's hacking must have drawn attention from the FBI, CIA, and Interpol, at the very least—we were no further along than we had been six months ago when this whole ludicrous idea was conceived.

"Is she gone?" My mother's voice came from the empty space to my left. How had she done that?

Lost in thought, I'd almost forgotten she meant Mona. "All clear. Can you teach me that spell?" I asked when she appeared to step out of the wallpaper, clapped her hands, and dropped the rest of the illusion.

A pair of bulletin boards hovered, notes tacked to their surfaces with magical pins, along one wall. Sylvana's having to do with her obsessive search for my father, mine holding information on a few odd events I'd attributed to Diana Diamond until investigation proved they hadn't. Red lines ran between seemingly connected events, each one with a big black X marked on it.

Despite the overwhelming evidence backed up by six months without a confirmed sighting, my gut insisted Diana still lived. Flix and Sylvana thought my gut was an idiot, but each went along with the search for their own reasons.

Flix to keep himself busy now that he didn't have a bevy of fawning clients hammering down the salon door, and Sylvana wanted me to help find my father and considered it quid pro quo.

"Simple camouflage enchantment. Honestly, Lexi. Have you not even studied the most basic spell books?"

"Save the lecture." I waved away further comment. "Did you check out that bird sighting in Philadelphia?"

Not only did my mother look enough like me to be my twin, but we rolled our eyes exactly alike. I found the experience unnerving in a Freaky Friday kind of way. I also made an internal vow to banish that expression from my face forevermore.

"An emu escaped from the zoo. It wasn't Diana because she's dead." She flicked away my concern with an impatient wave of her hand.

"You're sure?" As its keeper, my relationship with the Balefire is somewhat symbiotic. The keeper feeds the flame, and the flame feeds the keeper, or so the legend goes. To keep the fire burning strong, I have to stick close to home unless I can get my grandmother to come and play babysitter while I'm gone.

Except since Clara and Cupid weren't fans of each other, and I knew she'd frown on my efforts to prove Diana Diamond was still among the living, I couldn't tell her the real reason if I asked for the favor.

I also couldn't lie to her because she'd see right through that, so I was on my own, and that limited my excursions to those of less than a day or so. Having never been to Philadelphia, I had no reference point for taking the witchy speed method of skimming. If I wanted to go, I'd have had to take the long route, and that wasn't an option.

Sylvana had said she was happy to go in my place, leaving her free to scout around for my father. She was getting more out of this deal than I was, and it was starting to grate on my nerves.

"I'm sure," she reiterated with another exasperated expression. "The stupid bird stopped traffic on the I-95 for half an hour while the zookeepers chased it around. You asked me to check out a lead; I checked, it didn't pan out." She slumped in the chair, stuck her booted feet out in front of her, and blew a dark curl off her forehead. "It's been six months without a single shred of proof Diana is still alive. Time to give up the ghost."

"I know that." But the pool of dread still swirled in the pit of my stomach. Just as I knew my eyes were green, my name was Lexi, and my left big toe was crooked, I knew Diana Diamond still lived.

My relationship with my mother had improved marginally in the months since Diana was last seen, an effect, I believed, of the bond created by sharing secret goals. Nobody else except Flix knew what we were really doing at FootSwept Matchmaking. I suspected the rest of the family thought I'd been passing the time by reversing the negative matches Diana had made all over town, but the truth was her effect began to wane on the day of the assault on her apartment and office.

Diana's dark matches reversed themselves with little help from me, which was one more piece of evidence in favor of her being dead. And yet, if the lightning strike at her apartment killed Diana, then why, my gut screamed at me, had there been a second strike at her office?

If, as Aunt Mag suspected, the lightning came from Olympus, wouldn't Zeus know whether or not he'd scored a direct hit the first time? Or did he hit the office out of pique? It raised questions, and both a witch and a daughter of Cupid, I'd learned to trust my instincts. Most of the time.

Hence the arrangement with Sylvana, who patently disagreed with my stance on Diana but wouldn't say so for fear that I'd back out of helping her find my father. Not the best base upon which to forge the mother-daughter bond we'd missed out on during her long absence from my life, but it was all we had.

With what she considered the non-issue out of the way, Sylvana perked back up. "The trip wasn't all for nothing, though," she said now, excited. "Look what I found."

From the inside pocket of the black leather jacket she'd still had on when Mona showed up, she pulled a small, round, bright red object. Before I had time to get a look at it, she lobbed the thing in my direction.

Automatically, I snatched what I thought was a rubber ball from the air, then stumbled as the weight of it bore my hand down.

"You could warn a person." Rebalanced, I took a closer look at what I now recognized as a balloon, blown up, tied off, and weighing a ton. My face registered shock, then dismay. "It's not full of prohibited spell ingredients, is it?"

Given my mother's history, anything was possible.

"Don't be an idiot. It's a lead balloon." A laugh trilled out of her. "I found it in the oddities section of a shop in Atlanta. Cute little place called Triple Witch. I'll have to take you there sometime."

The eye roll that broke my vow not even five minutes after I'd made it came with a little head shake on the side. "I'm glad you had fun." Annoyed, I slashed another X over the note about the lead she'd gone south to follow.

"I also got this." She pulled out a second parcel and unwrapped the brown paper to reveal a small vial. "So, it wasn't all fun and games."

"Is that—"

"The tear of a dying witch? Yeah. Damned near impossible to get and costs the earth besides." She cut her gaze away from mine.

We'd been working on a spell Sylvana insisted we could use on her locket to turn it into an item that would locate my father. The spell required a tear from a dying witch as the final ingredient. And not just any tear, either.

Oh no, this one had caveats on its caveats. The tear had to come from a witch past her second century and must be gathered during her final breath. Witches of that age don't die every day, and very few potions called for such a rare ingredient.

For the spell Sylvana wanted to cast, another set of rules applied. To be potent enough, the tear must also be one of regret, have come from the witch's left eye, and been gathered under the light of a waning moon.

Given the creed we live by—if it harm none, do as you will—witches very rarely die holding onto lingering regret. I'd agreed to do the spell only because I didn't think Sylvana would ever find that particular ingredient.

Still, the spell also called for two tongues of fowl flame, so unless she pulled a fire-breathing chicken out of her pocket, I was off the hook. You can't bottle fowl flame. It burns through glass like a hot knife cuts butter. Probably burns through pockets, too. I shuddered to think what vessel might be capable of holding it, but I had no doubt Sylvana would rustle something up when the time came.

"What did you have to trade for the tear, Mom? Don't tell me it was blood."

Money's only one method of payment in our community, and not even close to the most popular. When she still refused to look me in the eye, I knew I'd nailed it.

"How much and to who?" Even a few drops in the wrong hands could spell disaster. Before she and my grandmother moved to Harmony to run a coven and an antique shop there, Aunt Mag took it upon herself to treat me to a few educational lectures on the way of the witch.

Body parts not to use for payment was one of the ones I remembered most because of its grisly nature.

The things a goblin could do with a hank of witch hair and a fingernail would curl your toes.

"Relax. I didn't trade with Athena if that's what you're worried about. I'm not half the idiot Aunt Mag thinks I am." She rotated her shoulders as if to release some tightness lingering there. "Except I really am. Twice the idiot, to be honest."

Sylvana admitting to any imperfection wasn't typical of what I knew of her and shocked me speechless.

"Do you have any idea what it means to be a Balefire witch?" she asked out of the blue.

Since it looked like things were taking an existential turn, I plunked the lead balloon down on the table, ignored the creaking of the wood under its weight, sat on the sofa, and settled in. "I think I have some idea seeing how I waited an extra ten years to become one."

Sylvana waved that discussion aside. "Lousy mother. Banished to prison. Fell down on my duty. Blah, blah, blah. That's ancient history now."

"Guess we wouldn't be getting any tears of regret from you if today was your day to pass into the Summerlands," I muttered.

"What I'm saying is we Balefire witches take our power for granted. You'd know that if you spent more time among your kind."

"Thanks for the not-so-subtle dig, Mom."

Hot words rolled around in my head, but I held back from saying any of them. She hadn't exactly been a perfect princess in her day, and it was mostly her fault all the witches in Port Harbor had studiously avoided me save for their necessary parade through my parlor to collect their piece of the Balefire flame every year on Beltane.

"I've been all over the country this past month, visiting covens and sitting at no less than three deathbeds."

Did she want me to pin a medal on her chest? Or maybe throw her a party? The way she was acting, you'd think she was Florence Nightingale reincarnated—wending her way across the country offering surcease to witches in their time of need.

The ringing in my ears might just be my BS meter going off.

"I got this from a water witch named Bessamina Shadowbend, but folks called her Swampwater Bess." My mother ignored my resting witch face and told the story in dramatic tones. "Bess and her partner Shyla Darvon lived in a little cabin on the edge of the wetlands. Bess harvested plants for Shyla to brew into healing potions, which they'd sell or trade with the non-magical."

While she talked, she twisted and turned the vial. The tear danced almost hypnotically inside the glass.

"How did she die?" Exploding cauldrons are the leading cause of death among young witches. Or so says my familiar, Salem, every time I get mine out.

"Snakebite." Sylvana sighed. "And when her time comes to pass into the Summerlands, I suspect Shyla will shed a regretful tear for not brewing a strong enough antidote."

Witches lead long lives, but we're not indestructible.

"Get to the part where you paid in blood, please." The look she flashed me could have wilted a mighty oak.

"It's not that big a deal. The snake bit Bess while she gathered herbs for Shyla to use in a healing potion for a gravely ill child living nearby. Did you know less powerful witches have to abstain from magic for weeks, even months, to build up enough power to brew strong potions?"

I had to admit I didn't.

"Of course, Shyla used her stored-up magic trying to save Bess, and had none left over for brewing the potion, so Bess died thinking her death had also doomed the boy. Hence the tear of regret."

"Okay, that's a really sad story. Now tell me about the blood."

"Fine, if you must know, I used it to boost Shyla's magic. Okay?"

My eyebrows shot up. "How? You didn't use any of the black, did you?"

"I did not, and I resent the implication." Sylvana tried to burn me with a look, but I'm a fire witch. It didn't take.

"It's not much of a leap given what you're planning to

do with that tear, so excuse me for jumping to a natural conclusion."

"I stoked Shyla's hearth," she said in tones that could chill an igloo, "with three drops of Balefire-infused blood. It won't burn low, not even in the days before Beltane, and it enhanced her magic enough that she was able to help that child and will be able to serve any other who needs a touch of healing."

In the face of such an altruistic—if uncharacteristic—moment, I felt like three kinds of a jerk.

"Sorry. I didn't know."

"Well, now you do, and it's high time we got on with things. Shyla told me where there's a flame fowl nest, and I think we should go check it out. If there's even a slim chance Diana's still out there, the sooner we find your father, the better."

And there it was, I thought condescendingly: my mother's staunch conviction this whole mess could be solved with the aid of a man and proof she was using me for her own ends. There was a little more to it, even I could see that through my haze of condescension, but I couldn't help wondering what had happened to her womanly pride.

We Balefires tended to have it in spades, but perhaps Sylvana had left hers behind when she escaped the Nexus.

Or maybe—and the thought was both sickening and repellent—my father really was that much of a stud.

Goddess, help us all if that's the case. I wisely kept the thought to myself.

"I can't go tonight," I said with a shake of my head. "I need to check in on Serena, and I refuse to break another plan with Kin. Tomorrow, after work. I promise."

It took some cajoling, but she finally agreed, and if I took some small amount of pleasure in making her wait another twenty-four hours, well, I'd take whatever punishment the karma fairy wanted to deliver.

CHAPTER

FOUR

I hadn't always been on the best of terms with Serena Snodgrass. That's actually putting it really nicely. At one point, I hated her with a fiery passion, and though I probably would have peed on her if she'd been on fire, I might have taken a moment to think it over.

Today, though, the oddity of our friendship didn't cross my mind at all. I was too busy thinking how adorable my little nephew Kaine would look in the tiny pair of sneakers that had somehow, despite being outrageously overpriced, ended up tucked inside my purse. Things had changed so much, and I knew I had every reason in the world to be happy. I just wished my heart would catch up with my mind.

"Serena!" I called, letting myself in and appraising the kitchen with a raised brow. Ever since her father had quietly moved into one of the buildings he owned downtown and her mother had gone on an extended "business trip" to the Andes, Serena had set about arranging her childhood home to reflect her personal style.

What there was of it, anyway.

Given our history, I'd have never pegged the woman

as a neat freak. A place for everything and everything in its place was Serena's motto—not a difficult task when you can wave a fingertip and force the broom to sweep of its own accord.

Usually, you could eat directly off her floors, but today the entire kitchen was a disaster. Cheerios coated the tile like a crunchy, honey-colored carpet. Strands of spaghetti clung to the tray of Kain's highchair, sauce spattered clear to the ceiling giving the impression I'd narrowly missed some sort of Scarface-style marinara massacre. At least three half-full cups of tea littered the table and sideboard, not one having been drained to the dregs.

My breath caught in my throat and, my voice verging on panic, hollered again, "Serena!"

Scenarios played through my head, each one worse than the last. I couldn't bear the thought of losing anyone else important to me, and that irrational worry was one I couldn't seem to shake. All the time, at any moment, I half expected to find myself in the middle of a Final Destination movie, death seeking out all of my friends and family, leaving me devastated and alone.

I pulled myself out of the morbid fantasy with an effort and tried to calm down. Except, the last time I'd seen Serena's house in such disarray was when Kaine's powers had emerged, and Serena had been helpless against the will of her adorable little hellion, unable to leave the house without attracting an entourage of adoring fans.

Then there was the time when she was pregnant with him, ready to give birth and trapped in her bedroom by my jerky half-brother, Jett—her former lover and Kaine's father, who thought he'd been doing the right thing at the time. He hadn't, and Serena had blown a hole in the wall to escape. While the thought she could take care of herself ought to have calmed my nerves, it didn't.

Until recently, I'd considered Serena to be somewhere just above the level of a slug, and our newly discovered trust bond hadn't entirely eclipsed our history.

Furthermore, I'd seen enough evil deeds to know that nobody—not even the most kickass chick in the world—could outrun every big baddie forever. Call me a fatalist if you must. You'd be correct. Someone has to worry about these things, and it sure isn't going to be my near-immortal faerie godmothers or my devil-may-care mother. Even Aunt Mag, who had lost her youth fighting against darkness, kept telling me to lighten up.

What sinister fate I thought Serena faced at that moment is irrelevant given it had no basis whatsoever, in reality. I bulled my way up the stairs shouting her name and finally burst into Kaine's bedroom with wild eyes, my hair standing on end.

I caught my reflection in the mirror over the little guy's dresser but couldn't focus on what a disheveled mess I was over the five-alarm screech that sucked whatever breath I had left right out of my lungs.

"Are you kidding me?" Serena hissed during the

silence that fell when Kaine ran out of air and stopped to refuel. Her eyes were wide and filled with ice. There also might have been another word or two inserted into the middle of the question, but I'm more of a lady than she is, so I'll keep my recounting PG-rated.

By then, the baby's face took on the shade of a severe sunburn while he continued his assault on the senses. Serena thrust him into my arms and, not for the first time, I might add, abandoned me with what might as well have been an angry banshee. My nephew is a cutie and everything, but not when he's screaming at the top of his lungs.

"What's the matter, little man?" I asked in what I hoped was a soothing voice, shifting Kaine in my arms and bouncing him up and down the same way I'd seen Serena do when he'd gotten his proverbial diaper in a bunch on several other occasions.

What I got for my efforts was a loud, wet load dropped into his actual diaper. It didn't take long before stinky brown sludge started dripping down my arm, and I realized the front of my top felt sticky beneath Kaine's chubby thigh. I'm not sure if it was the sense of relief he must have felt after that kind of release, or the expression on my face, but suddenly he stopped screeching and let out the tiniest of giggles.

One thing you have to know about Kaine is he's more like me than we thought he'd be. That is to say, he's half witch and half grandson of Cupid, meaning he got the Fate Weaver gene. If you haven't been following along, that means he's been blessed with the ability to make matches just like I do—and a whopping dose of, well, let's just call it charisma.

Long story short, he can manipulate the emotions of everyone around him, which is why when Serena came back into the nursery a few minutes later, she found me standing over a guffawing baby, wielding a wet wipe and wearing a particularly ironic type of grin.

"Who's a handsome little Fate Weaver?" I cooed, cleaning the last of the worst of it off his creamy baby skin. "Yes, you are, of course," I continued, finally tearing my gaze away and meeting Serena's sardonic grin. In the process of changing Kaine, I'd removed the object of focus —a button sewn into his clothes—that dulled the effects of his happy mojo, and she knew I'd done so without considering the consequences.

"He needs a bath, but he's not disgusting anymore," I said, handing the squirming bundle of cuteness back to his mother.

Once he was out of my arms, I came back to myself rather quickly, and the smile vanished. "Holy Hecate, Serena," I said, scrunching my nose in Kaine's direction. "What are you feeding that kid anyway? I need a shower, and I'm probably going to have to burn these clothes," I snapped.

"Oh, Holy Hecate, truly, Lexi," she retorted with an exasperated sigh. "You're the keeper of the ever-loving flame, and you can't fix this? Will you ever remember you're a witch, or what?"

She was right, of course. It had taken me so long to come into my full magical ability I still wasn't accustomed to calling on it to solve even the most mundane problem. I closed my eyes and concentrated, though it shouldn't have taken any amount of effort, and wished myself back to normal.

Serena swore again, a sharp inhalation of breath followed by an exclamation that caught me off-guard. "You look exactly like what you were just covered in. What the hell is going on with you?"

I glanced toward the mirror again and realized, in my haste to rid myself of any traces of baby poo, I'd inadvertently dropped the glamour I'd been wearing around beneath my clothes like a pair of magical underwear. It had been months since I left the house without it, and though the faeries pretended not to notice, I wouldn't have expected that sort of nonchalance from Serena even if I'd let my guard down on purpose.

"Thanks bunches, Swampgrass," I replied dryly, reverting to my old nickname for her even though there was no sting to it. "I'm fine. Just a little stressed out is all." Even I didn't think I sounded anything close to assured, and Serena certainly didn't buy it.

"You look strung out," she said. "Not like dark magic strung out, like actual street drugs strung out, and I know that's not the case. What's up?" she demanded, her tone brooking no refusal, and honestly, I had to admit I was sick and tired of pretending. I put the glamour back up all the same. I might consider Serena family now, but that didn't mean I wanted her to see me at my absolute worst.

"Hand me back Mr. Pooper Pants and put on a kettle. I'll tell you everything," I said, taking a deep, calming sniff of powdery baby head when she did as I asked. Half the world's woes could be cured by that smell, and as I inhaled, I vehemently wished my current ones were on the list.

Serena fixed me a cup of fragrant herbal tea—her favorite mix of lavender, verbena, and who knows what else designed to calm my ragged nerves. It worked, as always, and I loosened slightly. Still, she didn't give me a chance to speak before she hit the nail squarely on the head.

"You're still beating yourself up about Delta, aren't you?" she asked gently.

"Yes, and no," I said slowly. "I'm gutted about Delta."

It was the truth, but only the smallest sliver of it. I'd yet to broach the subject of Diana still being alive with Serena, but I suspected she'd discussed the matter with Evian, who held the title of Kaine's official faerie godmother, and also agreed with her sisters that not even a demi-goddess like Diana could have survived the full onslaught of Zeus's rage.

"I thought I could keep everyone safe, and I failed." *Nobody was supposed to die.* Those were the words that had been running through my head ever since I'd watched Delta fall at Diana's hand.

The breadth and depth of my grief threatened to overwhelm; turned, as it tended to do lately, to a sense of rage I could barely tamp down. Rage toward Diana, plus a heaping dose directed at myself for not having stopped her—and still, I had enough left over to be angry at the gods for whatever they'd done to deprive me of the pleasure of murdering her with my own bare hands.

Serena didn't say anything, but her expression spoke a thousand words. They certainly hadn't been fast friends, but that hadn't stopped Delta from helping save Serena's skin on more than one occasion. I could tell by the set of her jaw those acts hadn't been forgotten.

"But mostly, it's Diana," I explained, abruptly changing the subject and leaving all the rest of my feelings regarding Delta locked up inside. You'd think I'd have learned not to do that, especially after what happened last time I compartmentalized, but I couldn't bring myself to say the words, so I focused on the more immediate, solvable problem instead.

"I don't think she's gone. I don't know how she could have survived an attack from Olympus if that's definitely what it was, but I just can't shake the feeling she's still got another trick up her sleeve."

"You think she'll pop up when you least expect it, so why bother trying to be happy or move on when you know it will all be ruined in the long run?" Serena proved again to be more astute than I'd ever given her credit for before. "You're an idiot, Balefire, but I understand."

I looked up quickly from my teacup and looked Serena square in the eye. "You don't think I'm nuts for believing she might still be alive?"

One of Serena's brows lifted into an arch. "Lexi, take a look at my life. I'm a witch; my ex-boyfriend, best friend, and son are all Fate Weavers, and I have to charm my kid six ways to Sunday just to be able to go out in public. In the last year alone, I've come into contact with more magical creatures than even I knew existed, and to top it all off, I just called Lexi Balefire my best friend. If you think for one second, I'm going to say *anything* is out of the realm of possibility, then you're not as smart as I think you are."

The first genuine smile I'd worn in I couldn't even remember how long spread across my face. If it wasn't as big as it could be, well, at least it was a step in the right direction.

"Once this is all over, maybe I can make peace with what happened to Delta, and when that happens, I'll finally have the chance to focus on the rest of my life."

Serena rolled her eyes, and the pendulum swung back in the other direction like I suspected it always would.

"You realize how stupid that is, don't you?" she said without mincing words. "What if she *is* dead? Is it worth spending years waiting for something that might never happen? I say, live your life now. Let yourself off the hook a little and embrace all the wonderful things you *do* have, like an amazing family and—lucky you—a man who adores you. Otherwise, you're going to push everyone away until you end up a lonely, bitter old hag, and if you do, please know that I will mock you endlessly."

I resisted the urge to send a bubble gum charm in her direction, only out of concern for Kaine, who bounced on her lap and instead tossed her a scrunch-nosed glare that failed to elicit anything other than a giggle from the baby.

"Speaking of lonely hags, what about you? Are you seeing anyone?" I blurted, momentarily forgetting my vow not to butt into Serena's love life now that she and Jett were no longer an item. Her threat to hex *me* all over town if I violated that promise had been duly noted and entirely honored. I knew she could do it and had decided it wasn't worth the trouble.

For once, she didn't glare at me the moment the question popped out of my mouth.

Instead, she shrugged and answered, "Nope, I've got my hands full with a male of the species already. The baby is a full-time job. More so, I think, than a normal kid would be, and I don't have time for dating right now."

Uh-huh. I'd heard that from clients before. Usually, about six months before that same woman trotted out a shiny new engagement ring. Serena's situation *was* unique, so perhaps it wasn't just lip service. Problem was, I couldn't get a read on her. I'd never been able to tell anything more than that Jett wasn't her perfect match.

"Besides, I have plenty of time." She was right on that count; my grandmother and Aunt Mag had both already passed the quarter-century milestone, and Gran barely looked any older than Sylvana and me. Perhaps Serena wasn't destined to find her mate until later in life. Still, I detected a sliver of uncertainty in her tone.

"Yes," I said slowly, "you do, but wouldn't it be nice to have a partner, especially now?"

Serena rolled her eyes and when they settled back on me, her expression was one of exasperation. "Because so many men out there are lining up to date a woman with a kid. Throw in that I'm a witch, and my kid has magical powers, and guess what? I'm a catch!" she exclaimed sarcastically. "Seriously, Lexi, I'd need to find someone from the community because I just can't see any regular guy taking my situation in stride. The Kins of this world are in short supply. Romance just isn't in the cards right now."

I gave in and admitted she made some valid points and renewed my vow to stay out of her business. When she was ready, I'd help her, if for no other reason than the alternative was to let Kaine pick his own step-daddy, and that was just a little creepy.

CHAPTER
FIVE

Evening sun filtered through banded layers of clouds, all orange and pink and spectacular. Ocean waves crashed against the shore under the sunset sky, and a gentle breeze blew through my hair.

Kin's fingers entwined with mine as I leaned back and rested against his chest. For that one moment, I hadn't a care in the world. I felt light in body, mind, and soul. I should have known the feeling wouldn't last.

A keening thrum of magic descended from the western sky and made me press my hands to my ears for protection. When Kin did not follow suit, remaining calm and unaffected, I remembered we hadn't actually gone to the beach.

This was a dream.

It had to be because not only was the porch we were sitting on entirely unfamiliar, but Kin didn't so much as flinch as the clouds darkened and rolled ever closer.

"Kin!" I yelled, grabbing for his hands and realizing it was too late when mine passed through him as if he were a ghost. My eyes searched his face, and it was then that I noticed he wasn't the Kin I knew; it was an old man who looked back at me now, the wrinkles between his eyes deepening as he finally took in my panicked expression.

A force stronger than any I'd encountered before—mystical or otherwise—pulled him from my grasp. His mouth opened and closed without sound, and then he was gone. I felt the light drain out of my heart, felt the darkness take over as I let out a bloodcurdling scream that finally broke through my subconscious.

I woke, tears streaming down my face, and jumped half out of my skin when Kin's arms went around me for real this time.

"Lexi, Lexi, sweetheart," he murmured, stroking my hair in an attempt to stop my heaving sobs. "It's okay. It was just a bad dream."

Over and over, he whispered those words that were supposed to be a comfort, and I declined to remind him that rarely are my dreams ever only dreams. Kin's mortality—and my lack of much in that department, given witches could live for hundreds of years—was a touchy subject for me and one we tended to avoid. The thought of losing him had been, of course, the impetus for my current nightmare, and it shook me to my core.

"I need pancakes," I said finally, after extricating myself from his embrace and searching for a tissue to blow my nose. "Terra's blueberry. If we stomp around in the kitchen long enough, maybe we'll wake her up."

Having seen enough of the wreckage caused by angry faeries, Kin appeared skeptical but padded down the stairs behind me anyway. As it turned out, we needn't have worried too hard. Whether they'd been up all night or were getting an early start, I didn't know, but when we arrived, my godmothers were busy tucking into a feast fit for kings.

"Felt peckish," Terra said, answering my unasked question. "It's four-thirty in the morning. What are you doing down here?" She handed me a steaming cup of coffee, and I could have purred.

"Bad dream," I said lightly, then changed the subject. Talking about the nightmare would only cement it in my memory.

"Do you three have a job to get to or something?" The party planning business the godmothers started a few months ago had grown more quickly than anyone (except me) had expected, primarily due to their habit of using magic to make their events over-the-top special. Vaeta's involvement had waned ever since her demon boyfriend, Rhys, had convinced her to join him in working with the IMA (Inter-Magical Alliance) full-time. The rest of the faeries had been left with no choice but to pick up the slack, and I got the feeling they were a little peeved about it.

"Red Hat Society annual tea," Soleil explained while blowing on a stack of pancakes that had already cooled. When she handed the now-steaming pile to me, my stomach gurgled so loudly my cheeks pinked. She smirked and continued. "Those old biddies are hilarious, and we're going to give them a party they'll never forget. With or without Vaeta's help."

And, there it was. The undercurrent of irritation I feared would eventually turn into Faerie Armageddon #2,578.

"Ah, speak of the devil, and she shall appear," Evian said as Vaeta blew through the front door and into the kitchen.

"Sorry I'm late. I was up north checking out a tip about some missing honey pixies and lost track of time."

Before she could get started on the story, I excused myself and dragged Kin back upstairs. Now that the pancakes had driven away the bad dream fog, maybe we could catch another hour or two of sleep. It was going to be a long day, and I'd need as much rest as I could get.

CHAPTER

SIX

Besides our faces, my mother and I also share a love of two-wheeled conveyances. She drives a Harley, and in the summer, I tool around on a vintage scooter, but we both wear helmets, so that's gotta count for something, right?

"Your jacket's still smoking." I spat on my glove and used it to pat out the singed spot near her left elbow that still carried a tiny ember.

"We should have stopped at my place and cleaned up before we came here," she said. "Your godmothers are going to smell fowl flame on us, and then we'll have to break the lie of omission you've been telling for the last six months."

Enough snark was present in her tone to let me know Sylvana still held some resentment toward the four faeries who'd become my parents in her absence.

"And be late for dinner?" I balked, ignoring her comment. "Flix and Carl are coming tonight to talk about their wedding. Terra's serving some dishes she thinks they might like, and if we screw up her timing, she'll toss the faerie version of a hissy fit. After the day we've had, I can't deal. Just put on your glamour, and I'll dash up and change before they see me like this." I'd rubbed my face half raw with tissues, but bits of soot still clung to my skin.

Fowl flame.

Seems like someone could have told me about the smell.

To collect fowl flame, you must first find a flame fowl. They're not as hard to track down as you'd think. Just look for anyplace there's been a forest fire roughly every fifty years, and chances are, you'll find yourself a nest.

Fifty years is the incubation period for a flame fowl egg, and the hatching generates a lot of heat. Or so Sylvana informed me as we hiked about five miles in the middle of nowhere.

Once you've tracked your flame fowl, which looks like —you guessed it—a burning chicken, it's a fairly straight-forward process to extract the tongues.

No, you don't cut them out of the bird's mouth. That would be disgusting, and, in any case, they're not that kind of tongue. The harvesting takes two people. One to catch the fowl and hang it upside down by the feet, which puts the bird to sleep.

That's when the fun begins.

The second person's job is to poke the sleeping bird in the...uh...butt area to startle it awake. If you do it right, the fowl will squawk and spit out a tongue of fowl flame. As it turned out, there's a special container rugged enough to hold a lick of the stuff, a container which Sylvana had smugly pulled out of her proverbial hat at the very last minute.

This business of being a witch isn't all about cute nose-wrinkling and wand-waving. Potions are a lot more work than people think. By the way, guess who got the hot chicken poking job?

That's right, it was me.

Funnily enough, my mother didn't bother to say a word about the other unfortunate consequence. I gave the bird a quick prod, it farted, and I fell over. On my way down, I waved my arms and knocked the fowl out of my mother's hand.

Chaos ensued.

When I said I wasn't aware chickens could fart, my mom informed me that magic fire chickens don't play by the rules. When I asked why no one warned me about the farting, she pointed out that I would have known if I studied even the most basic texts. We argued; it wasn't pretty.

Basically, a typical day with my mother.

Twenty minutes later, the fool-the-faeries plan seemed to be going pretty well. After a speed-shower and fresh clothes, I passed the sniff test, and Sylvana's glamour was one of her best spells, so it looked like we were in the clear.

If Kin gave me a strange look when I entered the dining room, I chalked it up to a coincidence. I knew he couldn't see through the glamour, but every so often, I half wondered if he was one of those people who observes more than he ought to. Kind of like Mona.

It never occurred to me that perhaps Kin's expression had more to do with the one I wore. Glamours can cover a lot, but they don't make you look happy when you aren't.

"How was your day?" he asked after grabbing me and drawing me into a kiss that turned my knees to butter. I suspect there will come a day when that feeling is a distant memory, and so I choose to lean in and relish every second of my time with him.

That my mother looked on enviously was just a bonus. Maybe if she didn't keep my deadbeat dad hoisted on top of the tallest pedestal ever created, I'd feel sorry for her. My boyfriend might have been spelled to forget he was ever in love with me, but at least he hadn't turned his back on me of his own accord.

She'd be better off going on one of those online dating apps and finding herself a new man, which is saying something coming from a matchmaker who abhors technology. Believe me, I'd tried to find my mother's perfect match and had gotten a whole lot of bubkus for my troubles. Cupid's bow seemed somewhat reluctant to cooperate. That inclination, at least, I understood.

You can see why we have a volatile relationship. Our individual baggage could fill the cargo hold of a 747 and don't even get me started on the shared portion.

"My day was fine," I lied, coming back to myself and

answering Kin's question. I'd tell him the truth later. "Same old, same old. How about yours?" I made sure to put a little extra oomph into it and managed to look like the doting girlfriend he deserved.

Kin beamed, and his lips turned up into a mile-wide grin. "You remembered! Honestly, I'd thought it had completely slipped your mind."

Remembered *what?* I wondered, panicked and feeling less than an inch tall. Kin was the best man I'd ever met, and he deserved my full attention—something he actually got a lot less often than he should.

"The meeting was a boon, and Capricorn Black booked my first slot of studio hours! It's not a lot of money, but it's a start."

Of course, Capricorn Black. That I'd forgotten proved I was indeed the worst girlfriend in the world, off searching for supernatural deviants while he was trying to build a business and a life for us. A life I desperately wanted to live.

Funny, that. I'd spent so much time wishing for magical powers, and now I had them, part of me longed to hand them back. I suppose that's what they call irony, but to be honest, I could have done without the life lesson.

Somewhere in the middle of Kin's statement, the air at our end of the dining room shimmered iridescently and where, only a moment before there had been nothing, Flix and his fiancé, Carl, appeared.

"The deal's a go?" Carl asked excitedly, having heard

the last bit of our conversation during their dramatic entrance.

Kin replied in the affirmative, setting off a complicated bro-style handshake evidencing just how much time he and Carl spent together at the gym. Neither Flix nor I minded in the least, as we were the lucky two who reaped the rewards of their efforts.

Flix smiled thinly at me and muttered under his breath so only I could hear, "Remember the dozens of times you've said, 'Flix, I owe you one'?" His impression of me was a bit whiny, and I shot him a dirty look. "Well," he continued, ignoring my reaction, "I'm calling in all my favors."

My stomach dropped, momentarily, all the way to the tips of my designer shoes. Ironically, they'd been a gift from Flix himself. Of course, at the time, there'd been no mention of quid pro quo, but the fact he'd gone through all the trouble (and also happened to pick my favorite pair from the spring collection that year) meant he was a better friend than I probably deserved.

It's entirely possible I'd given him a handmade coupon for a free movie night on his last birthday. I use the term 'handmade' loosely; something tells me *napkin scribbling* isn't going to become the latest arts-and-crafts fad.

Was there anyone in my life I hadn't let down in one way or another?

"What do you need me to do?" I asked just as surreptitiously as he was acting while attempting to remain cheerful. I'd had a long day, and I didn't even need my spidey senses to know Flix wouldn't call in all his favors if the task wasn't something I'd abhor agreeing to under normal circumstances.

"Talk Carl out of the ridiculously ostentatious horse-drawn Cinderella carriage made out of real gold." Okay, that was the last thing I'd expected him to say.

My eyebrows shot into my hairline, and I smirked. "You need *me* for that? What happened to your powers of persuasion?"

"Evidently," Flix replied testily, "Carl and I have moved past the point where he considers my masculine wiles utterly irresistible. I promised I wouldn't use my *actual* powers on him, and I'm not going back on my word, especially this close to the wedding." Flix looked like he wanted to cross himself, and I couldn't help but giggle.

I swear, the look he pierced me with could have bored through me, the floor, and all the way to the other side of the world.

"The entirety of the wedding is based off that blasted carriage," Flix cursed and then, even quieter than he was already keeping, muttered something that sounded like 'groomzilla' and sighed a dramatic faerie sigh.

"When he came up with the idea, I figured it was just phase one, and he'd tone it down. Turns out I was wrong. I heard him talking to someone in Belgium about a troupe of acrobats who agreed to perform over each table while the entrées are being served. If anything dangles over my mother's haute cuisine, the entire reception might turn into a bloodbath. Literally."

Leaning in, I wiggled my brows. "It doesn't take that much heat to melt gold, you know. And your Best Woman does happen to be the keeper of a really hot flame."

"Subtlety is definitely not your strong suit, Lexi Balefire," Flix retorted with the first genuine smile I'd seen out of him since he'd popped into the dining room. "Let's call destroying the object of Carl's obsession a last resort, alright? And remember, I might need to do the same for you one day soon."

"Kin would never."

"You sure about that?"

The smile I'd been happy to see a moment before now turned to a smirk as Flix nodded his head toward our respective mates. I couldn't tell if Kin's story had ended naturally or if Carl had hijacked the conversation prematurely, but it didn't seem to matter because Kin appeared enthralled.

His eyes sparkled as they flicked between Carl and me, and I made an effort to tune in just in time to hear Carl say, "Every decent place in town, dude. At least a two-year wait. Just a warning, if you were thinking about booking a venue anytime soon. You know, for any sort of...big event."

Carl was about as subtle as a sledgehammer.

Furthermore, I didn't need a reminder that Kin was chomping at the bit to get married. Have I not mentioned any of this before? Well, ever since we broke Diana's spell and Kin got all his memories of us back, he's been dying to put a ring on it.

Actually, he *did* put a ring on it. What he's really keen to do is set a date and start the planning process. Problem is, I'm not so keen. Not just yet.

Don't get me wrong, I love the man with every fiber of my being, and I have no qualms about being tied to him for the rest of my life. I've even, on occasion, thought about what I'd want for my wedding. I *am* a matchmaker by trade; of course, I've thought about it, and it would be spectacular, let me tell you right now.

For most of my life, though, my side of the aisle would have been pretty empty. I'd no family save for Terra, Evian, Soleil, and a scant handful of friends since the witch contingency of Port Harbor had treated me like a leper up until I gained my power.

Now, my side would be full to bursting, and part of me wanted to run down that aisle and throw myself into Kin's arms. Another wanted to hit the airport, hop a flight to Vegas, and get married by the first Elvis impersonator we saw.

So why, do you ask, did I hesitate? Why had I been avoiding Kin's yearning looks and thinly-veiled hints?

Two reasons.

First, I struggled with the concept of allowing myself

to spare a moment of thought on a happy occasion knowing there was still work to be done. In my head, it felt like I had miles to go before I could sleep and too many problems to count.

Second, when I said I'd be thrilled to be married to Kin for the rest of my life, I really mean for the rest of his. How ridiculous that I couldn't be happy for our beginning because I couldn't stop picturing the end?

What I should have done was realize it never does any good to wait for the "right" time to do something. There's never a perfect time to get married or buy a house or get a nose ring; we can always think up some excuse to wait. That's why most of the time, we ought to stop dilly-dallying and just get on with whatever it is that will make us happy.

I'm not saying you should marry a jerk or get sucked into a seller's market, mind you. And definitely don't go for the septum piercing unless you're sure you can pull it off. But Kin was a solid investment, and I knew it. If I hadn't been mired so deeply in my private pity party, I might have had the good sense to listen to Carl's suggestion and set the damn date.

"We'll cross that bridge when we come to it," I said lightly, instead, refusing to meet the prying eyes of my godmothers or Kin's puppy-dog stare. *Just a little longer*, I promised him silently, launching into a diatribe about the negative environmental impact of gold mining in an attempt to dissuade Carl from his over-the-top wedding plans.

He appeared underwhelmed by my comments and wasn't the only one at the table to look at me like I'd grown a second head.

Luckily, the conversation got derailed when appetizers began emerging from the kitchen on a series of floating silver platters.

Strips of prosciutto shaved so thinly they were nearly transparent rested in delicate ribbons atop slices of pear and made my mouth water.

Then came a beautifully arranged assortment of nuts, dried fruits, and cheeses that, in a rainbow mosaic, formed Flix and Carl's entwined initials. It was, unfortunately, too beautiful to ruin by eating.

A variety of crostini was more than I could take, and I snagged one topped with cream cheese and crab before Salem bogarted the entire tray.

Poor Flix. He might just have to suck it up. That's what I was thinking when the tasting turned from upscale to southern comfort with an edge, and Carl's eyes bugged out of his head.

Even he couldn't deny that the fried chicken with savory waffle pudding, maple mousse, and pepper jelly was just as elegant as roasted quail with mushroom and truffle stuffing. Even so, there was a long way between foie gras and fried green tomato sliders.

"Oh. My. God," I moaned after the first bite. "You

should totally have these. In fact, you could plan the whole event around this dish: refined rustic. I'm envisioning shades of cream, stemless wine glasses, a million tiny fireflies lighting the hall. It could be beautiful," I finished, knowing my enthusiasm had fallen on deaf ears.

After that, an argument ensued regarding whether "rustic" was a term Carl wanted used in conjunction with his wedding, and he refused to budge. I could almost see a thought bubble above his head with the absurd golden carriage flashing like a neon light. This was going to be more difficult than I'd imagined, and I decided not to discount the option of simply disappearing the thing.

"Ladies," my mother said to the godmothers as she interrupted the discussion, laid her napkin beside her plate, and pushed her chair back a little. "You've outdone yourselves. Colonel Sanders couldn't hold a candle to you in the fried chicken department."

Terra smiled. "Who do you think gave him his recipe? The poor man was only using nine herbs and spices when I met him."

Kin snorted out a laugh at what he thought was a joke, then cut it off when Terra raised an eyebrow at him. "On behalf of the world, I thank you for passing on your secret recipe."

"Please," Terra huffed. "I didn't say I gave him my secret recipe, only that I helped him perfect his. I use fourteen herbs and spices in mine. Sixteen if I'm not serving mortals and have to leave out the ones your systems can't handle."

"Don't go taking all of the credit," Soleil chimed in. "Your flavors are good, but my technique for flash frying is what keeps the meat juicy."

Not to be outdone, Evian offered, "And let's not forget about me, shall we?" She buffed her fingernails against her chest—a motion that didn't go unnoticed by Kin. "Controlling the moisture content goes a long way when you're looking to get a mouthful of succulent meat."

Kin swallowed hard, his face going slightly red as Evian's silky voice delivered the comment. She hadn't meant to sound all sexy; she just couldn't help it. Evian's human appearance came courtesy of a glamour that toned down her natural beauty by a factor of at least ten, and she still ended up with supermodel-level looks. All of the godmothers did, and most of the time, Kin managed to keep his tongue from rolling out of his mouth and his eyes from bugging out cartoon-style. But every now and again, one of them caught him off-guard.

I'd learned to live with their effect on men, find it amusing, and even grow a healthy self-esteem. No mean feat, I'll tell you.

Unfortunately, being new to the family, my mother hadn't totally picked up on the dynamic and got all offended on my behalf.

"No matter how succulent you think it is, you'll want to keep your hands off Kin's meat, thank you very much," she said, letting a bit of her magic trickle into the room. Not enough to make the floor open and swallow me whole, so I had that going for me.

Evian frowned as Sylvana's meaning didn't get through right away. Kin shifted in his seat, his face going red.

"Mom! Take it down a notch. Evian doesn't poach, and Kin doesn't stray." Unless he's under a spell, I didn't add.

Another burst of magic oozed from Sylvan's pores. Dark power.

A white bolt of balefire flame shot out of the fireplace, arrowed through the kitchen door, and slammed Sylvana in the chest. Hot and bright, the aura surrounded her body, burning Sylvana-shaped spots into my retinas before toppling her over backward, chair and all.

A gout of water fountained from Evian's outstretched hands and doused the flames, leaving Sylvana shivering, soaked to the skin, and sitting in a puddle. Her glamour fell in the process, but Evian's bath had cleared off the last of the flame fowl soot.

"That was completely unnecessary." Sylvana sputtered.

Evian offered a cheeky grin. "You were on fire. It was my civic duty to put you out."

"Civic duty, my ass." Looking bedraggled, my mother scrambled up just as Soleil directed a burst of heat in her direction. Think human-sized blow dryer set on high. In seconds, my mom went from dripping to dry. If her hair looked like it had been styled with an industrial-sized teasing comb while driving seventy miles an hour in a convertible with the top down, wasn't that just too bad? She should have minded her own business in the first place.

"There now," Soleil said, her lips twitching only slightly. "Isn't that better?"

While the other two faeries delighted in messing with my mother, Terra's lips firmed in a straight line, and her eyes narrowed as she watched events unfold.

It goes against every rule in the handbook for a witch to be raised by her very own faerie godmother, but when she'd found me seemingly orphaned, Terra didn't give the rules a second thought, and neither did her two sisters. They gave up a lot and put themselves in a bad light within the fae community when they decided to stay in our world. More, probably than I'd ever know. In the mother comparison game, Sylvana came off two points behind the spread.

Still, if she and my grandmother hadn't tossed a butt-load of magic around in the witch fight to end all witch fights, one of them wouldn't have ended up in a portal prison and the other a stone statue.

We all make our choices in life, and we all have to live with them. Sylvana's jealousy was entirely of her own making. Terra's refusal to hide her opinion of my mother didn't help things, and she could say as much with a look as with a thousand words.

In this case, a pointed glance from Sylvana to the bale-fire was all it took to set off the beginnings of a showdown.

I tensed and prepared to get between them. Why couldn't the women in my life, just for once, talk things out over a cup of tea. Hell, I'd be happy if they'd all get drunk together, go to a male strip club, and bond. Whatever worked to get them past the three-steps-forward-two-steps-back stage they'd been stuck in for months.

"You two..." was as far as I got.

CHAPTER

SEVEN

If she hadn't already been driven mad by her own machinations, the banging and scraping sounds coming from behind the blackened window would have sent Diana Diamond over the edge.

"Idiots. Morons. Living their tiny lives in their tiny hovels." Spit slid from the corner of her mouth to dribble unheeded toward her chin. No one who'd seen the impeccably dressed and coiffed mistress of wayward hearts on TV would recognize the gibbering creature curled into a ball on the dank and dusty floor.

Hatred seethed through her bloodstream, turning every vein and capillary to a river of black that, under skin gone white and paper-thin, gave her the appearance of having been chiseled from marble.

Once thick and richly dark, Diana's hair stood out like dried grass on a wintry hummock, her scalp showing through the grayed and brittle strands.

As she lamented and railed at the turn of fates that had brought her so low, she scratched at the floor with torn, claw-like nails, leaving deep furrows in the wood.

Caught halfway through the mirror portal when it

struck, the diving lightning had thrown Diana clear across her hidden room, slapped her into the far wall, then sealed the opening behind her. Locked in a prison of her own making, Diana wouldn't die in a blast of righteous fire but instead with agonizing slowness. Most people who'd known her would call it a fitting end.

There was neither food nor water to be had, but Diana was beyond the need for such mundane forms of nourishment. Hate had fed her body and soul for far longer than she should have lived, even as the deep well of it sucked her down, sucked her dry.

Her time was nearly gone.

How humiliating, she thought, to die alone—and yet, being the self-centered thing she was, Diana either couldn't see or wouldn't admit the irony in the fate she'd earned for herself by consigning others to die unloved.

Moving closer to that death with each slowing breath, Diana huddled in the tattered remains of the clothing she'd shredded while she wore it and turned over, away from the blanked mirror, to find a more comfortable position. At least she would go out with her back to the world she hated above all else.

Diana pressed her cheek to the floor, felt a sliver of wood slip into her skin, and angled her chin so it went deeper, drew blood. As she reveled in the pain, her gaze fell on and then passed over an odd, dust-coated shape jutting out of the crack where the floor met the wall. Another self-pitying eternity passed before the shape caught her eye again. When it did, she frowned and blinked.

A spark of interest caught, guttered nearly out, then flickered to life. Gathering herself, Diana rolled onto her stomach and lifted her head for a better look.

"Probably a dust bunny," she said, her voice hoarse from disuse, but she inched her way toward it, scraping both elbows and knees on the floor until her shaking finger hovered over the dusty artifact. Six or seven inches long, vaguely pointed on one end, and covered in dust, the thing hummed with quiet power.

Such power that anyone with half a brain would have pulled their hand away, but not Diana. Even in her diminished state, the lust for more and better was enough to overwhelm common sense. Besides, what did she have to lose? The final minutes or maybe hours of life? Better to die fast and clean than by inches.

With that thought in mind, she tore a shred from her tattered clothing and endured the sting and buzz that shot up her arm as she swiped cloth over the outer layer of dust. Gold-tipped light shone through the clean spot, nearly blinding her after so much time spent in darkness.

Not waiting for her eyes to adjust, Diana worked the rag over the shaft until bright red shone through her closed eyelids. Slowly, she slitted one eye then the other, opening them just enough to realize what she'd found.

Rejuvenated by hope, Diana rose to her feet, the gauntness of her frame filling out as life flowed back in.

She grasped the shard, endured the pain as she raised it over her head, and laughed until her muscles ached. This was power like she'd never known. A shard of lightning made solid, and there was only one place from which it might have come. Mag Balefire's theory had been correct.

"Oh, mighty Zeus. Your granddaughter thanks you," Diana cried to the heavens.

Using the shard as a knife, she tore her way out of the sanctuary-turned-prison, sending a wave of magic across the land.

CHAPTER

EIGHT

Ripples of magical energy cut the air like rings from a stone dropped in calm water. Each one tugged at the back of my throat, sending vibrations up through the earth until my feet tingled as if they'd been asleep. The sensation spread to my knees, then rushed up through me to steal my breath.

"Terra!" With difficulty, I turned to what I thought was the source of the problem. It wouldn't have been her first fury-born earthquake, particularly while lobbing magical bombs back and forth across the house like she was doing now, but something about this one felt different.

Terra shook her head. "It's not me."

We both looked at Sylvana, who had stopped mid-argument. Now, with one hand braced the table and a concerned expression on her face, she appeared slightly stunned.

In its hearth, the balefire roared and shot a pillar of angry red up the chimney. The whole event lasted only a few seconds but seemed longer.

"Is everyone all right?" Evian's voice trilled from the kitchen.

I turned to check on Kin. Over the buzzing in my ears, I heard him say, "What was that?"

"I don't know." Terra's brow furrowed, and she held her hands up in a helpless gesture that spoke volumes.

Whatever it was had packed a magical wallop. I felt like I'd been turned inside out and then back again. Around the table, a sea of paled faces let me know I wasn't the only one affected.

I reached into my pocket and, hands shaking, fished amongst the contents for a coin I often carried. Giving it a little rub helped calm my nerves, and not because the motion was somehow soothing but because I knew that in moments reinforcements would arrive.

Simultaneously, the front door slammed open, and the house phone pealed out its strident tones.

After poking her head in and scanning quickly to make sure everyone was okay, my grandmother, Clara, said, "I'll get it." While she fielded the first of many phone calls from the local coven members, Aunt Mag's cane beat a tattoo on the hallway floor.

Salem skidded into the foyer on all fours, his ears perked excitedly, and weaved between Gran's feet looking, no doubt, for her familiar, a Siamese beauty named Pyewacket. When he didn't find his crush, he slunk back out dejectedly, and my heart went out to him just a little. Despite Salem's tendency to needle me about my studies, he only had my best interests at heart, and I'd been a bit harsh with him lately.

"Everything okay? Anyone hurt?" Mag asked—or rather, demanded. The elder witches hadn't wasted any time getting here, just as I'd trusted. Aunt Mag still had on her bedroom slippers and flannel pajamas—she tends to be an early sleeper. "What happened?"

"We haven't a clue, Margaret," Terra explained, the lines that had appeared between her eyebrows growing deeper. "If it was an earthquake, it was the biggest one in Port Harbor history, I can promise you that. Did you feel it all the way in Harmony?"

Mag ignored the question and instead headed toward the dining room, where the smell of the faerie's leftover feast still lingered. "Is that fried chicken I smell?" she asked hopefully. "I could eat some chicken."

Terra sighed and followed Aunt Mag. "Help yourself," she offered ruefully.

Mag took a seat, nodded a friendly hello to Flix and Carl, her hand already closed around the bone of a drumstick, and finally answered Terra through a mouthful. "We felt a little rumble. Probably just a cauldron mishap. I remember this one time, Maryanna Pingrey tried to curse her cheating husband's new secretary. She thought it would be a good idea to add *quadruple* the number of giant's warts and ended up blowing the whole second floor off their beachside condo. I felt the blast from that one clear to the Fringe!"

"That's nothing," Salem scoffed. He'd seen enough cauldron mishaps to be considered an expert. "My first witch's demise created a crater the width of a football field. The humans still haven't figured out what caused it."

Mag swung round to stare incredulously at Salem. "You're not talking about the Patomskiy Crater in Siberia, are you?"

He nodded, clearly satisfied with his ability to impress the venerable Mag Balefire with a bit of witchy trivia, and I vowed to come back around to that conversational tidbit at a later date. It was more than he'd ever shared regarding the eight witches he'd served before me; all he'd ever done was implore that I be careful since my life was tied to his ninth and final one.

For now, though, I had more important things on my mind. What we'd all experienced had felt like a surge of immense power. Even the balefire had reacted, something it had been known to do in extreme circumstances. The devil on my shoulder whispered that Diana Diamond must be involved.

"They're right," Sylvana said, eying me sharply with a warning look as though she might be reading my mind. "These things happen all the time."

The angel on my other shoulder agreed with my mother and reminded me that the balefire didn't react exclusively to negative stimuli. Its color tended to change like some sort of mood ring, and it always put on a lovely magical light show for Kaine whenever Serena brought him over to the house.

All of the faeries appeared satisfied, but I couldn't shake the feeling that we should be doing something more. That is until the telephone stopped ringing and Gran emerged from the parlor.

"Hecate's petticoats, the coven is in a tizzy!" She rolled her eyes—eyes that mirrored mine and my mother's so closely we looked like a living version of a set of nesting dolls—and flopped into a seat across from her sister.

"Oh, blast the coven, Clarie," Aunt Mag said with a wave of her hand. "You're not even in charge anymore. Shouldn't they be calling their high priestess with their questions and concerns?" To be fair, Mag was ornery for a reason, and that reason had to do with the way the witches of Port Harbor had treated me throughout the years—and how they'd reacted to Clara when she'd come back from being stoned and wrongly accused of killing my mother.

My life is a little complicated, didn't you know? Regardless, I'd gotten over all the slights and was finally on half-decent terms with most of the witches hereabouts —and so was Gran. She wasn't the type to hold a grudge and simply ignored her sister.

I had to wonder what the dynamic was like in the little house they shared in the riverside village of Harmony. The two of them, sisters for two and a half centuries, living together again. Gran had primarily stayed mute on the subject, but I suspected there'd been a few bumps in the road. None of that was important at the moment, and I feared I had bigger things to worry about.

Like magical earthquakes that cause the balefire to belch showers of sparks out of my chimney. Old Mrs. Chatterly next door was probably having a hairy conniption. I suspected she'd called the fire department and activated some 70's-era phone chain, but when I peeked through the curtains, her windows were, for once, completely shuttered.

"It's Tuesday, right?" Clara squinted. "Cleo Rathmore's triplets turned fourteen today. I'm betting they all got their magic at the same time."

"Triplets? Is that a witch thing?" My eyes rounded.

"Not unless they run in your family."

It seemed that was all there was to it, and slowly, the party began to disperse. Flix and Carl, sensing the evening of wedding planning had been effectively ruined, left first.

"Don't worry about it, Lexi," Groomzilla insisted before the pair skimmed out. "We're both stuffed to the gills and have so many options to consider it's probably a good idea for us to take a breather. You don't suppose there's any more of that lemon creme mousse cake left, do you?" he asked, appearing crestfallen when I said I'd seen Aunt Mag lick her plate clean of the last slice.

"It's probably for the best if I want to fit into my tux," he said, but I swear I saw his eyes narrow in Mag's direction. *Good luck, buddy. She'd eat you alive and clean her teeth with the bones.*

Salem scampered off, supposedly to check with his familiar cronies, though I suspect the lack of his paramour had him looking for a reason to bail. Even though he'd just consumed a metric ton of the godmothers' canapes, I knew they served all-you-can-eat fish and chips at his favorite pub until midnight, and I'd no doubt he'd saved room.

Kin caught my eye from across the table, tilted his head to one side, and raised his eyebrow in a question. I made my way over to him and whispered in his ear, "Give me some time with Gran, and I'll pop over later," then kissed him soundly and watched him exit through the front door.

Out of the lot of them, Gran was the one who made me feel most like the little girl whose lifelong wishes had all come true. I'd wanted for nothing growing up with Evian, Soleil, and most of all Terra—they'd lavished me with love and affection, and for a long time, I felt guilty for wishing I'd known my mother.

Gran, however, had been frozen in stone across the street for the first twenty-five years of my life, presumably in punishment for killing Sylvana in a magical rage. As such, I'd always believed her a villain and therefore had never longed for her presence.

Imagine my surprise when it turned out she wasn't guilty after all. I'd found a way to save her, and she'd returned, all sweetness and light, around the same time my pedestal-occupying mother came out of the wood-work and then subsequently betrayed me. To say they'd switched places in my hierarchy of affection would have been a gross understatement.

All that was water under the bridge at this point, but you can imagine how bizarre it was to sit at a table with the two of them. Bizarre and at the same time wonderful. Wonderful enough to, at least for a few moments, make me forget about the earthquake and Diana Diamond, the two decades I'd pined away, and even my secret actor crush, the glorious Chris Pine, who ought to be the one immortalized in stone.

CHAPTER

NINE

Later that night, I decided to take Serena's advice literally and at least make an attempt at relaxation. We witches incorporate ritual into many aspects of our daily lives, and one of my favorites was that of a nice, hot bath.

So, I raided the sanctum's stores, tucked a handful of salt and an assortment of herbs into a small satchel, and sprinkled it with a few fragrant essential oils.

I lit some candles, set the water to a nice warm temperature that wouldn't have me come out looking like a steamed lobster in the end, and then tossed in the sachet.

The scents of frankincense, lavender, and ylang-ylang hit my nose with a bang, and I let out a hum of appreciation before lowering myself into the warmth.

As I soaked, I felt my muscles unkink and loosen, and in the process, my mind began to wander. Surprisingly, it landed on what I would have thought was my last priority: Mona's friend's love life. I should have known better. Matchmaking was my job for a reason—several reasons, actually—and it should have been higher on my priority list.

I made a choice right then to put my best effort into helping Nadia Hale. I wasn't sure how long I'd be able to keep FootSwept going in its current incarnation, and Flix and I had discussed closing up shop once we'd put a lid on the Diana situation once and for all.

No formal decision had been made, but the truth was I didn't need the offices and the staff and the whole nine yards to do my job anymore. The Bow of Destiny worked pretty well at cutting out the middle man, which in this case, was me. Nadia might well be my last official client, and therefore she would get the premium Lexi Balefire treatment.

I got out of the tub the expected shocking shade of scarlet, but I let at least a portion of my woes wash down the drain.

A tapped-out text message sent post-haste to Mona suggesting a "chance" meeting with Nadia cemented the task into my calendar. One decision made, and I'd call that progress.

CHAPTER

TEN

After the fifth time I woke that night with my heart racing for no good reason, I decided I needed a good talking-to.

Gran was right about the triplets causing that ripple. After all these months, it couldn't have been anything else, and especially not the she-beast from hell. You need to pick yourself up, Lexi Balefire and move forward with your life. Starting right now.

I'd finally fallen asleep for good about two hours before I needed to get up. The next morning, I took one look in the mirror and slapped on a double coat of glamour before starting my day.

Flix had the office under control, and so I took to the streets, Bow of Destiny in hand, just itching for a match to affirm my new beginning.

No matter how many times I check my stance, fit a heart-tipped arrow to my bowstring, and sight in on my target, there's a piece of me that still can't get used to aiming a pointy weapon at a fellow human being. Even if that person has a neon heart symbol flashing over their head to help guide me towards their perfect match.

It's a far cry from the days when I did my job—and did it well—running on intuition and an inherent knack for correctly judging the compatibility level of two people.

Firing the Bow of Destiny lacked the personal touch, though, and I missed the hands-on aspects of my former methods.

However, over on the plus side, I could put more couples together than ever before, so I supposed I ought to be grateful I'd found it and—sort of—figured out how to use it. The bow carries a special brand of magic that allows me to shoot people in broad daylight and not get arrested, so it has that going for it.

Even so, my eyes still snapped shut every time an arrow hit.

I'd just finished putting one into the heart of a lovely older woman—the bowstring hadn't even stopped vibrating—when my phone dinged loudly, and I jumped nearly out of my skin.

I'd almost forgotten about my undercover meeting with Mona and her friend Nadia, but luckily Flix had thought to add a reminder to my calendar. For once, I didn't have to resist the urge to throw my beeping phone straight into a garbage can—that is, until I noticed he'd added another task for me to complete: *Get Carl to come to his senses!*

I silenced the alert with a grimace, gathered my wits, and put the bow back in its magical holster. Which, weirdly enough, was *me*. That's right, the thing lives inside me, and somehow its arrows are made out of my bones. Don't ask; I don't know much more about it than the next person.

Three blocks over, I stepped through the doors of a little bistro catering to the health-conscious, smirked at the thought of consuming anything comprised almost entirely of kale, and made a show of looking around for an empty table.

When I got to within a few feet of her, Mona called out to me.

"Lexi, hey!" she said, waving. "Fancy meeting you here. This is the woman who introduced me to Mark," Mona explained to her companion—presumably, Nadia Hale—whose eyes narrowed immediately. A feeling of déjà vu hit me. It seemed Mona only wanted me to match friends who wouldn't have, under any circumstances, voluntarily asked for my services.

"Nice to meet you," I made with the pleasantries, but Nadia declined to extend her hand and make my job a piece of cake. Unless I'm holding the bow, I have to touch a person to turn on my LPS—Love Positioning System— and this girl was having none of that. Maybe she was a germophobe, or maybe she just didn't trust Mona any more than she should have.

I'd figure out a way to brush against her during lunch, which Mona was busy inviting me to invade despite the irritated look on her friend's face. Sure, if all else failed, I could pull the bow back out, but I'd made a vow to do this particular match the old-fashioned way, and damn it all to spell, that's exactly what I intended to do.

I did, it turned out, recognize Nadia from the bus bench ads all over town, just as Mona had promised. Except, today, she didn't look quite like the same woman. Her eyes were faintly red, with some puffiness around the lids as though she'd been crying, and there wasn't a bit of makeup on her pretty face.

Perhaps Nadia's current state had something to do with why she and Mona were tucked into a table at one of the far corners of the restaurant and why she didn't relish the idea of lunching with a virtual stranger.

Still, she returned my polite greeting and even attempted a smile as I settled into my seat. "Please, don't let me interrupt your conversation," I said with a wave of my hand. Better to listen, anyway, get a beat on this woman before I set about the task of connecting her with her match.

"Oh, we were just chatting," Mona assured. "Nadia, why don't you tell Lexi about your waterfront listings while I use the restroom for the fifth time since we sat down. I think she might be in the market for a beach house."

The words *beach house* made Nadia wince, and I raised a surreptitious eyebrow at Mona. Perhaps this whole endeavor wasn't going to be so simple after all. Nadia was still mourning her relationship, and I'd be willing to bet good money she hadn't reached the rebound stage yet.

Leave it to Mona to completely jump the gun. Not much of a surprise since she idled at high speed. No crystal ball needed to see that one coming.

Cupid's—or actually right now, they're mine—arrows aren't sharp in a literal sense—but they pierce their target's hearts, creating an opening for love to grow. Of course, it's not always as simple as point and shoot. The heart tends to have a mind of its own, and it's my job to gauge whether aiming my bow is the best course of action.

I could already tell Nadia wasn't ready, and the last thing I intended to do was force her, but I'd need to make contact to know how to proceed. And so, I set about getting her to first open her mouth—I'd worry about the rest later.

"Hey, I recognize you," I said excitedly, as though Mona hadn't already briefed me on everything from Nadia's rural upbringing to which brand of tampons she preferred. That's not a joke, and I'll save you from reliving how we happened to get from point A to point—pardon the pun—o.b.

"You're on the bus bench near my office! *Keep calm and call a Realtor*, right?"

A shadow crossed Nadia's face for the briefest of moments, and she nodded, making an attempt at a smile. "That's me," she confirmed somewhat reluctantly.

"Did I get it wrong?" I asked, thinking it would be just

like me to stick my foot in my mouth and kill any chance of ingratiating myself to the woman.

"No, no," she waved a hand. "It's just—and I don't know why I'm even telling you this—but I don't really like that slogan. In fact, I hate it."

I tried to smooth the situation over, but it seemed as though Nadia was having some sort of epiphany. For a moment, I wondered if I *had* actually used magic on her but then remembered what a mess I'd been during my brief breakup with Kin. Shortly after he forgot I existed, I burst into tears in front of a bank teller, then proceeded to tell her half my life story before she was forced to inform me I'd need to let the line move forward.

"It's not a bad slogan, really. I thought it was cute," I offered lamely.

"It was my boss's idea," Nadia replied, then shook her head as if to dislodge the unpleasant thought.

No, I decided, I hadn't accidentally put her under a truth spell. This woman was just in her own little world, and coming from me, that's saying something.

"What are you looking for in a house, exactly?" Nadia asked, professional now, though a bit less guarded than she'd been before. Whatever worked, I supposed and thought about how to answer.

What tumbled out was a description of the home I'd been fantasizing about for Kin and me—if we were entirely different people with entirely different lives.

Unless I wanted to relocate the Balefire out of my

existing fireplace—the one it had resided in for more than two centuries—I wouldn't be moving anytime soon.

My ancestors were able to transport the flame across the Atlantic, so a few more miles probably wouldn't be an insurmountable feat, but something about the idea just felt wrong.

"A bungalow would be lovely," I gushed. "One floor, three bedrooms. My boyfriend is a musician, so he needs a place to set up a small studio." They say it's best to stick as close to the truth as possible while lying, and whoever *they* are is right—I sounded completely natural.

My efforts amounted to little because Nadia had a one-track mind. At the word *boyfriend*, her lip curled, involuntarily it seemed, into a snarl. She had it bad, let me tell you. I could feel the pain and loneliness that surrounded her, enough to turn my arms to gooseflesh.

"Is there anything I can do?" I asked, reaching for Nadia's hand. She moved it just as I was about to make contact and smiled thinly.

"No, I'm fine. Embarrassed is all. I don't know what's wrong with me today, but it looks like Mona's already told you I was recently dumped. As usual, she's meddling." It seemed I wasn't the only one who had a line on our mutual friend, though to be fair, Mona was far more conspicuous than she believed herself to be.

"You seem very nice and everything," Nadia continued, "but I don't need a matchmaker." Her cheeks pinked when the word came out sounding like a slur.

Deftly, I waved away her concern. "Half my clients feel the same way. Mona's a good friend, but she's so happy in her relationship, it makes her overzealous when it comes to love. I'm certainly not in the business of forcing hands —or hearts, however you want to look at it. What I *am* exceptionally good at is listening." I tossed her my best sympathetic smile, but Nadia still appeared skeptical.

I might have actually considered sending a little wisp of magic in her direction for the sole purpose of loosening her lips and getting to the point. Patience and kindness aside, I had a job to do, and I needed to start somewhere.

Salem would have hissed disapprovingly at me for even deliberating about taking liberties, but I brushed away the thought just as Mona returned from the restroom and rendered the notion moot.

"I see you two are hitting it off," she commented smugly. Nadia shot me a conspiratorial smirk, which finally broke the ice between us.

The expression on Mona's face as she perused the vegan menu made me want to laugh out loud, but for once, I restrained myself. It started out hopeful but concerned, and by the time her eyes had traveled down the page, had turned to disgusted and desperate.

Evidently, the restaurant choice had been Nadia's, so I turned to her and attempted to garner some more good-will. "Would you recommend the cashew cheese ravioli or the marinated tempeh?" I asked, even though they both sounded absolutely revolting. I thought I saw Mona's face literally turn green at the words "cashew cheese," but she dutifully remained stoic.

"Neither," Nadia replied. "You'll be wanting the ginger teriyaki stir fry. Trust me, it's to die for." It did sound like the least vile thing on the menu, so I focused instead on my umbrella-bedecked mocktail. Hey, it was lunch, and it wouldn't have been fair to Mona to imbibe when she couldn't, but it's my personal opinion that the notion of an alcohol-less cocktail is positively depressing.

I set the glass down on the wrong side of my plate, right next to Nadia's ice water, and waited until she reached out to take a sip. All I needed was to make contact. Just one strategic move and bingo!—I'd know exactly what to do.

Unfortunately for my best-laid plans, Nadia didn't touch her drink until halfway through her entree, and if she did, I didn't notice, distracted as I was by how tasty my meal had turned out to be. The tofu had been marinated, sliced into strips, and flash-fried to create a crispy crust and a chicken-like interior. I still wouldn't be trying cashew cheese anytime soon, though. Just yuck.

Finally, I got my chance when we both reached for our glasses at the same time. The second my fingers brushed against Nadia's, I felt the familiar tingle of magic as a blinding vision swam behind my eyes. Except, this time, it felt like my gut was tied into a knot—a knot square in the center of a raging game of Tug of War. I thought my insides were going to split in two and doubled over from the pain.

"Lexi, are you all right?" Mona asked, alarmed. I nodded and held onto my stomach in an attempt to avoid witnessing seeing my lunch in reverse.

"I think so," I said, my eyes wide and trained on Nadia. "But that tofu isn't sitting well," I lied. "I think I'd better go home. I'll call you later, Mona," I promised, then barreled out of the restaurant and around the corner into the alley. There, my stomach finally gave out, ruining a perfectly good pair of wedges. Sure, I could magic them back to rights, but they'd never be the same again.

I wasn't sure I would be, either, because the vision I witnessed when I touched Nadia was like no other I'd had since gaining my powers, finding my father's bow, and putting my goddess and witch halves back together.

The woman was an enigma, I discovered while I watched her futures play out. That's right, futures plural, and not the delightfully easy-to-decipher kind I used to get while battling Diana Diamond for the hearts of lonely hopefuls. Then, the symbols told their story, and all I'd had to do was tell a black heart from a pink one. Easy peasy.

This, though—this was entirely different and completely disorienting. Nadia had two possible matches —strong ones. So strong, either of them would have tripped my radar under normal circumstances. They pulled at her, and by extension, me, with a brutal force.

Was it me, or was it her? Was my magic on the fritz, or did this woman have multiple personalities or something?

Neither Garrick nor Fritzroy—two of the last living fate weavers who I'd had to track down to help Serena keep a handle on Kaine's burgeoning powers—had mentioned anything about multiple matches in their description of their own experiences. Then again, they weren't Balefire witches, and they didn't have enough power to wield the Bow of Destiny.

I could ask them again, but something told me they weren't going to have the answers I was looking for. Cupid might, and the notion that I might actually need to find good old dad for reasons other than my mother's romantic fantasies wafted through my head and made me want to hurl again.

Perhaps, I decided, it was time to start listening to Salem and do some brushing up on my heritage. Tomorrow, though. Because tonight, I had a date with Sylvana, and if we were successful, I might even get the chance to ask my father for advice on what to do about Nadia.

The thought of that made my stomach churn again.

CHAPTER
ELEVEN

The old car bumped over ruts and stones as we drove through the tree-tunnel shadows of an old dirt road, the headlamps barely lighting our way under the darkness of a new moon. Just because I'm a witch doesn't mean I don't get creeped out by spooky places, and this was as spooky a place as I'd ever been.

"Where are we? Are we even still in Port Harbor?"

Hunched over the wheel, her eyes scanning both sides of the road, Sylvana answered absently, "I don't know. Probably not. Watch your side; we're looking for a sign—"

"You mean the one with the pentacle on it? We passed it a minute ago."

I rocked in the seat when Sylvana slammed on the brakes. "You could have said something."

"Sure, because I knew where we were going and all." When in doubt, sarcasm is always the way to go.

I'm pretty sure her smacking me when she put her arm along the back of the seat to look over one shoulder and drive the car in reverse was not an accident. My stomach lurched from both fear and the effects of the motion at the speed we were traveling. I get car sick if I can't see where I'm going.

"There." Gravel made plinking sounds against the car's underside when she hit the brakes, and we slid to a stop. "That's it." She nosed the car into a clearing barely big enough for it to fit. We had to stand on the edge of the dirt road to open the trunk. "We'll walk the rest of the way."

"We couldn't have done this closer to civilization?" I did not whine.

"Carry the cauldron. I'll get the rest." All business, Sylvana jammed a bundle of firewood into a medium-sized cauldron. Probably a number 3, as it looked like it would hold about two gallons of potion. It weighed a good twenty-five pounds and banged against my leg with every step. She shouldered her backpack, then pulled out a large thermos jug and a metal toolbox. "Get the trunk."

Leaving me to do so, she flicked on the penlight from her keychain and headed off down an unmarked trail. I banged the trunk lid hard enough for the clunk to echo off the surrounding trees and followed her into the living shadows of the forest before she left me behind.

Twigs cracked under our feet, leaves rustled in the puddle of darkness—all sounding louder than they should have. We walked along the downward-sloping trail for hours, or for less than ten minutes—seemed the same to me—before I felt the ground begin to change beneath my feet and heard the tinkling sound of water running over rocks.

"Watch your step." Sylvana's motherly warning grated a little. She hadn't been around nearly long enough to earn that spot in my life. Plus, based on our history, it was a safe bet if I ever found myself on the road to going astray, she would be the one twirling the baton and leading the parade.

We came out on a low precipice overlooking a narrow brook. The cauldron feet rang out against sedimentary stone, the sound echoing off the cliff rising across the water. I put a hand to my lower back, arched to work out the kinks while my mother used an athame to cast a circle of protection. When finished, she placed ceremonial candles to the north, south, east, and west, lighting them with her breath and her intention.

"You could at least get the fire going." Sylvana gestured toward the cauldron.

"With what? I don't have any matches."

I couldn't see her expression in the darkness, so I only had to imagine the way her eyes rolled when she said, "Aren't you the keeper of the sacred flame?"

"Oh," I said, but I meant duh.

"Honestly, Lexi."

I fired up—both literally and figuratively—kindling balefire in my cupped palm. "Hey, no thanks to you. I spent most of my life without magic. Sue me if I haven't had time to adjust to all of the perks."

Responding to my mood, the balefire flickered green for a moment before settling into a more normal hue.

"Wah, wah. You had no magic. I rotted in a prison cell. Cry me a river." Sylvana made a fair point. "We're here now, so let's just get on with this, okay?"

I sighed and jammed my hands in my pockets. "Sorry." Sometimes, I wondered if we'd ever get past our past. "What do you want me to do?"

She pointed toward the thermos jug. "That goes in first, and make sure you don't get any on you."

Dutifully, I popped the cover and poured. And then, I gagged, and my eyes watered. "What is this? Essence of puke mixed with septic tank sludge?"

"Something like that." She wasn't giving details, and I really didn't want to know. In fact, the less she explained about black magic, the better.

Balefire-driven, the sludge in the cauldron began to boil before I finished pouring. Bubbles rose to the top, burst to release foul steam. I backed away and checked the vial in my pocket. After a thorough examination, aunt Mag had filed the piece of Diana's card on a shelf in the sanctum. Of course, she wouldn't be pleased if she ever found it gone, but I figured if the spell worked for finding my father, maybe it would work for finding Diana Diamond as well. Two birds, one potion. Or something like that.

Sylvana opened her pack and tossed more ingredients into the stench-laden cauldron with a flair that would have made her millions as a cooking show host. The two tongues of fowl flame sparked and sizzled as they slid below the surface. The brew turned from a dull brown to a pale green. So far, nothing appeared poised to stain my soul with blackness.

Relieved, I took a deep breath and let it out on a sigh. It felt good to relax, so I took another as my mother added the next ingredient.

The tear of regret gathered at the lip of the vial, glittering in the firelight as it fell. The potion swallowed the drop, the surface roiling as if there might be something hungry lingering beneath.

"I don't see what all the fuss was about." I gestured toward the steaming cauldron.

Sylvana grabbed my hand before I could snatch it back. Then, quicker than I'd ever seen her move, she pulled out a penknife, slashed it across my palm, and while I stood in shocked silence, did the same to hers.

"Ow," I winced, and as slapped her cut palm against mine, hovered our clasped hands over the cauldron and squeezed. Our blood mixed together. Hers to mine. Mother to daughter. Witch to witch.

"Whatever happens next, remember who you are."

Chanting ancient words with a deep intonation, Sylvana tipped our hands to let three drops fall, one after the other.

As the first one hissed into the potion, the balefire flared blood-red to match the crimson offering.

I was named for the sacred flame, and I am its keeper. The witch feeds the flame, and the flame feeds the witch, or to be specific, the flame feeds all of witch-kind. My job shouldn't be taken lightly, and I don't. It didn't occur to me that using the Balefire to monkey around with black magic might have far-reaching consequences until the third drop fell and the fire turned black.

But when I felt the draw of the magic we'd wrought, I didn't care anymore.

Deep and rich and powerfully strong, it showed itself to me in a heady rush of temptation. I laughed.

Okay, now that I'm thinking back on it, I cackled. I'm not proud of that, but at the time, I didn't care.

Nothing mattered except for the sheer force of power within my grasp. To touch it, to take it in, would feel better than sex. It wanted to fill me until magic wasn't just something I could do. I could become magic; let it take me over. Take me under, really.

Every blade of grass, every leaf that swayed in the breeze would live or die at my command. I could end them all if that was my will. I could end Diana Diamond with a whisper of power. End her, and return to the source. Bathe my final thoughts in the black flames, and let them burn me to ash. All I had to do was open the door and let it in.

I wanted to open the door, to throw it wide, and take the power shrouded in the type of darkness that blackened souls. I'd waited so long for my birthright; why shouldn't I jump at the chance to have every ounce of the magic I'd been owed for all those wasted years? Black or white. It all amounted to the same thing—control. Control of my own fate. If I gave myself to the power, I could control my own destiny.

Take the magic, said the voice in my head. *Who deserves it more than you? Feed yourself to the flame and be reborn.*

Seduced, I reached toward the dark fire that wanted me like nothing and no one ever had.

"Lexi!" Screamed the voice of the goddess who also lived in my skin. She was no witch, I thought. What did she know of arcane power? I ignored her, hunkered down, and put my hand out to the flame.

"Lexi Balefire, I'll slap you into the middle of next week if you don't get hold of yourself," said the voice in my head.

I'm half witch and half goddess, and I've worked hard to reconcile my pieces and parts into a cohesive, mentally balanced whole. But every so often, I have a moment of duality, and this one saved me.

Distracted, I batted at the equivalent of the mosquito buzzing in my head, and that was enough to clear away the miasma, to pull me back to myself enough to realize what I had been about to do.

Frantic, I looked for Sylvana. She was the one with all the experience, the one who was supposed to be in charge of the spell, the one who should never have let things go this far.

Her face set in both ecstasy and pain—a mirror of what I imagined mine had been only seconds before—my mother crouched beside the cauldron, her hand mere inches from the dark flame. There wasn't time to get to her, to dig through her pockets for the locket my father had given her—the locket she'd planned to use as the focus for the spell.

Instead, I reached for the only thing in my possession that had belonged to him.

Yes, I realize how colossally stupid it would have been to apply dark magic to the Bow of Destiny. But, at the time, I wasn't thinking that clearly. Or half of me wasn't, anyway. My inner goddess fought me like a wildcat as soon as my hand touched the stave.

Have you ever seen anyone walk into a cobweb and freak out? Then I'm sure you can imagine the tussle I had with myself as my mother drew closer to utter destruction. In the end, the goddess won, but I came out with something, too. Cupid's compass reverted to necklace form when I snatched it from the bow. It flipped end over end as it fell into the cauldron along with the shred of one of Diana Diamond's playing cards.

Breath whistled in my nose as I inhaled, and then the world turned to heat and strobe-like flashes, and then to darkness. Or that's how I remember it, anyway: a flare of black flame, then something boomed like a cannon going off. I think it was probably the cauldron cracking in half. Then a shock of white light that hurt my eyes, and my mother's body flying past me, limp as a rag doll. The thump when she hit the ground. The buzz in my ears and the feel of damp soil against my cheek.

Somewhere in there, I could swear I saw my mother's eyes go black, but once I dragged myself up and wobbled over to check on her, she opened them, and they were the same color as my own.

"Don't move," I held her down when she tried to rise. "I think you slammed into that tree. I need to make sure you haven't broken anything." Seemed likely since I'd found her crumpled at the base of it.

"I'm fine." Sylvana batted my hands away but groaned a bit as she pushed up to sit with her back against the rough bark. Her hands went to the locket she still wore. "What happened? Did it work?"

What was it about Cupid that kept her spinning and pining for him? He must have a really big...personality to engender such devotion. The more my mother wanted him, the less I wanted to meet my father. I'm not sure what that says about me.

Because I needed a minute myself, I settled down beside her and surveyed the aftermath of the spell. "I have no idea."

Surrounded by a puddle of spilled and stinking potion, the balefire burned green again—a sure sign it wasn't happy with me. Hey, some people get to wear mood rings; I live with a moody fire. Welcome to my world.

"You could have warned me," I said in the sullen voice of the bitterly betrayed. "What sort of temptation I'd be up against."

"I did tell you to remember who you were." Sylvana brushed off my concerns with a wave of her hand. "It's different for everyone, and I figured your upright morals would carry you through."

Coming from her, that was an insult.

"Jeez, Mom, tell me what you really think of me."

To my surprise, she grinned. "I like it when you call me Mom."

"I'd probably do it more often if you acted like one," I muttered and wiped the grin off her face.

Excuse me, but I get cranky when she talks me into doing things that might end in disaster, and this certainly qualified. "Do you have any idea how close I came to turning wicked just now?"

I'd grown up thinking the witches in my family were all wicked, and I'd probably end up the same. To be fair, I hadn't had the entire story, but still, when it looks like your grandmother killed your mother during a magical duel and got turned to stone as a punishment, assuming you come from wickedness isn't that big of a leap.

I felt my mom's shoulder shrug against mine since we sat side by side. "Never happen," she said. "You're made of goodness and light."

If there'd been the least hint of snark in her tone, I

might have been tempted to give her a demonstration to prove her wrong, but her sincerity disarmed me.

"Your father's doing, not mine."

"I'll be sure to thank him when I see him." My tone carried the counterpoint to her sincerity, and since I didn't want to go any farther down that conversational path, I rose and went to take a look at the aftermath of the spell.

I found the compass hanging from a branch, the light from the fire glinting off the glass as it spun in the gentle breeze.

"Then again," Sylvana squatted next to the remains of the cauldron, tapped the cast iron with her index finger, then leaned forward to sniff the puddle of brew. "You might have more darkness in you than I thought."

My heart lurched, then went into double-time. "What do you mean?"

"Your blood is the only unknown ingredient that went into the brew."

"So, this was my fault?" I gestured at the destruction around us. "Could it have been the compass?"

Sylvana shook her head. "No. Only something truly dark could have caused a reaction like that."

Like Diana's card.

I opened my mouth to tell her what I had done but closed it again without speaking. Let her think whatever she wanted. We'd both come out of the experience in one piece. Maybe she'd leave me out of her next crazy scheme.

Except this crazy scheme wasn't even over yet. When

Sylvana reached for the compass, I tucked it under my shirt and insisted we clean up the mess we'd made.

"The cauldron is just iron. It'll rust away eventually," she argued.

"I am a witch, and I was raised by an earth faerie. I don't litter." Couldn't if I wanted to because if Terra found out, she'd probably curse my underwear to give me a perpetual wedgie. Nobody needs that in their life.

"At least give me the compass to hold. I can look at it while you hug trees and commune with mother earth."

"Fine." I pulled the chain over my head, winced when some of my hair caught in the links, and pulled. "Take it."

Out of the corner of my eye, I watched her grip the compass tightly and close her eyes while infusing it with her desire. My mom might tease me about communing with the earth, but I'd learned a trick or two from Terra since I'd earned my magic, and it only took a minute of focus and a hint of power to send the cauldron deep below the earth where it would, as Sylvana had pointed out, rust and return to the elements. Then, I stowed everything else in the toolbox and picked up my pack.

"Anything?" I asked.

She shook her head, handed me the compass, and took the toolbox. Then, stiff-backed, she went on ahead of me up the trail, stowed the box in the trunk, and drove in icy silence back toward the city. When the streetlights made it possible, I pulled out the compass and cupped it in my palm.

"How is this supposed to work?"

"You tell me," Sylvana snapped. "The compass is your thing, not mine. The locket would have worked like a pendulum, but you decided not to use it."

"Excuse me for being too distracted to consider every tiny detail while I was saving us from turning into evil hags." I put the compass in my pocket. Given the spectacular backlash from using the shard of Diana's card, I'd be lucky if I hadn't ruined it entirely.

My mother mumbled something under her breath that I didn't even attempt to decipher, then drove off after booting me unceremoniously out of the car, without so much as a 'good night.'

CHAPTER
TWELVE

Kin found me, fifteen minutes late for our dinner reservation, covered in musty book dust in the sanctum behind the Balefire hearth. The second I walked in, the room had shifted to accommodate my personal tastes. Lately, with all the witches coming in and out, it seemed to be having some sort of identity crisis and would rearrange itself for seemingly no reason at all.

For me, there were far more book-lined shelves than what appeared for the rest of my family. I'm sure by now you know the reason; falling down on the job, blah, blah, blah. The area for potion making took up half the space it did for Aunt Mag, though in all fairness, that was more encouraging than it sounds.

I wasn't a complete null when it came to alchemy, but divination was the only one of my skills that felt particularly intrinsic. To that end, there was a tidy little nook with an uncommonly clear quartz crystal ball and several decks of tarot cards. Having watched Diana wield hers, those had been left untouched by me.

Earlier, I'd spent a solid hour staring into the crystal, concentrating on Nadia Hale and hoping for some kind of miracle that would illuminate which of her two paths would be the best choice.

Whether because I didn't actually *want* to make choices for her—I'm far more comfortable with simply setting the universe's plan in motion—or for some other reason, I'd come up with bubkus and had instead taken to the stacks.

"Did you forget about me?" Kin asked when he'd entered and enveloped me in a heavenly, musky-scented embrace that made me feel all the grimier. He planted his lips on mine, and like always, I felt the rest of the world fall away. When I finally pulled back to earth, I let out a gasp.

"We had a date! I'm so sorry. I have this deeply unsettling situation with a potential client, and there's been more drama with Sylvana. I came in here to do some research and completely lose track of time." It wasn't not like me, and I felt terrible. Kin was always getting the short end of the stick.

As usual, he took it like a champ. I've often wondered how I'd gotten so lucky as to bag a guy like Kin, but for some reason, this time, the notion made me sad instead of happy. "I'll go upstairs and change right now. Just give me fifteen minutes."

"Why don't, instead, you sit down and tell me about your client and the drama. We'll order in and go back to my place for a movie. Sound good?"

"It sounds like you're the best boyfriend in the world,"

I said, kissing him enthusiastically once more before sinking onto the ancient settee that had helpfully scuttled up behind us. Evidently, even the furniture thought I ought to keep scouring the ancient volumes, or perhaps it just knew I needed to take a load off.

Kin rubbed his thumb in circles against my aching arches, and I would have purred if I hadn't been intent on explaining why I was knee-deep in the mythology section, looking for clues about the intricacies of my father's powers.

"I thought I was done being thrown off by my magic, but this chick is really getting to me," I said miserably, running my fingers through my already tangled hair. I probably looked a sight.

"Two soul mates is a conundrum," I explained, "but it's not entirely out of the realm of possibility. I've seen plenty of cases where, after the death of one spouse, the other finds true love with a new partner. That's different, though—the matches didn't exist at the same time. I can't wrap my head around it. Maybe it's some sort of glitch, or maybe I really am going insane."

"Or maybe," Kin hedged, "your father will be able to provide some clarity. Have you uncovered any valid leads?"

My nose crinkled, and I shook my head. "Why does everyone think Cupid is the answer to all questions like a real-life Magic 8-Ball? If he'd been any better at this than I am, Diana wouldn't have been able to escape her cage in the first place."

Kin raised one eyebrow while I ranted—a gesture meant to mildly chastise but, given how it made his lips curl into a suggestive little bow, rarely did anything more than distract me from whatever had elicited the diatribe in the first place.

"We're no closer to finding him than we've ever been, or Diana either for that matter. I'm starting to wonder if everyone's right—maybe she really is dead, and I'm chasing a ghost." It wasn't something I would have admitted to anyone other than Kin, mostly because I knew he wouldn't hold me to it and expect me to stop looking. I couldn't stop, wouldn't until I found either Diana or her rotting carcass and ensured she'd paid the price for what she'd done to Delta.

"Add it to the list of my failures. If only Delta were still here, maybe she'd know where to start. More likely, she'd say something cryptic and smart-assy, like *you already have what you need to locate Cupid, just look inside yourself for the answer.*"

I must have made another, even more pathetic face because Kin's eyebrow returned to its natural position and his mouth turned down into a sympathetic frown. "Maybe you do already have the answers." I shot him a glare for that one, my contrition waning and delivered a halfhearted kick to his midsection.

"If I have all the answers, maybe we don't need my deadbeat dad at all. Did anyone ever think of that?"

"I don't know why you're snapping at me," Kin said then, his voice taking on the mildly sulky whine that let me know I'd gone to the other side of crabby. "I'm on your side, you know."

I relented. "I do know. I'm sorry, and I love you for it. You're amazing, and I should be thanking my lucky stars I have you in my life."

Kin's lip began to quiver into a smile, though he made an effort not to crack completely.

"Without you, I'd be bereft—" I said with mock desperation, my hand fluttering to my forehead like a damsel in distress—"lost, an island unto myself—"

He cut me off, finally breaking, and covered my face with kisses in one of those moments you want to freeze frame and remember for the rest of your life.

"All right, my little comedian. Your crabbiness is forgiven. I know this has been difficult for you, and I want to give you everything you need." Kin shifted, his face serious again. "Just...don't forget about me. There are things I need as well."

I knew exactly what Kin was referring to, and my fingers immediately went to the diamond ring resting on my left hand. Kin knew what he wanted, and I'd promised to give it to him. Except, something made me stop short every time the conversation turned to setting a concrete date.

Don't get me wrong. I love Kin with all my heart, and ever since we shared the big TLK, I've wanted nothing more than to drag him down the aisle and lock him in before he comes to his senses and runs for the hills.

What's more, the ring he gave me well, let's just say it's spectacular. No, on second thought, spectacular isn't enough. It's by far the most perfect piece of jewelry I've ever laid eyes on: pave setting in silky rose gold with a princess-cut rock the size of a small glacier nestled in the center. Seriously swoon-worthy.

Not only is the ring absolutely to die for, but the way he popped the question could have been scripted into a romance movie. Really, you haven't heard this yet? I tell practically everyone I meet.

All right, if you really want to know. It was almost six months ago now, mere days after Diana's spell was broken and Kin's memories of our relationship were restored. Delta had just died, and I was like an old rubber band—stretched to the max and ready to snap at the tiniest provocation.

Of course, I was trying to keep that fact to myself. I'm not the kind of girl who usually wears her emotions on her sleeve. You try living with four elemental faeries who can't keep their feelings in check, allowing them to instead bleed out in the form of enormous fights that tend to require reshaping of the backyard down to the earth's core.

I'm the sensible one. I'm the one who calls forth her

inner goddess to take the reins so she can hide inside her sorrow. *Not anymore*, was what I told myself after that debacle, but there we were just a breath later, and all I could think about was escaping the pain of Delta's loss.

Kin, smart man that he is, decided to kill two birds with one stone. He could have gone to the faeries and asked them to help make a spectacle out of the proposal. He could have had us skimmed to Paris, to the top of the Eiffel Tower, or to Rome or Venice. Another man might have chosen to hire a skywriter or arranged for the question to appear on the big screen at a baseball game.

Not Kin, though. Kin knew, just as he knew the ring would make me swoon, that even though I love my designer shoes and abhor the idea of camping, I'm still a basic witch at my core. We'd had an audience for our unprecedented *two* True Love's Kisses, and so he correctly presumed that our engagement ought to be a private moment.

How he managed to keep it a secret is beyond me, though I've already admitted to having been unusually distracted, so perhaps I missed all the clues—and who knows what else besides. Anyway, that night Kin arranged for us to have dinner at a new rooftop restaurant I'd been dying to try, and that promised the best views of Port Harbor.

My beloved city is not what you'd call a sprawling metropolis, nor does it boast any skyscrapers worth mentioning in Architectural Digest. Mostly, it's full of historical buildings with lots of charm and a few taller ones that make for an impressive but understated skyline.

He did not put the ring in my drink or in my dessert, for which I was thankful. With my luck, I'd have ended up breaking a tooth. And he didn't go down on one knee. Instead, he took my hands across the table and disarmed me with simple words.

"I never thought my life was dull until I met you. Lexi Balefire, you are the fire in my soul, the color in my eye, and the music in my heart. I want to spend the rest of my life singing your song. Will you marry me?"

I could hardly breathe, but I know I said yes because the next thing I knew, I was wearing his ring.

"How'd I do?" Kin had asked when afterward, still floating on air, we reached the street level. The diamond twinkled in the light from the streetlamp overhead, and my cheeks hurt from smiling so hard. I'd leaned into him then, my hands wrapped around his arm and my head on his shoulder.

"Oh, you hit it out of the park. Absolute perfection. You must be a mind reader or something, Mackintosh Clark," I'd assured.

His smile had widened further. "No, just a good listener. I remembered you saying the city's lights were your stars, guiding you to where you needed to be. Luckily for me, they seemed to have been pointing in my direction tonight."

And there you have it, ladies and gentleman, the

perfect man. You can remind me I said that in twenty years when I'm still magicking his socks into the hamper, but for the time being, I can't think of anything better than that proposal.

Now, back in the sanctum, I refocused on his eager face and reiterated the promise I'd made that night. "I will give you everything you've ever wanted, Kin. Everything—marriage, babies, the whole shebang. Just give me a little bit more time, and then our life together can begin."

"Our life together already *has* begun, Lexi. We don't even have to have the fancy wedding if that's part of the problem. I'm not a golden carriage kind of guy. All I need is the words and the promise."

I looked at him like he'd gone bonkers. "Oh, right," I mocked. "Because we do so well with understated around here. The faeries throw a ticker-tape parade every Flag Day for crying out loud. And besides, I *want* the whole to-do. That's part of why I want to wait. So nothing is hanging over our heads."

Kin looked skeptical, but he shook his head as if he understood. "Why don't we dispense with the maudlin and find a movie that will make us laugh so hard we cry?"

Just then, I heard the door to the sanctum begin to creak open, so instead of answering, I kissed Kin soundly on the lips and skimmed us instantly around the block to his place. We landed on the sofa in the blessed quiet of his bachelor pad, and not for the first time did I envy him for being able to live alone.

CHAPTER
THIRTEEN

As it sometimes did when I elected to stay at Kin's place for the night, the Balefire invaded my dreams, leaving me with the comforting feeling of being bathed in its warmth and light. The safety and strength that flowed from me to the flame became magnified and then returned. All part of the symbiosis I enjoy as its keeper.

It wasn't always that way, and when Sylvana told me her tale of the young witch without enough magic to heal, she had no idea how much I sympathized. As much as she wanted to feel slighted and whine about having to live up to Clara's expectations, my mother got to enjoy the upbringing I always wanted. One steeped in the promise of the magic she would one day command.

Was I jealous? Yep. I can admit to that.

The dream pulled me in deeper, the crackle and hiss of the fire like a spate of words in a language I couldn't understand.

That was new. Usually, the Balefire communicated through changing colors to match its mood. This was the first time it had used sound as a means of communication.

"Talk to me," my dream self ordered as she settled cross-legged in the middle of the flames. "I'm listening."

Tongues of fire, white at the base shading to yellow, then orange, then red at the tips whirled around me in a twisting dance, tickled as they tasted me, gave me a sense of peace. I breathed into that feeling, let it carry my mind where it wished, let it bring memories that weren't my own.

They came in a rush, dragged me along with them at speed as they pulled me into a new reality.

I became the Balefire. I became the nascent spark kindled by a breath of power to smolder and smoke on the forked end of a long branch of sacred wood. I became the single tongue of hungry flame coursing over bark, singing as I went. Thrust into a tangle of fuel, I tasted. Devoured. Grew.

Magic filled me, and at first, it felt good. Powerful, strong, aware.

More, then more. I became engorged, pregnant with power. Painfully so.

At the peak of pain, a figure stepped near, drew off her dark cloak, and held hands out toward my warmth.

Inside the dream, inside the fire, I recognized a face like my own but was helpless to stop myself as I roared and took her.

She screamed, but not with pain, lifted her arms wide, and walked right into my center, bathing herself in the fire. Uncontrolled magical fury engulfed her, but she took it in, feeding on it and taming it as she did and sending it back in a smooth stream of energy.

I fed. She fed.

We became one.

Symbiotic.

Within the dream, the Balefire retreated, and I was just Lexi again, sitting within its circle.

"That was intense."

A flicker of blue shading to green was the response. I took it as agreement.

Feeling safe among the flames, I wasn't prepared for it when cold dread stole over me and began to grow.

Outside the ring of safety, I sensed rather than saw the shadowy, cloaked figure moving closer.

The dream popped, leaving me shaking and chilled.

"You okay?" Kin's voice was rough with sleep.

"I think so." I burrowed into his warmth, but it was a while before I slept again.

FOURTEEN

For all the ribbing I receive about not having mastered every one of the basic skills most witches my age have been practicing their whole lives, there are a few aspects of my power even Salem can't criticize.

I hold the household title for scrying, as determined by one of the more interesting family game nights held in the Balefire backyard. Combine that with my built-in LPS, and there was no hiding from me, particularly not within the Port Harbor city limits.

I'd been keeping tabs on Nadia Hale—you know, in between avoiding having to search for my dad and putting out faerie fires—waiting for an opening to run into her in an accidentally-on-purpose, movie-style meet-cute. I needed more information, and to get it, I'd have to get close to her. It wouldn't be easy, but I'd been up against worse odds.

When the mirror on my desk at FootSwept showed Nadia walking into Bliss, the best spa in town, my lips curled into a satisfied smile. How often do you get to write off a ridiculously pricey pamper package as a work expense? None of their treatments were speedy; after all, the point was to relax and let a team of estheticians and massage therapists shoo all your troubles away, so I had time on my side, plus a little something extra.

"Flix, I've gotta run. There's a thing I have to do—Mona's friend's case. Can you hold down the fort while I'm gone?"

He took a break from spinning in his barber's chair and pinned me with a glare. "Sure, Lexi," he said testily, "and you can count on me. When *I* say I'm going to do something, you can bet that something gets done!"

I wasn't sure at first what his problem was, but I suddenly—and a moment later than I should have—realized he'd been quiet all morning. Sulky, even, and I'd barely noticed. "Is this about Carl?" I asked, already knowing the answer.

"Ding ding ding, folks! She wins the prize!"

I rolled my eyes and picked up my purse. "I don't have time for this right now. I'm sorry. And I'm sorry I haven't talked sense into Carl yet. I'll get to it, I promise."

I wouldn't, but he didn't need to know that. I vowed to, as soon as possible, shunt this particular Best Woman task onto the faeries. It was their job to deal with crazed bride or groomzillas they could handle Carl and his ridiculous desires, and besides, I had an idea I just knew was going to work, I just needed to get Terra on board.

Flix grunted but didn't try to stop me from leaving,

and I hustled out the door without another word, pulling into a space in front of Bliss with scant moments to spare.

I'd matched the front desk manager with her partner, and as such, it took hardly any cajoling at all to secure a mani-pedi station right next to Nadia's. My cuticles were in dire need of attention anyway, and if all went well, I'd come out of there with pretty fingers and toes and some useful information about Nadia's special case.

Normally, I might have lingered near the entrance fountain to watch the koi fish flit back and forth beneath the surface of the water like a choreographed ballet. I might have even taken the time to feast my eyes upon the spectacular backside of Leonardo, the masseur, as he bent down to pick something up off the floor near the beverage bar.

Hey, I said feast my eyes, nothing more. I may be taken, but that doesn't mean I've gone blind.

Today, though, I didn't even spare a passing glance. Instead, I quickly approached the reception counter and checked myself in, making it just in time to get settled before Nadia, fresh from her previous treatment and blessedly bleary-eyed, entered the mani-pedi room.

I'd beaten her there, which granted my presence some validity. Trust me, the subterfuge was necessary. Uncomfortable clients can smell a coincidence a mile away, and I've found that one appears less conspicuous when one is happened upon as opposed to being the one doing the happening.

Prospective stalkers, please, follow me on social media for more helpful tips.

I pretended not to recognize my target, buried my head in an issue of People magazine, and waited for her to make the connection. Judging by how long it took for her to notice me, I concluded Nadia's previous treatment must have been with good old Leonardo from the lobby. She had that glazed-over, jelly-bones look about her, but eventually, she returned to herself and did a double-take.

"Lexi?" she asked, giving me the in I needed.

"Oh, hello. It's Nadia, right?" I asked as though I might have forgotten our somewhat bizarre lunch experience. If only she knew how entirely impossible that would have been; the vision of Nadia and her two soul mates, plus the memory of physical pain that came along with it, was still fresh. Truth be told, I wasn't looking forward to touching her again, but unfortunately, it was the main reason I'd come up with this whole clandestine-meeting scenario in the first place.

"How's it going?" I asked casually.

It's interesting how when people know what I do, they assume love is all I can talk about. Sometimes, like with Nadia, they jump to that conclusion with frog-like reflexes.

In her case, she hopped right down my throat when she snapped, "Still single. Still not in need of a matchmaker." She at least had the decency to blush a delicate shade of pink and look down somewhat contritely while adding a perfunctory, "no offense," but the damage had already been done.

If that's how she wanted to play it, fine. It would have been more fun for me had Nadia resembled our mutual friend in any way, but it seemed she and Mona had very little in common, particularly a sunny demeanor or a willingness to ask for help. Mona had felt no shame in coming to me, but Nadia was a total DIYer.

It didn't matter anyway. All I needed was a little skin-to-skin contact, not to become the woman's BFF. Granted, I had been looking forward to a little old-school match-making—the kind where I get to know and often even like the client before sending them on their way toward happily ever after.

"None taken. This is how I spend my days off," I replied breezily, reaching over to pat her on the arm and bracing for the flood of images to wash in front of my eyes.

The experience seemed to span days, but in reality, it lasted mere seconds—a short enough time Nadia didn't perceive my touch as lingering or decide I was a total nutjob.

Not that she'd have had any room to talk about being abnormal because, let me tell you, there was something seriously wonky going on with her: I'd just picked up a read on a tertiary match.

That's right, three separate possible soul mates. Apparently, Nadia was even more special than I'd initially thought. I'd never encountered anything like it in my time as a fate weaver, and certainly not prior to awakening my witch powers. Back then, it had just been my gut guiding me, and I'd never felt a pull toward anything other than a single match.

I'd also never been faced with making a choice for a client, and that's exactly what it felt like I was expected to do. If fate weaving meant violating Nadia's free will, this wasn't the gig for me. What if I picked wrong? All three of the matches felt the same kind of right, but it shouldn't be up to me to decide, and the visions only made things worse.

Perhaps you've been misled by my succinct and relatively panic-free retelling of the story, but when I dove into Nadia's future, it was one of the most excruciating sensations I've ever experienced.

Once it was over, I could no longer remember the pain, only the idea of it, so I guess that was a plus. What I did recall, however, were the images now seared permanently into my skull.

You probably think this is a no-brainer, and I could just take the easy route and go with the first random match I ran across, but everything in me screamed that would be a disservice not only to Nadia but to fate weaving itself.

While I reeled, the minutes had passed in a silence I wouldn't necessarily call companionable, but at least Nadia wasn't glaring daggers at me anymore. In fact, her irritated expression had completely softened, and her smile was friendly when she caught my eye.

"You wear heels all day, too?" she asked, nodding ruefully toward where our feet soaked in swirling tubs of gloriously hot, rose-scented water. Each revolution of the massaging jets ebbed away a scrap of the tension I'd been carrying in my arches and reminded me to put aside my concerns for my job and just listen to Nadia. Maybe she'd give me a shred of useful information.

"We should get hazard pay for walking around on those stilts," I agreed wholeheartedly with her unspoken statement that heels suck. "It's too bad I'm addicted to Manolo Blahnik."

Nadia surprised me by deadpanning, "We're both in the same shoes."

We chuckled simultaneously, and the tension finally dissipated.

"Sorry if I was rude earlier," Nadia apologized. "I'm not really in the market for a boyfriend right now. Dean and I just broke up and I'm already sick of all my friends trying to set me up on dates. Honestly, what happened to a mourning period anyway?"

She wasn't wrong, and I knew it from personal experience. I spent a few months being separated from Kin, believing it was the end of us, and there was no way I could have attempted to date another man during that time. Yet, I couldn't help but stare at Nadia as though she'd grown a second head.

Her statement that she wasn't in the market for a boyfriend right now contrasted so completely with what my intuition—and the blinding vision—was telling me. I took a sniff, tested the air to see if I'd missed something magical with regards to her lineage, but there wasn't so much as an inkling of supernatural coming off her.

"You're right," I replied to her rant. "It's your decision and yours alone whether or not to wade into the dating pool. Quite honestly, I wouldn't have taken you on as a client anyway. Not, at least, until you actually asked me to find you a match. I'm not in the business of chasing people down. Who has time for that?"

Me, actually. I had time for it, and in fact, it's what I spend most of my workday doing. Tracking people down. Followed by a little meddling in their love lives. They're happier for it, and usually, it was as easy as pie. Not today, though, and that was Nadia's fault, so I took some pleasure in the look on her face when she registered my somewhat snarky comment.

"Sorry. I just assumed."

I shrugged. "People do. Seriously, I could clear half a stadium by simply standing up and announcing what I do for a living. I'm used to it by now."

"I never thought of it that way," Nadia frowned. "But I get it. I really do." She held up both hands in a warding off gesture, shook her head. "My house is not for sale, and I'm not looking." Then she grinned. "That's what I get most of the time. If they haven't hauled out of the room like their pants were on fire."

It was a bonding moment that revealed a bit more about her standoffish ways.

"Sounds like you need more than a spa day. If you really want to blow off some steam, why don't you come to Driven on Friday? My fiancé will be playing, but it can be a girls' night. And, I promise I won't even point out a cute guy if one walks by. First glass of wine is on me."

"I'll think about it," Nadia smiled, tilted her head to assess my veracity. "It sounds fun, and I sure could use some of that."

"You and me both, sister."

We both settled back to let the heated foot bath do the rest of its job.

Heat and the weight of Kin's arm slung across my hip brought me slowly out of sleep. Well, that and the sandpaper tongue sliding along my cheek.

"Salem," I slit one eye open, tilted my head back slightly to bring his face into focus. "Lay off."

In response, he turned and flicked his tail in my face. An eloquent gesture, which he repeated until I finally groaned and dragged myself out of bed.

"I hate you."

Not true. Mostly.

But enough to take my sweet time getting dressed before I joined him in the hallway with one last, lingering look at the man in my bed. There are better ways to wake up in the morning than a cat kiss. I'm just saying.

"You're not supposed to be in the bedroom when Kin's here," I said. "You know the rules."

Between one step and the next, Salem's feline shape gave way to his human one. "I'm not supposed to sleep in the bedroom when Kin's here." Salem's voice was as silky smooth as the eggplant-colored shirt that billowed back from his muscular shoulders. "I didn't sleep there."

"It's too early to argue semantics. I need coffee."

When I moved to detour into the kitchen for some, he blocked the door.

"There's coffee in the workshop." Under a cocked brow, his blue eye dared me to argue while the green one glinted with amusement. I don't know how he does that, but I find it unnerving at times. "And your mother's already there."

"Great." I didn't remember making plans with her, but I followed him toward the fireplace, steeling myself as I reached into the flame to activate the handle that opened the secret door to the sanctum. I know the fire won't burn me, but a lifetime of conditioning takes a while to overcome.

"Get in here," Sylvana said when she saw me. "We're burning daylight."

"It's ten minutes after dawn." I'm not a morning person.

"It's after eight. Drink your coffee, eat your pancakes, and stop whining."

Pancakes?

"I wasn't whining," I mumbled, wondering why even a mother who hadn't been there for my formative years could bring out the rebellious child in me. "And the pancakes are probably cold by now."

Sylvana slapped her hands on her hips and gave me a

look that could wither dandelions. "You are a fire witch. Heat them up, for Hecate's sake, Lexi. Didn't those faeries teach you anything?"

She turned away, and I did not roll my eyes and make a face at her.

"I saw that."

Okay, maybe I did.

Two hours later, curled on the sofa with a stack of musty old books on the floor beside me, and Salem sprawled across my feet—which would have been more comfortable for me if he'd been in his feline form—I came across something interesting.

"You lied to me," I cast a glare at Sylvana.

"Not that I'm aware."

"Don't give me your innocent face, you lying liar." Heat rushed across my skin. "According to *Pembroke's Treatise on Tactical Potions*, I didn't have to poke that flame fowl in the backside. There were other ways to scare it awake."

It didn't help my mood when she smiled and nodded. "All of which would have been far less entertaining for me. But you wouldn't have fallen for it if you'd taken time to study your craft."

"Very funny, Mother."

"Anything useful in there?"

"Not so far," I said. "Do you think we're looking at this the wrong way? I mean, we've been looking for a tracking spell all this time. Should we have been looking for one to summon him instead?"

Sylvana frowned, and began to offer an automatic dismissal, then stopped and thought about it a bit more. In the end, she shook her head.

"Too dangerous and probably wouldn't work unless we found a way to reverse the spell that banished him. The whole thing could boomerang on us."

Spell that banished him? What was she talking about?

"Mom, there was no spell. He chose to walk away."

Balefire witches have an affinity with fire, but we don't actually shoot it out of our eyes. If we could, I'm pretty sure Sylvana's would have burned me to ash where I sat.

"I was there, Lexi. Your grandmother banished him." She paused, her eyes widening, then narrowing craftily. "Now that gives me an idea. If I cut off the power to her spell, he'll be able to come back on his own."

"Cut off the power? What does that even mean?" I blinked back the dire image forming in my mind. "I thought you were getting along better. You're not thinking of hurting your own mother?"

Salem had reverted to feline form at the beginning of the conversation. I glanced in his direction and then toward the exit. I had no problem using him to tattle if Sylvana decided to do something drastic.

"Un-bunch your panties. I'm only talking about

binding her powers for a minute. Just long enough to break the spell. Nothing major."

Nothing major, she said. Clara would not be amused. Someone would get hurt.

"You're out of your mind."

Sylvana ignored me while she pondered possible ingredients for a binding spell.

"I'd need a length of gallows rope. Not something you find just lying around the house."

"You'd need your head examined, and it wouldn't work because he walked away of his own accord."

"I'm sure that's what my mother told you, but I was there, Lexi, and I'm telling you he didn't."

"There was no spell. Your beloved walked away. I saw it happen."

"You were a baby. You couldn't possibly—"

"Yes, I could." Hadn't I told her the story of my trip back in time? "I thought I told you about this already, but I wasn't a baby when I saw it, and I can prove it."

I grabbed the book I'd been poring over, turned back a few pages to a spell I'd read earlier. All I needed was a bowl of water or, better yet, a large mirror. Something shiny to cast the spell against. Something shiny. I knew just the thing.

"Follow me."

Books scattered as I launched from my place on the sofa. I let them lay where they fell because I'd had an idea that might just rival one of Aunt Mag's impressive feats of magic. Passing through the sanctum, I gathered what I'd need for the spell, then led the way back up to my bedroom.

Sylvana said little with her mouth, letting the sardonic arch of her left brow do the talking while I set up candles, sprinkled some herbs, and inscribed a circle on the floor.

Ignoring her, I pulled a DVD out of my movie collection.

"Sorry, Ferris Bueler, you're getting sacrificed to the cause."

Magic welled inside me—something I hope I never take for granted—as I focused on the memory of my trip back in time, then rushed out to bind with the shiny plastic.

"Here goes nothing." I popped the DVD into the player, turned on the TV, and hoped for the best.

In white against a field of deep blue, the words A Balefire Production appeared. The spell—it seemed—had worked. I grinned until the theme music kicked in. You know the song, the one they played when the witch showed up in Wizard of Oz. Probably didn't bode well.

"Should we have popcorn?" Honeyed sarcasm dripped from her tone as the camera panned across treetops before zeroing in on a grassy clearing where two women stood off against each other.

"Get away from him." Sylvana's scream shot out of the

TV speaker, her voice sharp and edging toward hysterical. "You vicious old witch. Leave him alone."

White fire lanced from her fingertips, arrowed toward her mother's body. Clara batted the sizzling flame away with as much attention as she would have paid a fly buzzing around her ear.

I watched my mother watching herself as she threw a temper tantrum on screen. Her jaw clenched, but that was her only reaction.

My voice coming from the TV called my attention away from my mother.

Calm in the face of Sylvana's rage, Clara's attention remained focused on the man who was at the crux of this fight. Or, technically, the minor deity: Cupid. The one and only god of love who carried a bow and heart-tipped arrows but was as far from a winged cherub as a donkey is from a goose.

Chiseled perfection from head to toe, there was nothing baby soft about him. It was no wonder Sylvana had fallen for his...charms. She stared at him now, her face carefully blank but for the occasional twitch at the corner of her mouth.

I'm Lexi Balefire, daughter of Sylvana, granddaughter of Clara and Cupid? Well, he's my dad. I know; it shocked me, too, when I found out. And not in a good way.

Apparently, I would be the narrator for this little piece of cinema.

Oh, goodie.

CHAPTER

SIXTEEN

"Tell me what you really think," Sylvana said. The real one, not the one on the TV.

Even if I wanted to, I couldn't. Too many thoughts crowded each other for space in my head. Did my voice really sound like that? Would TV me say anything to tick my mother off? Why had I ever thought this was a good idea?

While the fight raged, I was the squealing infant tucked into a carry basket and left forgotten on the grass. Paradoxically, I also played the time-traveling interloper watching the biggest mystery of my past play out before stunned eyes.

This was the pivotal moment that would leave me virtually orphaned, send my mother to hell and my father to who-knows-where. In a few minutes, nothing would be left except a black scar on the ground, my grandmother's body turned to stone, and me, a crying infant who would grow up with the stigma of having hailed from wicked witches.

TV me said, "I wasn't sure I could watch, but I knew I couldn't look away." Talk about deja vu.

"She doesn't know what you did, does she?" Clara Balefire's wrath curled around Cupid like a living thing that might strangle him if she gave full reign to her temper. "Just how many lies *did* you have to tell to get my daughter to let you put a baby in her belly?"

More white fire arced from Sylvana's direction, to be deflected with a twitch of Clara's finger while my father's burning gaze rested on my grandmother.

"Of course, he told me. Didn't you, baby?" Sylvana purred at Cupid, then spat at her mother, "We don't keep secrets."

Cupid declined to comment, and even now, I could see the secrets in his eyes. I glanced over to see if current Sylvana saw them, too. If she did, she didn't let on.

"The child has promise. At the right time, I will teach her how to make the most of her gifts." His voice reminded me of a French horn, tenor with a deeper resonance underneath. His glance strayed toward the baby, and I had trouble wrapping my head around the fact that *she* was *me*.

"This one carries the potential to be the strongest of her kind. I would not allow her to take on that burden without guidance."

"How very noble of you." Clara's sneer turned the words to knives. "Do you even know her name? Or is she just a thing to you? Something to mold and shape."

Cupid's lack of interest deflected the cuts as surely as if he'd worn forged armor.

"You presume too much, Clara Balefire. I protect what's mine and Alexis," he placed emphasis on my name to prove a point, "is mine."

"Like you protected Beatrice and Reginald? Like you would have protected my sister if she'd been stupid enough to let you have your way with her? Alexis would be safer if she never realized that potential. You're willing to put a target on her back out of a sense of inflated ego."

The image on the screen whipsawed from the adult standoff back to the crying baby. Real Sylvana flinched. Maybe the motion made her sick, but I'd like to hope her reaction had to do with seeing the way she focused all her attention on her lover and ignored her infant daughter.

"He loves us." TV Sylvana leaped aside to avoid a spell that boomeranged back on her when Clara, without even looking in her direction, deflected the curse with a single finger. "We're going to make a family together, and we don't need you to be part of it. Just leave him alone and let us go."

"Did he tell you that in so many words?" Disdain put a sneer on Clara's face. "Did he tell you how he's been trying to bed a Balefire woman for centuries? First my mother, then my sister, and now my daughter, and who knows how many before that? And all to make a new and more powerful Fate Weaver."

TV Sylvana thought about it for half a second. Real Sylvana's mouth set in a grim line.

"Shut up, you old cow. You're wrong about him—he loves us, you'll see."

Old cow wasn't an accurate description of my grandmother, nor would I have dared to blithely show such disrespect to a family member. Then again, growing up without my true family had given me a different perspective on its sacred nature.

Watching it all play out again, this time with a bit more perspective on the players, I couldn't help seeing certain similarities between the fighting women. And I didn't mean only in the looks department.

There's a certain expression both women can claim when they're stubbornly clinging to the notion that they are right. I wouldn't be surprised if I carried the same one for the same reason at times.

Eyes trained on my father, Clara slammed a barrier to close TV Sylvana out of the conversation. Real Sylvana leaned forward to hear what she hadn't on that fateful day.

"Are you even capable of love?" Clara asked.

Cupid turned his head, showing only the curve of one cheek half covered by the edge of the Bow of Destiny. All gold and shining, the weapon's string chimed soft notes against the light breeze.

"Love is my business."

Next to me, Sylvana's body stiffened when he skirted the question she hadn't heard that day when everything went to hell; no handbasket needed.

The bow looked like a liquid blur practically leaping into Cupid's hand, the strings screaming a tune of willingness.

I flinched when the compass around TV Lexi's neck erupted into sound.

Dark was the bowsong, with honed edges that cut and sliced. The compass played a series of discordant notes that grated across my nervous system.

Cupid bore the brunt of the onslaught coming directly off the weapon in his hand but ignored the warning. Ultimately, the Bow of Destiny is still a weapon and one that my father appeared ready to use on my grandmother with deadly intention.

"No, don't." Real Sylvana said.

On-screen, Clara heard no bowsong. Neither did Sylvana. Maybe if either woman had, things would have turned out differently.

"My daughter's happiness is mine." Fast as a striking snake, Clara crossed the space and, before my father realized her intent, snatched the bow from him, fitted arrow to string, and took aim. "If your will is what makes this thing work, then my own should remove the blinders and help her see her way clear."

She dropped the barrier and dodged as my father made a grab for her.

Silence fell like a stone when the arrow flew straight and true on a course for Sylvana's heart.

Faster than a human can move, my father covered the

distance between himself and Sylvana. Clara's arrow slammed into his backside with a solid sound that made real Sylvana gasp.

Clara's triumphant shout ended in a roar of, "Nooo."

The force of the blow slammed my dad into my mom, and she hit the ground hard enough to be stunned. Staggering and struggling to regain his footing, Cupid yanked the arrow out of his flesh.

"Stupid witch. Do you have any idea what you've done to me?" He grabbed the bow from Clara and then tossed it away as if the bright gold had turned to searing flame. Whether it burned or not, the bow did something to Cupid he hadn't expected. His face altered from robust perfection to a haunted pallor so quickly it reminded me of watching a movie on fast forward.

By the time he turned and walked away without so much as a backward glance at Sylvana, my father had become a shadow of his former self.

If you asked me, he'd earned his fate.

"He would have killed her." I kept my voice neutral as I hit pause on the recording. "Is that what you remember? Is that what you wanted?"

Wicked fury twisted my mother's features, the expression flashing so briefly I later wondered if I had imagined it.

"Play it out."

I didn't imagine the twitch of her eyelid as Sylvana

turned back to the TV and made an impatient gesture with one hand. I hit play.

"Look what you did." TV Sylvana practically levitated off the ground, fury oozing from every pore, hands twisting to form dark magic.

Black fire ate daylight and grew between her palms to a crackling mass so large she could barely hold it. The green in her eyes flickered to black and then back to green.

TV me sprang into action. You could tell by the dizzying shift of perspective.

"Stop. You have to stop this right now. Look what you're about to do to each other. Look what you're about to do to *me*!" My narrator voice went raw with effort.

The moment drew out long and pregnant with magic I could feel even now. Sylvana railed and cursed Clara with every filthy name she could pull to her lips.

"Think what you like. I only want you to be happy."

Clara's quiet statement hit the two Sylvanas with very different results. The one sitting next to me let out a small sound that might have been a sob while TV Sylvana went over to the dark side.

Everything after that happened at high speed.

Sylvana let the seething magic go with all the force she could muster. Clara spoke a few short words, her reaction a half-second too late.

The Bow of Destiny went up in a cloud of smoke. Knowing where it ended up, I assumed my grandmother had wasted precious seconds ensuring my father's legacy would remain safe.

"Ligabis, Ostium, Carcere." Clara's second spell rippled through the air and turned to a set of shadowy ropes. A binding spell.

Halfway between the two women, Sylvana's crackling, ebony flame crossed with Clara's spell and mingled.

Sylvana's witchfire absorbed the binding spell and hit Clara, who tried to throw up a shield but failed. Face fierce, hair floating on the breeze created by the force of Sylvana's intent, I watched the spell bust through the feeble beginnings of a barrier and turn my grandmother to stone. Inch by painful inch.

Sylvana's moment of glee quickly turned sour when the evil she'd sent out bounced off the feet of the stone effigy and returned to her before she had time to duck. A flash, a sizzle, the scent of ozone, and a scorch mark on the earth marked the end of the show.

The credits played against the soundtrack of a crying baby.

"She put a spell on the bow," Sylvana said even though the evidence to the contrary had played out in clear detail.

"She didn't because it wouldn't take. Trust me on this one, I've been carrying the thing for months now, and I know. It's not possible, and even if it were, she'd have meant the spell for you. Your mother never wanted you to walk away from her."

Ignoring the most logical explanation, Sylvana snatched the remote from me, reversed the DVD, and watched the scene again. And again, and again until I finally left her there. Maybe with enough repetition, she'd see the truth.

When I later returned, I discovered she'd left without saying goodbye.

CHAPTER
SEVENTEEN

The only thing marking the transition from our world into the neutral area called the Fringe, where many worlds touch one another, is a built-up line of dead leaves, pebbles, and other debris bisecting a narrow alley in downtown Port Harbor.

You have to know it's there and cross with intention, or else someone might stumble in there accidentally and never find their way back. Or worse, they would and tell everyone what they'd seen.

There's a horror writer from my neck of the woods who, if you ask me, certainly writes like he's crossed the line a time or two.

Before I stepped over, I double-checked my pack for the proper currency. Dollars and cents only bought certain things at Athena's, and I'd run out of one or two more sensitive potion ingredients. Besides my walled, my pack held a plastic container of toenail clippings, a small Ziplock bag with two of Salem's whiskers inside, and a coin purse carrying seventeen bottle caps. I should be fine.

Once on the other side, I took the scenic route to avoid the circus atmosphere lining the main street. That kind of thing is a lot of fun if you have plenty of time to kill, and I didn't.

"Hey, Athena, what's shaking?" I said to the proprietress as I swung through the front door. The interior of Athena's Attic defied all logic as well as the laws of spatial dimension by being many times larger than the exterior.

Gleaming mahogany shelves spiraled from floor to ceiling in a circular space at least fifty feet in diameter and three stories high. A complicated series of ladders suspended on rails allowed access to thousands of books on the third floor. Foot after shining foot of brass hardware sparkled as though freshly polished.

As usual, nothing was shaking. Athena wasn't the most talkative of elves. I picked out a few odds and ends while I was there, then asked, "Did the minotaur milk come in yet?"

"Half a shipment, but it's gonna cost you extra this time. Little problem in the extraction process."

Since I didn't want her to tell me any details whatsoever about the extraction process, I agreed to the bargain without haggling and handed over four bottle tops and two toenails. "Keep the change," I joked. Athena didn't see the humor.

"Hear anything weird lately?" Just about everyone who passed through the Fringe ended up at Athena's for one thing or another, and while she wasn't much of a talker, nothing got past her notice.

"All manner of things." My toenails went into a box

under the counter to be dried, pulverized, and sold as a powder to other witches who didn't care for the DIY option.

"No weird bird sightings?"

"Sold some burn balm to a rock troll last week. He wanted to know if it would work on a mountain dragon. Weird enough for you?"

The news gave me a little tingle. "What kind of fire burns dragons? Aren't they immune to fire?"

Athena shrugged. "One would think."

When she refused to elaborate, I took my bottle of milk, went home, and unexpectedly walked into a level three party-planning freakout.

Six hours before the event, the venue's manager had called to cancel when a broken plumbing pipe caused a flood.

They'd figure out something; they always did. As I headed over to stash the milk in the back of the fridge— we have a special shelf for inedible ingredients that require cooling—Terra noticed me.

"We missed you at breakfast."

"I had to go pick up something from Athena's. Thought I'd get an early start."

Soleil and Evian began to discuss whether anyone would notice if they popped over and used their collective magic to clear up the flood damage. "I can get rid of the water, and you could dry everything out. Bam, the party's back on."

There were several flaws in that plan, which Terra was required to point out. Before she did so, she said to me, "When all this is over, can we take a minute to talk?"

"Of course, is anything wrong?"

Her smile was for me, but her eyes were on her sisters. "No. It's nothing like that. We'll talk later."

As I turned to leave them to it, she called out, "Oh, and your plan for dealing with Carl is moving along perfectly."

At least that was one piece of good news.

CHAPTER

EIGHTEEN

After ten texts and two voice messages went unanswered by Sylvana, I turned to the one family member in my life who wouldn't bug me about my studies or heap more drama on my head.

"Hi, Gran." She looked up from pricing jars of salve meant to relieve the itch from bug bites. I picked up a jar and took a sniff. "That smells really nice. What's in it?"

"Tea tree oil, a couple drops of frankincense, some lavender for soothing, in a coconut oil and beeswax base. Quite a simple recipe, but effective." Priced, the last jar landed on the shelf, and my grandmother turned to me with open arms.

How did she know exactly what I needed?

And how did her embrace feel like a warm blanket, a cup of tea, and a good book all at once?

"Ah, I needed that." I let her hold me for a few extra moments, then pulled back to kiss her cheek.

"To what do I owe the pleasure?"

"Can't I just want to visit? Maybe look around the shop a little?"

Part antique shop, part apothecary, Balms and

Bygones reflected both sister's interests perfectly. Gleaming surfaces and jewel-toned bottles invited shoppers to browse through the entire store to keep from missing anything.

There's no fooling Clara Balefire. "What's wrong?"

"Nothing special. Just stuff with mom. We've been in a *two steps forward, two steps back* phase, and I'm worried we'll be stuck in this uncomfortable place forever."

If anyone could understand my situation, it would be Clara because she'd been there and done that for way longer than me.

She sighed. "Never tell your aunt I said this, but she's right. I spoiled your mother shamelessly. But under all that bravado—"

Mid-sentence, she trailed off as if listening to something only she could hear.

"Something's triggered the alarm at Shadow Hold." Rounding the counter, she flipped the open sign to closed, then yelled up the stairs to rally her sister. "I'm sorry, Lexi, I have to go right now. It's part of my duty."

"I understand. I'm going with you," I insisted. Too many dangerous objects resided in the confines of Shadow Hold for me to contemplate what might happen should the wrong person get their hands on any one of them.

Because it seemed the thing to do, I texted my mother to let her know we would be converging. Aunt Mag made it down the stairs, and as a threesome, we skimmed across space to land as close to the repository's outer entrance as possible.

My mother leaned negligently against a tree.

"What took you so long?"

The acerbic comment went ignored.

"The wards have been compromised." Eyes closed, Gran hovered her fingers an inch or two over the knot in the tree that triggered the doorway guarding the entrance to Shadow Hold. Whatever residual energy she sensed there put a look of foreboding on her face that gave me chills.

Aunt Mag stomped forward. "How bad is it?" She repeated Clara's actions, yanked her hands back, and rubbed them on her skirt as if to clean them, then answered her own question. "Bad as bad."

Coming from her, that was saying something.

"Dark magic. Black stuff. Lucky you checked before you touched it. I reckon it might have put you down." Mag flicked a glance at Sylvana.

My eyebrows shot up, and so did my pulse. "What do you mean by *down*."

Offering nothing but a stony silence, her lips in a straight line, Mag answered my question, and I shuddered to think what might have happened.

"Do, Sister Dear, make me out to be an idiot." Clara injected a wealth of scorn into her tone. "As if you're the only witch with an iota of talent in the family."

Family squabbles are the bane of my existence. Most

anything can set them off, and it always falls to me to diffuse the situation.

"Gran." Gently, I appealed to the sister most likely to achieve calm first. "I don't think Aunt Mag considers you inferior. She just has a weird way of showing concern, is all." I gave the witch in question a quelling look and trod on her foot when her eyes lit, and she opened her mouth to protest. "If we all work together, I'm sure we can fix the damage."

During the entire exchange, my mother stood back from the rest of us, rolled her eyes several times, and sighed once or twice as if bored. Clearly, she was still mad at me. What else was new?

Between the cranky sisters and the petulant mother, it felt like the faerie wars all over again. I wanted to tell them all to grow up, but I'm not stupid enough to invite that sort of retaliation into my life. I mean, really, who needs chronic foot fungus? Not me, and I knew they could do worse if they wanted to.

A tense moment passed before the animosity ebbed away.

"Yes, you're right." As expected, my grandmother gave in first and with enough grace to allow a smile to play over her lips. "Shall we, Maggie?"

Still looking grim but no longer confrontational, Margaret Balefire set about doing what she did best— taking on dark magic. If I'd hoped to be included in the working, it only took a moment to realize that wasn't happening. Nor was my mother, but that seemed to be by her choice since she stayed far enough away to hear nothing of the hastily whispered debate between the sister witches over what was the best spell to handle the problem.

"What do you mean you don't have a mirror?" Clara's voice rose as she glanced down at the fanny pack her sister habitually wore. "You have every other damn thing in there."

"Excuse me for not powdering my nose every five minutes."

Despite their visual differences, a mere two years of true age separated the sisters, which accounted for the bickering and probably for Mag's acid tone. During my visit to the past, I'd seen Aunt Mag as she'd been before the unfortunate accident. Even then, she wasn't what you'd call a girly girl.

"I have one," I pulled a small compact out of my bag and handed it over. "Concealer is a necessity."

"You have a face like a baby's backside," Aunt Mag pointed out—without judgment, I might add. "What could you possibly need to conceal?"

"You get between two feuding faeries sometime; see if you don't end up with a pimple or two." That came out more defensive than I wanted. Being the pivot point between my blood relatives and my adopted family can sometimes be a delicate balancing act. I suppose every family has its thing, though.

"Just get on with it," Sylvana piped up, earning a hot look from her mother and a quelling one from me. Not that I didn't agree with the sentiment, but her tone wasn't helpful. We Balefires are not the most biddable of witches, but eventually, we do get the job done. If the knot carried the faint scent of burnt wood when the forest rearranged itself into the path to Shadow Hold, Clara had reset it to trigger a stronger warning should anyone try to mess with it again.

Grim-faced, she marched forward, leaving the rest of us following behind.

We arrived at the top of the gentle slope overlooking a cluster of cobblestone buildings with stained-glass windows. At a glance, nothing seemed amiss. I knew from experience the more dangerous artifacts rested in the round structure at the center of the compound, a series of shorter rectangular buildings circling it like the rays of the sun.

"You have a special pass, or a key, or something, right?" I came up beside my grandmother as she paused at the top of the hill. "I mean, we won't have to do the whole three-tests thing to get in, will we?"

My first visit to the hold ranked right up there with some of my more unpleasant memories.

"Hush, child." Clara lifted her face as if sniffing the air, then proceeded down the hill at a faster pace than before. By the time the path circled to where we could see the door had been blown right off its hinges, she'd broken into a run.

Torn between adjusting my own pace and hanging back to make sure Aunt Mag arrived safely, I made it to the clearing a few seconds behind Gran, and just in time to hear her let loose a string of curse words worthy of a sailor.

Or of her sister, who arrived a bit out of breath and repeated the performance with only slightly more panache.

"I'll need to call in the rest of the team, but first—" Clara pulled a dog whistle from her pocket and blew into it three times.

To my utter shock, a dog shimmered into view. A black dog with red eyes, no less.

"Is that a hellhound?"

Clara nodded. "Her name's Trixie."

Trixie looked like she'd been hit by a car as she limped toward my grandmother and let out a small whine of pain.

"The poor thing." The next shock of my day came when my mother surged forward and sank to the ground next to the injured dog. "She's been hurt." Sylvana petted the night-dark fur, sympathy evident on her face. Trixie licked her hand. Somehow, I'd have thought a hellhound's spit would be made of poison or something.

Aunt Mag's face mirrored my mother's. "Burns," she said. "They're deep, but the wounds are clean." Her motions were spare and clinical as she began to pull vials of this and that from her fanny pack. "I've got something that will help. Sylvana, can you hold her?"

Whatever they planned to do, I didn't want to watch. I joined Clara at the door where she stood, hands moving in an intricate series of gestures.

"Do you think it's safe to go in?"

Behind us, Trixie yelped once, then the whining stopped. I whipped around to check on her, thinking the worst had happened. Relief set in when I saw her whip of a tail slapping the ground. For a dog meant to strike terror into the hearts of mortals, she seemed fairly cuddly.

My grandmother finished testing the open doorway to Shadow Hold just as Mag and Sylvana joined us.

"Trixie?" she asked.

"Needs a bath, but she'll be fine." Aunt Mag began to repeat the same gestures Clara had just made, then stopped when her sister jammed an elbow in her ribs. "Ow!"

Having, apparently, deemed the entrance clear, Clara shot her nose in the air and stepped through the doorway, leaving Mag to grumble about shoddy treatment and thankless sisters. Loathe to step in front of her, I hung back. Lucky I did, too. Hearing a whistle from inside, Trixie nudged my aunt nearly off her feet as she shoved past, and if I hadn't been handy, the elder witch might have fallen and broken a hip.

Being wiser than I look, I refrained from pointing that

out to her, though. As I made sure she was steady again, my mother huffed and strode past us.

Shadow Hold objected to her presence.

Strongly.

Sylvana hit the doorway and stopped short as if the opening were made of glass. Her face bounced off the boundary three times before a flare of light shot through and blew her off her feet as if she were no more than a plastic bag caught in a breeze.

She rolled twice, landed on her back, and just laid there.

"Mom, are you all right?" I rushed over, falling to my knees at her side.

"I'm fine." The chilled fury in her voice shivered over my skin, teased goosebumps to taut, prickling life. I helped her up.

"I guess I'll stay out here and play lookout," she said. "You go ahead inside."

Her features schooled into an enigmatic mask, Aunt Mag watched the whole exchange without making one of her snarky comments. I'd have asked her about it if Gran hadn't poked her head back out to demand we hurry up.

I glanced back as I followed the elder witches inside, but Sylvana's smile looked genuine enough as she offered an encouraging nod. I let the trepidation I'd been feeling fall away. Shadow Hold was more than just a building. It was a building with spells on its spells and a repository of dangerous things.

Going in with Clara meant I didn't have to run the worthiness gauntlet, so I had that going for me as I followed her voice and a flickering, red light deeper into the hold. The flickering light turned out to be a pool of fire. Horrified, I watch Trixie skirt the edge.

"No!" I shouted. "You'll fall in."

Too late. Though, to be fair, she didn't fall so much as dive in. I turned my head and squeezed my eyes shut to avoid the carnage, only opening them a slit when I heard Aunt Mag snort out a laugh.

"Hellhound, hellfire," she pointed out the obvious affinity and made me feel like an idiot for not figuring it out for myself. "The fire will complete the healing."

Made sense, and she didn't point out this was information I would have learned in my studies, so a point for her for exercising discretion.

Trixie's fate no longer in jeopardy, I finally took a moment to get my bearings. This wasn't my first trip to Shadow Hold—or even my second, but Clara didn't know that, and things were always changing here.

In my haste, I hadn't really noticed the path of destruction leading off in the opposite direction of the hellfire pool. But then again, as part repository for dangerous things and part junk storage, the hold tended toward shambles on a good day.

This was not a good day.

"Oh, my," Clara repeated in a muted tone as she assessed the damage. "My goodness."

"What?" Mag tapped her cane against the floor. The sound echoed unnaturally loudly, a sure sign she hated being left in the dark. "What's been taken?"

Clara ignored her sister, continued to mutter, and climbed up on the high seat of an oversized throne made from bleached bones that sat in front of a tall shelf. The throne boasted a pair of human skulls as finials on the back of the seat. Absolutely shudder-worthy.

Stepping up on the arm of the monstrosity, Clara rose to the tips of her toes, stretched high to quest fingertips into dark recesses of a narrow cubby. I shuddered again as I pictured spiders or something worse lurking in the murky depths.

"It's gone."

"What's gone?"

"A length of gallows rope."

Did someone dump a bucket of ice water down my insides? No? Could have fooled me.

"What's it used for?" I didn't want my mother to be the one responsible for breaking into Shadow Hold. "And are you sure it was there before?"

Clara shot me a raised eyebrow over the fact I'd dared question her knowledge of the hold. "Your great-grand-mother cut that rope from the gallows at Salem after the first witch hanging. It can be used to bind a witch's magic."

"I carried a length of it in my former life," Aunt Mag said.

Clara's face was grave. "Devastating in the wrong hands."

"Aunt Mag knows a spell that might help us find out who was here."

A fact I was not supposed to know, and so, I got a dirty look from Mag this time.

"I mean, Aunt Mag knows so many spells. She must have one that would help."

"None of which will work here," Mag said. I detected the faint aroma of sour grapes.

We followed Clara deeper into the hold, helping set things to rights as we went. The magic humming in the air made the skin between my shoulder blades itch.

"Don't touch that," Clara ordered as her sister reached for a shallow brass bowl that had fallen. "It's a bleeding bowl."

"I can see that for myself, can't I?" Aunt Mag took offense. "You do remember I run an antique shop. I sold one that looked just like it last week."

Since the pair of them ran it together, the question was rhetorical.

"I sold it."

"Well, it was my stock." Aunt Mag didn't add the *so there*, but I heard it anyway. My question about the state of their relationship while sharing such close quarters had been duly answered during this little excursion, that was for sure.

"This one," Clara said as she pulled a pair of white

gloves from out of the air, "has a spell on it. Touch it with your bare hands, and you'll be leaving bloody prints on everything you touch for a month."

"Pshaw," Aunt Mag scoffed. "A month. That's nothing."

"A month because that's how long it will take you to bleed out and die." Clara picked up the bowl, sent it on a cushion of magic to nestle back on the high shelf from which it had fallen. Staring her sister down, she removed the gloves by pulling on one finger at a time, then used an extra flourish when she put them away again.

Mag snapped her mouth shut, once more proving she could exercise discretion when she wanted to.

"You and your self-appointed protector cronies can come back later and clean up. For now, just figure out what else, if anything, has been taken."

So much for discretion. Aunt Mag didn't entirely disagree with the need for putting dangerous items away, just on the definitions of what was and wasn't safe for witchly consumption. However, now was not the time to debate the merits of censorship, so I smoothed things over and got my grandmother moving again.

A minute or two later, the path of destruction abruptly ended at a stone plinth with a stand worked into the top. Whatever had been on the stand was gone.

"Looks like this might be ground zero," I said. "Any idea what was here before?"

"Yes. I know exactly what's missing." My grandmother turned to me, her face gone pale. "A branch."

"*The* branch?" Mag wanted to know.

Clara nodded.

"What was it doing here?"

"I put it away for safekeeping. Good thing I did, too. Can you imagine if it had been in the house during my unfortunate stoning?"

"Right," Mag waved her cane. "Because it wouldn't have been safe in the hidden room our mother designed while an actual Balefire lived in the house." She rolled her eyes.

"You couldn't think Lexi would have kept it any safer."

"What branch? I'd had enough of the verbal tennis match and that last crack seemed like an insult. "And you might remember I was the one who saved you from your unfortunate stoning."

"None of this is your fault, and I didn't mean to belittle your achievements." Clara took a calming breath then smiled at me.

She was wrong, though. No matter if it was Diana or my mother behind the break-in, I was the one who'd set them both free. Everything that had happened since— good, bad, or indifferent—was my fault. Gram must have seen the worry on my face because she came over to give me a one-armed hug.

"The missing branch is the one that was used to light the first Balefire."

"So, it's more of sentimental value?" I could only hope.

"Not exactly," Clara began, only to be interrupted by her sister.

"It's a branch from the Tree of Life."

Oh. That explained a lot. And nothing at all.

We three were quiet as we returned to the clearing where Sylvana waited. While we toured the hold, she hadn't sat idle.

"I got bored, so I fixed the door. You'll have to mount it, though, and cast your wards because I'm not in the mood to get magically hammered again." She never asked what we'd found inside, which did not bode well.

There were other ways of getting magically hammered. Maybe I could tease a bottle of Twinkleberry wine out of Terra. That stuff would loosen her tongue for sure.

NINETEEN

"Tropical," Terra said in a tone that suggested this was the final word on the subject.

Evian leaned back in her lawn chair and flicked an indolent finger, replacing the lush trees and brilliant flowers surrounding us with craggy fingers of blue and white. "Ice cave."

"Enchanting." For once, I detected no sarcasm in Sylvana's tone.

Not that her intent mattered because the faintest whiff of her approval brought out Terra's stubborn side.

"Tropical." The trees and flowers returned. This time with the addition of bright birds and a painted turtle perched on a rock.

"Ice cave." The decor switched again.

"More wine?" I held up a bottle of the Twinkleberry variety, made a show of refilling my own glass even though I hadn't actually taken a sip, and waited for my mother to hold out hers. If I had any hope of remembering any secrets I managed to pry out of her, I needed to abstain from the potent brew. Now was not the time to repeat past mistakes, and spending the next three days in a haze, committing crimes of embarrassment, was not on my to-do list.

Besides, with the decor flashing from green to blue around us, I already felt slightly woozy.

"How long will this go on?" Sylvana asked in a low tone.

I shrugged and then made the gentle suggestion. "Perhaps a compromise?"

Terra and Evian exchanged looks, and it was at that point I realized they'd been showing off more than engaging in a dispute. Evian winked at me, and Terra let a smile twitch at the corner of her mouth.

"Tropical ice cave it is."

Happy with her handiwork, Terra orchestrated the earth to create a granite basin with a ring of seats all around. When she was pleased with the shape, she gestured to Evian, who filled the tub with water so clear it magnified the glittering flecks embedded in the stone.

Finally getting a chance to contribute, Soleil leaned down and touched the water, heating it until it steamed gently.

"I can't stay," Vaeta said. "Some of us have work to do." She dipped a finger in the water and loosed a stream of her element, air, into it to set it bubbling. "Enjoy your night of debauchery."

"Who died and made you the morality police?"

I didn't catch which faerie muttered the question, and

I also didn't point out that police work required no death in the line of succession.

"An hour of R&R wouldn't hurt, would it?" I thought Vaeta looked a little worn around the edges. So did Terra, it seemed when she conjured a bottle of oil and poured a generous helping into the water. The top note of roses was soothing enough I couldn't wait to sink down into the bubbling depths and let the concoction take my cares away. Underneath that, I detected hints of lavender, comfrey, and basil.

"Just an hour, Vaeta. Surely, you can spare that much time." Always the earth mother, Terra wheedled her sister shamelessly. "We've hardly seen you lately."

Vaeta sniffed and closed her eyes in appreciation. "You know I can't resist a rosewater bath."

"Seemed the right choice for the evening, but you're free to leave if you feel you must."

"I suppose I could manage an hour."

Soleil caught my eye, gave me a wink as I set the wine bottle within easy reach, slid my legs, and then the rest of me into fragrant water heated to the perfect temperature.

Beside me, Sylvana's sigh echoed mine.

"Refill?"

"Don't mind if I do." My mother held out her glass, and with no shame whatsoever, I filled it almost to the brim.

Well into her third glass, I envied Sylvana for her ability to hold her magical liquor. I'd have been chasing imaginary butterflies by now. In the nude, and probably while singing show tunes. Laugh if you must, but I've been there, done that, and though I don't have the T-shirt, I do have humiliating video proof. Proof that cost Flix his favorite cell phone, which I hexed when he showed me the video. Unfortunately, he'd backed it up on the cloud, so the evidence of my shame lives on.

Even now, my face flushed at the memory, so I pulled my attention back to the conversation.

"You'd think Voldemort was on the loose with all the reports coming in lately," Vaeta said. "I feel like a pinball bouncing from place to place trying to keep up with the onslaught."

Vaeta had my attention as she described a series of seemingly unrelated incidents among the magical community. From a missing colony of honey pixies to a dead gnome, there didn't seem to be a discernible pattern. No wonder she looked like she could use a good night's sleep.

"Someone killed a gnome?" Terra snapped her fingers, produced another bottle of wine. Living primarily below the surface, gnomes fell under Terra's specific sphere of influence. "How?" She leaned forward, eager to hear.

"Not just any gnome. One of the crystal tribe. Slagged to death."

Shocked faces met that piece of news, though mine wasn't one of them. I'll confess to possessing limited knowledge of gnomes with absolutely no shame.

"What does that mean?" When they all stared at me, I elaborated. "I know slagged means melted, and I know gnomes are mostly made of stone. Or at least, of stone-like…stuff."

More stares.

"Excuse me for not knowing the technical term, but it sounds like you're saying something or someone melted a crystal gnome to death. What could even do a thing like that?"

Dark and full of foreboding was the tone when Soleil, mistress of fire, gave the answer. "Magical fire. It's the only way."

"Balefire type of magical?"

"That's one possibility," she admitted, her eyes going dark as cinders. The temperature of the water rose a degree or two.

"So, you're thinking a witch killed a gnome?"

"Not just any witch." Terra carefully avoided meeting my gaze. "Only one with more power than most and an affinity for fire could generate enough heat to do the deed."

That narrowed the list down to…um…me and the rest of my family. I knew I hadn't murdered a gnome, but I couldn't speak for the others.

"You don't think it was one of us, do you?"

I leaned sideways to get a closer look at Vaeta's face while keeping my mother in my peripheral line. What reason she'd have to kill a gnome was anyone's guess, but if she did, I wouldn't cover for her.

"Could have been a coven," Sylvana ran a damp hand over hair beginning to go unruly from the tub's steam. "Or even part of a coven if they were all in cahoots. Or a dragon." She squinted as if running through a mental list. "Phoenix, chimera, ifrit, hellhound." She swilled half a flute of wine, swallowed hard, then waved the glass in the air. "Probably take two hellhounds to generate enough heat, but still an option."

Vaeta nodded. "You do know your fire types. There haven't been any dragon sightings in the area for at least two decades, but we're still looking into the other possibilities. That's what I should be doing now, in fact."

"What about—" I cut myself off mid-sentence. Bringing up Diana Diamond wouldn't do me any favors, and she'd never used fire magic in the past. "Never mind."

Warm water sloshed as Sylvana abruptly turned to set her wine glass on the stone rim of the hot tub. So much for my ploy to get her drunk and wring information out of her.

Terra rubbed her hands together until a small ball of mud formed, which she slathered over Vaeta's face. "You just sit still and let the treatment do its work. You'll thank me later."

"Mother knows best." The cheeky quality of Vaeta's response was a testament to Terra's skills, so it didn't come off quite as tartly as it might otherwise have done.

"When you get everything settled, you might consider opening a spa."

I caught the flare of Terra's nostrils and the glance Evian flicked in her direction. Before I could ask what was up, Sylvana's elbow jabbed me repeatedly in the arm.

"Ow," I muttered and turned to see her vigorously rubbing at a welt on her palm. It looked like the ones I'd come home from school with on rope-climbing days in gym class."

"Sorry," she said. "I think I picked up a case of poison ivy."

The fae can't lie—except by omission, but my mother certainly could. She kept on rubbing, so I moved over a little to keep from being jabbed again.

An odd and uncomfortable silence fell over the group, which might have had to do with Sylvana's presence since none of the godmothers liked her, or from Vaeta's subtle disapproval of her sisters. She'd wanted them all to join the IMA and hadn't been happy when they'd all declined.

Whatever the reason, hot tub time ended early.

CHAPTER

TWENTY

Deranged witches? Sure. Psychotic half-goddesses bent on draining themselves of their humanity? Sounds fun. Wrangling wild eaflocks with only a toothpick for a weapon? All right, fine. Not something I'd sign up for unless the prize was a closet full of Christian Louboutins—or if it meant getting out of even worse plans. Like the ones I had tonight, with Kin.

It was finally time to cross a major milestone off our list. I'd tried to get out of it, of course, even blowing him off on one occasion, rather rudely, in fact. That was one of the reasons I'd rather poke my own eyes out with a soup spoon than meet Kin's parents. I figured they thought I was a total flake, and I really didn't want them to figure out they were absolutely right.

Except I knew it had to happen, and I couldn't put it off any longer. We were officially engaged, had been for months now, and Kin knew every member of my family probably far more intimately than he'd have liked, so I owed him. Plus, it was the normal thing to do. Whether I had any frame of reference for the word was up for debate, but it didn't much matter.

Kin insisted I was acting both childishly and unnecessarily neurotic. His mother couldn't wait to meet me, he said. She was a lovely woman, he said. His father was a teddy bear, and they were both overjoyed at the prospect of a wedding. It all sounded a little fishy if you asked me.

I'd hemmed and hawed, and finally, my otherwise perfectly lovely fiancé insinuated that if I didn't cooperate, there would be consequences. He probably meant I'd be watching HGTV with him for a solid month, but the notion he might retaliate by informing the godmothers of my recent extracurricular magical activities briefly crossed my mind.

No, Kin would never be that duplicitous...would he?

Either way, I had no choice but to agree to his terms, and that was how I came to be sitting—with uncharacteristically perfect posture, I might add—across from Cody and Caitlyn Clark at brunch that Sunday.

"Oh, no, thank you, I certainly don't need another mimosa," Kin's mother said, waving away the proffered flute of liquid gold. Part of me wanted to snatch it away from the waiter and chug it like a fraternity brother would, while another part insisted alcohol was not what I needed right now.

She'd already had two and probably didn't want to look like a lush in front of her son's fiancee, but even if she'd had six more mimosas and ended up dancing on the table, I still would have been more worried about her opinion of me than the other way around. Had I chosen the wrong top? Was it too low-cut? Did I look like a harlot? Did she think I wasn't good enough for Kin?

That was the real question, wasn't it?

Truthfully, Mrs. Clark had been perfectly nice. When we'd arrived at the restaurant, Kin's father had greeted me warmly, even enveloping me in a short, enthusiastic hug. His wife had hung back and extended a dainty hand, reserving her affection for her son. At him, she had positively beamed, with a look of such pure adoration it made me feel both envious and as though I were intruding on a private moment.

"It's been too long since we've seen you," she'd said to Kin. If I detected a hint of accusation directed toward me, it was well-concealed because he merely grinned and replied, "You'd say the same thing if I'd seen you yesterday, Ma," as he kissed her on the cheek. "I've been busy the last couple of weeks."

"Mmm," Caitlyn, as she'd insisted I call her even though I couldn't fathom actually doing so out loud, replied, her eyes sliding between the two of us as Kin gallantly pulled out my dining chair. She didn't miss a thing, that was for sure. Her eyes stayed trained on me throughout the entire meal while she put me through the politest third degree I've ever experienced.

"Yes, I'm originally from Port Harbor. I've lived in the same house all my life," was what I said, but what she hoped I meant was, *I'm not a traveling grifter with my sights set on your son.*

"Of course, I'd be thrilled to spend the holidays at your country cabin." *I'm not a selfish harpy who wants to tear him away from his family.*

"Yes, of course, my mother will be attending the wedding, as well as the aunts who raised me." I reluctantly repeated the rehearsed lie regarding my godmothers' identities. *She's not a recovering drug addict or an ex-con who just got done doing hard time. Not technically, anyway.*

They weren't all the same run-of-the-mill, getting-to-know-you questions, and I was grateful when Kin took possession of the gauntlet. "Mom," he said finally, the beginnings of an edge to his voice, "we'll discuss children once we've actually said our vows if that's all right with you. We're in no rush."

"You've known one another for only a year, Kin—that counts as a rush in my book."

My eyes widened, and Kin's eyebrow rose into an arch. "Mother," he said, a warning in his voice.

"All right, all right," she acquiesced, holding up her hands in surrender. It didn't escape my attention that the crease between her eyebrows didn't disappear. "You're doing things your own way. I shouldn't interfere."

If I'd thought about something besides my own feelings, or my work, or my mother, or my magic—my my my!—for even a fraction of a second, I might have seen things from Mrs. Clark's point of view. There was her son, getting engaged to a woman she'd never even met. It would have been more out of the ordinary had she *not* been skeptical.

She didn't want him to get hurt, and she didn't want to be left out of our plans. Both of which were entirely reasonable fears and concerns under the circumstances.

Only, at that moment, instead of reassuring Caitlyn Clark that family—including herself and Mr. Clark, of course—was of the utmost importance, I let my own fears and concerns get the best of me. During the rest of brunch, I barely spoke, which, let me tell you, didn't do anything to further ingratiate me to the woman and only served to make Kin feel slighted and unsupported. His father was the only one seemingly unaffected by the drop in temperature, and I envied him just a little bit for it.

Once they'd been deposited into their car and had driven off in the direction of the I-95, Kin turned to me with a question in his eyes. A question and something else, something I'd rarely seen color his face: anger. Anger at *me*. We'd been in arguments before, of course, but he'd never turned this stony, not ever.

"What was that?" he demanded, his voice clipped. "I know she likes to ask a lot of questions, but most of them were fairly reasonable, I thought, under the circumstances. Honestly, I knew you were nervous, but I never dreamed you really didn't want to meet my folks."

"It's not that I didn't want to meet them," I fired back indignantly. "It's just—you can't expect me to be completely comfortable; I've never done the *meet the parents* thing before, and it's a lot of pressure."

Kin scoffed, "You've met *people* before, though, right? I mean, come on; you spend half your day making small talk with clients, charming their pants off. Where was *that* Lexi?"

I could have told him the truth, that I didn't know and that I was sorry. But instead, I jumped straight to the defensive. "I'm sorry I'm such a disappointment," came my sarcastic reply, complete with eye roll and jutted hip. A couple of passing pedestrians had begun to peer curiously in our direction, but I refused to back down.

"You *were* a disappointment today," Kin fired back without remorse. His words stung, but not as much as what he said next: "The excuse that you didn't have your parents growing up is just that—an excuse, and it's wearing thin. At least my mother didn't try to have you killed at brunch."

It wasn't exactly what had happened, but Sylvana *had* nearly let Kin die during one of our trips to Shadow Hold. She'd also saved his life when Diana Diamond's Balmorrigan puppets tried to kill us both, so I'd thought he considered her even at this point.

"At least my mother doesn't want to meddle in our relationship!" came my tart reply. I must have sounded like a petulant child, and I'm surprised Kin didn't laugh in my face.

What he did instead was say, calmly, but with an acid

edge that set my teeth chattering, "At least my mother cares how I end up. She's worried about me, and today was supposed to set her mind at ease, not make things worse."

We stared at each other for a long moment. I hadn't expected brunch to go swimmingly, but I hadn't expected this, either. It was our first big fight since getting back together—our biggest fight ever, actually—and I couldn't control the emotions coursing through me.

"Maybe your mother's right then. Maybe we're rushing into this," I said. I didn't mean any of it, and I wanted Kin to reassure me, but I still couldn't swallow my pride even when he did.

"To hell with what my mother thinks, Lexi. She doesn't know what we've been through in the last year, does she? This was never about getting her approval for us to be together. That's something only we can decide. I want you. Now. If you don't feel the same way, we have a serious problem."

TWENTY-ONE

Kin dropped me off at home and didn't even attempt to come inside. He said he'd see me later that evening at Driven for his band's gig, but that right then he needed some time to cool off. Well, he wasn't the only one, and so I let him go without further argument but muttered to myself all the way up the walk.

By the time I made it to the kitchen, I was in full-on temper tantrum mode. My godmothers found me there, slamming drawers and yanking the refrigerator door nearly off its hinges as I made coffee and put a Pop-Tart in the toaster oven. Give me a break, I hadn't eaten much at brunch, and I have a weakness for the raspberry frosted.

The noise had roused the godmothers. How I don't know because they'd been making plenty of racket over in their wing of the house.

"What's wrong?" Terra hit the kitchen with Soleil close on her heels. Evian must have been watching Kaine for the day.

There wasn't time to answer before a mighty wind tore through the house, sending small items skittering and teasing dust from cracks that Terra's magic cleaning hadn't reached.

When it settled, my fourth godmother, air faerie Vaeta, and her demon boyfriend Rhys stood in the center of the parlor. His breath came in short gasps, and Vaeta's hair stuck up in every direction. She had a smear of blood across her face; rips and holes riddled her clothes. That she immediately took a seat on the sofa rather than magically cleaning herself up spoke volumes and left my stomach tied in knots. The rest of us followed her in from the kitchen.

"You're hurt," Terra said, her beautiful brow furrowed over eyes gone fae. In human form, she opted for brown over her natural hues of the pinks and blacks found in granite. She began checking her sister for wounds, but Vaeta shooed her away.

"It's nothing. I'm fine."

"We were coming in on an easterly zephyr when one of those toy drones came screaming out of nowhere. We dodged a bit too zealously, threw ourselves off course," Rhys explained. "And botched the landing."

"*You* botched a landing?" Terra seemed surprised.

Vaeta grimaced. "I was distracted. Let's just say my day has been a little odd. By the way, you might want to send an anonymous donation to the Presbyterian Church. Looks like they'll be needing a new steeple. You'll also need to call in Mag and Clara. It's best if we only have to tell the story once."

At least it was late enough in the morning we shouldn't be treated to the sight of Aunt Mag in her jammies. I removed the summoning coin from the box on the mantel, used it to call them, and when the elder witches arrived, decided the tie-dyed skirt in shades of yellow and pea green wasn't that much of an improvement.

"Odd how?" Soleil demanded, pacing the floor until little wisps of smoke began to roil around her feet. I placed a hand on her shoulder and flicked my eyes down to indicate I'd rather she not set the hardwoods ablaze, and she calmed slightly.

Vaeta shook her head, "We're not sure, exactly. That's why we were hoping to bend Mag's ear. Her expertise in supernatural beings is unparalleled." Mag brushed aside the compliment, but I caught the small smile that flickered across her lips. Flattery would get you everywhere with Margaret Balefire, whether she would admit it or not.

"Well, don't dilly dally around then, and explain what we're up against," Mag said, her tone gentler than her words. She settled herself on the armchair across from Vaeta, propped her feet on the ottoman, and looked back and forth between faerie and demon with a raised eyebrow.

Rhys was the one who launched into an explanation. "Yesterday afternoon, the IMA received a tip from a witch up in Yarmouth who witnessed some sort of light show.

Since we were in the general area already, Vaeta and I volunteered to follow the lead."

The Inter-Magical Alliance was an age-old organization of supernaturals that I'd had no idea even existed until recently. With a goal of keeping the balance between good and evil in check, they'd amassed the most comprehensive catalog of mystical beings and objects on earth. Though they'd prevented countless uprisings over the centuries, the IMA's true allegiance was still somewhat of a mystery. However, Rhys had proved himself to my family during a confrontation with a witch and her murderous companion, so if there was something we could do to repay his kindness, we'd rise to the occasion.

"We followed a trail of strong magic into a warren of caves off the coast of Nova Scotia and," Rhys continued gravely, "and found—" Vaeta shivered, something I'd never seen her do before. It sent a chill up my own spine.

"It was a winged horse," Vaeta said, her voice filled with sorrow. "His name was Windborne, and he'd been attacked. Someone tried to harvest his tail hair. It took most of the day to convince him we were trying to help, but not before he took a few swipes at us. He was one of the most beautiful, majestic creatures I've ever seen."

"I didn't know a pegasus was a real thing," I spoke my first thought out loud and received several looks of surprise in return.

Salem let out a sound that would have been a hiss if he hadn't been in his human form and launched into a lecture. "There's no such thing as *a* pegasus. Pegasus is a name referring to the winged horse that was the offspring of the god Poseidon. I see it's not only the study of your witch heritage that you've neglected to pursue."

I shot him a glare in return. "So sorry I've been wasting my time, you know, trying to save the world and everything. I haven't had much energy left for boning up on mythical creatures."

"You've completely missed the point, Lexi," Salem replied silkily, in that righteous tone of voice that made me want to scream but demanded I remain as calm as he did lest I lose the upper hand. Not that it really was mine to claim since he was partially right, but it would have taken a whole team of winged horses to pry that admission out of me.

"Enough, Salem," Mag said, stamping her cane on the ground to create a mini earthquake that rattled the pictures in their frames. "You've both missed the point. Winged horses are rare nowadays. They've been hunted nearly out of existence. I met Windborne decades ago, back when I was a young woman. He'd stumbled upon a patch of burdock and had dozens of the thorny seeds stuck in his mane. I helped him, and in return, he nipped a hair out of his tail and gifted it to me. *That's* the point. The tail hair of a winged horse can only be given—not taken."

"Did Windborne describe his attacker?" I hadn't noticed Terra leaving the room, but she must have because she returned from the kitchen with a platter of finger foods meant to tempt her sister into eating something.

Vaeta shook her head definitively no. "He was enjoying a night flight over the Rockies, just minding his own business when something landed on his back and went after his tail. He only saw it from the back and described it as a humanoid form wearing dark clothes."

Aunt Mag huffed out a breath. "That could be anything. I need more detail if I'm going to help you narrow down the list of possibles."

"That's about all we have," Rhys said. "Except that his attacker used a fire weapon or heated blade, which left a festering burn on his flank. We did the best we could for it, but I have concerns about how it will heal."

The new information elicited a shrug. "Doesn't narrow it down much. Give me a day. I'll go talk to him and let you know what I find out."

"I'll go with you," Clara said. I have some salve that should help with the burn if you can talk him into letting me use it."

"Thank you," Rhys said, rising from his seat with a wince of pain. "You have no idea how much time you just saved us. We'd have spent days slumped over dusty old books in the IMA library."

"All in a day's work." Aunt Mag seemed happy to be deemed useful. "Come on, Clarie. No time like the present, eh?"

"Not just yet," Clara put a restraining hand on her

sister's arm. "A lot of weird things have been happening lately. Someone broke into Shadow Hold the other day, and I had a call this morning that one of the solitary witches in town went missing at around the same time."

"You think those two things are related?" Vaeta tilted her head.

"Maybe. Maybe not. But if you could keep an eye out for her, I'd appreciate it." Proving she was no slouch in the magic department, Clara conjured a holographic likeness of the missing witch. It hovered in the air long enough for Rhys and Vaeta to memorize the woman's features.

"Will do."

"Appreciate it." Mag and Clara kept their goodbyes short and were gone within a minute.

Looking down at himself, Rhys wrinkled his nose. "What do you say, Vaeta? I could use a shower and maybe a nap."

"You can use mine if you want," I said while my mind offered up an image of Diana Diamond swooping down on a flying horse. In my head, Windborne sported a horn, but no one had to know that besides me.

"It's okay. There are three bathrooms in the new place. We can just head over there and get out of your way." Vaeta had no idea she'd dropped a bomb when she held out her hand to Terra. "You said you'd make me a key."

"Vaeta," Terra thundered. "Could you ever be bothered to think before you speak?"

"What key? What new place?" I might as well have been talking to the wind.

Vaeta puffed up. "You said you were going to tell her. How was I supposed to know she still didn't know? Isn't the day after tomorrow the big moving day?"

"What's going on?" It was as if they were talking in code. "Are you moving out?"

Thoroughly annoyed with her sisters, Vaeta said, "Mrs. Chatterly's moving into an assisted living facility, and Terra bought her place because she thought it would be a good idea if you and Kin had your own space now that you're engaged. There, was that so hard to say?"

"Stupid air-headed faerie." Stepping close to her sister, Soleil got in on the deal by wagging a finger in Vaeta's face. "Always running off at the mouth."

As if summoned—and perhaps she had been, via one of her seashell communication devices—Evian blinked into the parlor and stared at the scene going on around her. It was a familiar sight, actually; three faeries squared off against one another, glaring daggers.

In an attempt to cool things down, Evian's water element turned Soleil's fire into steam and fogged up the mirror that hung above the fireplace. The Balefire danced, though the air was heavy—as if it were enjoying the show. Perhaps it was; I never really have understood the sentient thing that lit up my hearth.

Soleil took offense at the assault, and the fight was on.

CHAPTER

TWENTY-TWO

There are two types of faerie fights—the kind that build over time like pressure inside a champagne bottle waiting for the cork to pop. You can see the bubbles forming, and with a little luck and a bit of foresight, you can control the explosion, even keep all the champagne from fountaining out of the bottle. Sometimes.

Then, there's the other kind. Those are the ones that hit without warning—like a meteor streaking out of the blue. A flash of light, a lot of noise, and the next thing you know, you're staring at a crater of destruction with almost no memory of how it all happened.

Since the first kind was rarer than hen's teeth, I almost always had to deal with the second type, and this one broke a land speed record on its way from zero to Armageddon. The faeries opened with a lightning round of elemental spells that included actual lightning inside the house.

When Rhys moved, I assumed, to get between Soleil and Evian, I grabbed his arm and yanked him out of the line of fire. Then, I dragged him to the floor just in time to avoid having his head caved in by the flailing hooves of a flying pig. Guess that phrase was out of my lexicon now.

"Stay down. It's safer," I warned him.

"How do you figure?" Rhys scuttled into the hallway and shook his foot to dislodge several ants with oversized heads and huge pincers from crawling up his pant leg.

I guess it wasn't safer after all. "Find higher ground. The stairs should work. I'll take care of this."

"Not by yourself."

Maybe he wanted to protect me, or maybe he wanted to maintain his masculine reputation, but when it came to wrangling angry faeries, he was a lightweight and a newbie. Even if he was a demon.

"I've got this. It's not my first time." Or my fifth or even my hundredth. "Just stay out of the way. It's for your own good. In fact, why don't you go take that shower? This could take a minute."

Hearing the slither, I turned to kick a polka-dotted snake—the pattern bearing a marked resemblance to one of our dish towels—back toward the kitchen where they'd apparently shifted the fight. Why did these things always have to happen in the kitchen?

A blast of humid air carried the cries of animals that didn't exist in our world, along with the fetid scent of decomposing plants down the hallway. Rhys wrinkled his nose.

"This would be your basic, otherworldly swamp-fest," I said as I checked for quicksand or worse. "Rates somewhere around a four point two on the faerie fighting scale."

"Only a four point two? What rates a ten?"

When a fire-breathing teapot with stork legs strutted out of the fray, I amended the rating to a respectable four point seven. "That's new."

Apparently, fire-breathing crockery rated higher on the demon scale because Rhys could no longer contain himself. I could almost smell the testosterone as he rose, shoved past me, kicked the teapot shattered bits, and put himself right in the center of four fury-spitting faeries.

"Ladies, this isn't—"

It could have been the air of condescension in his tone or the term he used that sent the godmothers over the edge, but whichever it was, they ramped the fight up to a solid six.

I figured I'd better stop it before someone conjured up a dragon, which would land us in the seven or eight range, depending on the breed. We'd hit a nine once when Evian turned the entire property into the equivalent of a giant fish tank, and the backyard volcano still rated a ten.

Anything above an eight could get us featured on the local six o'clock news. Ask me how I know.

I could, I figured, leave Rhys to his folly. Him stepping into the fray might alter the dynamic from a one-against-three situation with Vaeta's energies turned to defense rather than attack, to an *each faerie for herself* scenario.

He'd be safer that way, but the results would be the same, and I didn't think Rhys would fare well.

But I still have to live with myself, so I set my sights on the patio doors and made a wide circle around the tangle of vines twining down from the ceiling.

You live in my house, you learn a few things. My back-yard is full of pretty flowers, but you sniff them at your own risk unless you want to spend a week drooling rain-bow-colored spit—or worse. In this case, I figured I was looking at the or-worse option. The vine had eyes. Pretty ones with long lashes that fluttered at me coquettishly while a tendril quested in my direction. Very cute. Probably deadly.

Beyond the vines, the dining room table danced on stiletto-shod feet that delivered a solid kick to my shin when I tried to dodge past. I let out a howl that attracted Soleil's attention. Even in a fury, the Fae possess uncommon beauty. Her hair a tower of flame, her irises black as coal and rimmed with ember red, her skin so pale it glowed, Soleil flicked me a wink and a half-grin and burned the table to ash where it stood.

They're my godmothers; they're always looking out for me, even when they're the reason I need looking out for in the first place.

The air pressure went up a notch, made my ears pop as I reached for the handle of the sliding door, but I managed to pull it open just before a mighty gust slammed me up against the glass. Pinned there like a bug on a windshield, I could only watch helplessly as a minia-ture tornado barreled past.

On the plus side, they took the fight outside. On the minus, when the pressure eased, and I got a look at the kitchen, I didn't see Rhys anywhere. Conclusion. He was in the tornado. Great.

Well, he'd asked for it.

But I still had to save him.

One of the godmothers— I'm assuming Vaeta—had the presence of mind to throw up a dome to contain the chaos within the backyard. Only problem, I was on the outside of it.

"You know what?" I said to no one. "I'm over it."

For the first time since I was a kid, I decided to let them work it out on their own. It wasn't the moving out that bothered me. I could throw a rock and hit Mrs. Chatterly's house from my porch. Hadn't she spent my entire life watching us from between the drapes?

A change in our living arrangements was way past due, even if we had to do it backward compared to most families where the younger generation moves out, not the older.

It wouldn't be my family if we didn't do things the weird way.

Without Terra there to maintain it, the swamp dried up and fizzled, leaving only a layer of soil to clean. On my way to the closet where we kept the vacuum, I passed the polka-dotted dish towel. It twitched, and I stomped on it.

Twice.

Mostly because I was annoyed, but a little because… snake.

An hour later, just as I dumped the last dustpan of table ash into the trash, four filthy fairies and one worse-for-the-wear demon appeared outside the sliding door.

Terra grabbed the handle to find I'd locked it behind me.

"Open the door, Lexi," she said in a tone that threatened reprisal if I didn't. For the first time ever, I stared her down. She'd hidden things from me, and while I'd been busy lately, that was no excuse. "We'll clean it up."

Ignoring the offer, I demanded, "Are you finished? Kin bought me that teapot when he played a gig in New Orleans."

I stared her down through the glass, something I'd never done before. Hipshot, one brow arched, I held eye contact until she looked away. Something she'd never done before. "And you lied to me."

A lie of omission, but even so.

"We're done. Now, open the door."

I did, but not before pinning each faerie with a look. "Apologize to your sisters and to Rhys." If they wanted to act like children, they should expect to be treated like children. "All of you."

After sullen apologies all around, I unlocked the door, slid it open, and stepped aside to let them in.

"Wipe your feet. I've just finished cleaning up your mess."

Turning my back on the lot of them, I headed upstairs to shower and change.

"Our baby's all grown up," I heard Soleil say just before I passed out of earshot. "You know what this means, don't you?"

I didn't stick around to hear what it meant. Getting away with flouting Terra (so far, at least) gave me a case of the giddies.

TWENTY-THREE

ater that evening when I heard the text message notification on my phone ding three times in quick succession, I figured maybe it was Kin deciding to forgive me. I was right in the middle of trying on every top I owned and had nearly decided I might have to switch skirts and start all over from scratch.

"Hand me that," I demanded, my voice muffled as I pulled a lavender peasant blouse back over my head and tried to figure out what I could have possibly been thinking to have bought it in the first place. Who was I, Little Bo Peep?

"I got it." Salem, lounging in the brand-new beanbag chair from Lovesac that had cost me more than the Gosselin family's monthly cell phone bill, reached out languidly and cracked one eyelid to read the message.

"Who's Nadia Hale?" he asked, both eyes now open a little wider. "She seems weird."

I shot him and indignant look. "And you say *I'm* the one falling down on the job. Isn't it your responsibility to have some idea of what's going on in my life? Nadia's my latest client; the one I've been talking about all week. And what do you mean, weird? What did she say? You know what, never mind. Give me that," I said, throwing the offending blouse into the growing pile on top of my bed and snatching my phone away from Salem's hands.

He held them up in surrender. "Fine, fine, I admit it. It's my job to guide you and obviously, if you think that chick has all her ducks in a row..." He still sounded doubtful, and I stuck my tongue out at him in reply.

Hey Lexi, Nadia Hale here. You know, the rude Realtor lady. Anyway, Mona gave me your number, and if your invitation still stands, I think a girls' night out might just be exactly what I need this evening. I'm all dressed up with nowhere to go, and I believe I've hit the anger stage of my post-breakup mourning period. You said it's at Driven, correct?

"What's the big deal?" I asked Salem "She's better off than a lot of women who've just gone through a breakup, and there's nothing weird about this text. She is a Realtor, and she was rude at least once."

"Pfft," he scoffed, but shrugged and settled back into his comfy spot. "Whatever you say," he murmured, his eyelids already beginning to droop.

I hadn't actually expected for Nadia to take me up on my offer and I realized I'd have to find at least one other female friend to invite along if we really were going to call it a girls' night. Mona wasn't an option, unfortunately; she was too pregnant for all that. I tried to ignore the ache in my chest when, for a split second I forgot about reality and considered calling Delta. She'd enjoyed watching Kin's band play, and could always be counted on to infuse a sense of adventure into an evening out. I shoved the pain down deep inside and shot Flix a text.

His response came back immediately and was a no, but at least it seemed like a cheerful refusal. The faeries must have put the plan for the wedding into action. That left one final choice. I went ahead and dialed Serena's number.

"What do you need *my* help for?" Serena didn't exactly jump at the mention of watching Kin's set, but she sounded vaguely flattered by my request for assistance.

"Reinforcements," I replied. "Just say yes. I'll be the designated driver, pay for your drinks, and even arrange a sitter for Kaine. What else do you have planned for the evening?"

Serena grinned, I could hear it through the phone. "Watching Peppa Pig until Kaine goes to bed followed by binge-watching a whole season of the Bachelor. My DVR is sad. All right, I'm sold. You'll send Evian over then?"

Oh, crap. I would rather have let Edward Scissorhands give me a haircut than ask Evian for a favor after the way we'd left things, but I realized the godmothers weren't my only option.

"Not Evian," I said, giving the Lovesac a little kick. "I'm sending Salem. He and Morana can watch Kaine for a couple of hours. What's the worst that could happen?"

Salem shot me the dirtiest of dirty looks, but when he

heard Serena's resounding "no" all the way across the room, it morphed into one of injured pride.

"I'm perfectly capable of keeping a small human alive; I'm 676 years old, you know." Apparently, the blow to his ego trumped his abhorrence for Sabrina's familiar. Morana had always had a *thing* for Salem, and she was incredibly...let's just say persistent. It made Salem entertainingly uncomfortable and in defense he'd taken to avoiding Serena's house like the plague.

"He's right, you know. It's all going to be fine," I said into the phone. "And Evian truly is only a whisper away if things get out of hand. Now, get dressed and stop worrying. I'll be over to pick you up in half an hour."

I worried that Kin might still be angry with me but when I arrived at Driven and we locked eyes across the room all the tension drained out of my body. Just looking at him I knew we were perfect for each other and that we'd work this whole thing out. I'd meet his parents again and do exactly what he'd asked me to do: charm the pants off of them.

Don't get me wrong, I still had some groveling in front of me. The set of his jaw and the way his smile didn't quite meet his eyes told me that much, but even so, I felt about two tons lighter than I had during the afternoon. Penance would be paid, with interest.

"You'd better wipe that lovestruck look right off your face before I puke on those cute sandals—that I'm borrowing, by the way—and your client decides she'd rather go home and get drunk by herself than watch you moon over your fiancé." One thing I both loved and hated about Serena was she didn't pull any punches, even if sometimes I wanted to punch *her*.

I scowled at her, to which Serena nodded in approval and said, "That's better," as she sat down and ordered herself a double gin martini with six olives. "What?" she asked when I looked at her like I was questioning her sanity. "I didn't have lunch, don't judge me."

Four olives down, Nadia arrived, looking very much unlike her bus bench image. That was Work Nadia; Nightclub Nadia was a smoke show. Legs for days, wide blue eyes enhanced with artful liner and thick black lashes, and a head of playful ringlets even I wanted to run my fingers through. This Dean guy was a total idiot.

"Wow," Serena said with a low whistle when I'd introduced them both. "I feel like Skipper standing next to Barbie right now," she quipped.

Nadia's eyes flicked downward and then back up in a roll. "I was trying to prove a point, but it seems that point is moot now," she said wryly and flopped into a chair. "Waiter!"

"To hell with men," I said after our drinks arrived, raising my glass of lime-garnished sparkling water and wishing vehemently I hadn't offered to drive.

Serena snorted and waved her half-empty glass in the air. "Nuh-uh, Lexi Balefire. You don't get to be the one who says that. You leave that up to us unloved and unlovable. You've got what every woman dreams about." She rolled her eyes in the direction of the stage, caught Nadia's eye, and clinked glasses.

Who could blame them? Serena had a point. I watched as she bonded with Nadia, swiftly and with seemingly little effort. This Serena was a far cry from the insecure girl she'd been for most of her life—and I'd known her all that time so trust me, she'd changed.

I let her coax Nadia into a retelling of the love story between her and Dean James, the deadbeat she'd dressed to the nines for tonight and who had dumped her the moment their relationship had gotten serious. It seemed the well had finally broken and Nadia couldn't fight it anymore; it all came pouring out. I let Serena do the talking and I did the listening.

Both women had been with men who'd hurt them and who, it was easy to believe, didn't deserve either of them. I'd learned though, during my time as a fate weaver, that there was a match out there for everyone no matter how vile. It wasn't up to me to judge. At least, I'd never thought it was until I'd met Nadia and been faced with making a choice—a choice in shades of gray and no clear path to guide me.

"He seemed so sincere," Nadia was saying when I tuned back in. "And I fell for it; hook, line, and sinker. I still can't believe it." Her eyes took on a faraway, searching look, as though she were flipping through the relationship in her mind, trying to figure out the missing linchpin that had allowed it all to crumble.

"It makes you question your judgment, doesn't it?" Serena replied, throwing her hands in the air. "It makes you wonder if you're blind, or just really, really stupid, or both."

I couldn't keep my next thought to myself. "You just have to keep believing. People come into your lives when you need them to, and sometimes they also leave when you need them to."

"So what, you think it's all just *fate*?" Serena asked with a raised eyebrow and a small smirk. "Maybe you're right but in my case, it seems fate enjoys taking its sweet time. You, though," she turned to Nadia, "should let Lexi do what she does. You might just be pleasantly surprised and forget all about this Dean guy."

Buoyed by the second round of martinis, Nadia corrected Serena. "That Dean *jerk* you mean. Tonight, was the final straw. I've had enough. Lexi, do what you do." She reached over to pat my arm and when her skin made contact with mine, I got pulled into another vision.

Maybe it was due to her lowered inhibitions; maybe it was because she really had hit her limit; or maybe, it was because Nadia had finally come to me instead of the other way around, but this time there was no pain or the disorientation of being pulled in multiple directions.

There was, however, the strangest sensation of being stuck inside a magnifying glass; Nadia, Serena, the rest of

Driven all curved in front of my eyes, went wonky for a few moments, and then swirled back into focus.

I blinked, and when I opened my eyes again a glowing symbol hovered directly above Nadia's head. It shook a little, flickered around the edges like the neon light it resembled, and I thought perhaps it might go out altogether. Panicked, I looked down at my hands and heaved a sigh of relief when I saw that I hadn't, in fact, pulled the Bow of Destiny out of its human holster in the middle of a crowded nightclub. Not that anyone could see it anyway, but still.

My head swiveled back in Nadia's direction, and I took a closer, curious look. The glowing shape above her head resembled a heart, but it reminded me of old 8-bit, pixelated video games.

Up close, it actually looked more like a puzzle piece than anything else, its bottom half jagged and notched, each of the semicircles comprising its top half curved in a different direction. I rolled my eyes skyward, cursing the gods—one in particular—for having bestowed on me such a confusing power, but stopped short when I caught a glimpse of the rest of the club.

The shape of Nadia's symbol still seared into my vision, I felt like I was in a science fiction movie, moving from person to person around the club, searching for a match in a rainbow of neon that flooded my peripheral vision.

Something didn't feel right, so I took a deep breath

and relaxed my eyes. The noise of the club had quieted, though I could sense my companions and the rest of the patrons still bopping along to the beat of the band. I was missing Kin's performance but I knew he'd understand.

I focused my intent and then my eyes and then nearly crowed when all the symbols that didn't match Nadia's shade of purple flickered and went dark. The ones left matched in color, but not necessarily in shape. I blinked again and eliminated anything that wasn't a heart, and yet there were still almost a dozen possibilities.

The barrage of visions was at least gentler this time, but even so I was treated to a jarring experience I can only describe as the opposite of the movie Groundhog Day. Any of these men could have been Nadia's perfect match. I watched a parade of the perfectly lovely lives she could lead if I had the guts to actually pull out my father's bow and choose a match for her.

In some, Nadia had a passel of kids and raised them in suburbia; in another she traveled the world with her exotic husband. Or, I could match her to a woman with whom she would share a family and a lovely life.

It was too much for me to absorb. Too much responsibility even if, as I was forced to admit, any of Nadia's possible futures would have been considered a happy ending. Did that make my job easier or more difficult?

Would that be the eternal question of Lexi Balefire's life? That's all I could think about as I claimed to feel a migraine coming on and asked the girls if they wouldn't mind getting a ride home with the band.

"I'm sure Kin will be happy to drive you. I'll just check with him on my way out," I promised.

Serena waved me away but the concerned expression on her face didn't escape my attention. I'd explain myself tomorrow, when this wretched day would finally be over.

CHAPTER

TWENTY-FOUR

Soaring low through the inky night, Diana scented water and magic. Not just any magic, the kind that set her blood to singing dark songs in her ears. Balefire magic. She dipped a wing, angled in for the landing. This form, she thought, wasn't half bad now that she had control over when she used it. Stupid Balmorrigan did her a favor.

But then, she was Diana Diamond. Hard, like the name she had chosen, with a brilliant shine that would never dull. She'd have buffed her nails against her chest if they hadn't been talons, and her legs would reach that high.

As it was, she used those talons to maintain balance when she touched down on still water. Compared to the fetid stench of decomposing plants stirred by her passing, the wood smoke from the nearby cabin's chimney smelled clean. Too clean.

Diana stepped onto firm ground shedding feathers and beak as she made her way out of the swamp and settled into her human form.

Inside the cabin, Shyla came awake, huddled more deeply under the blanket that suddenly failed to keep her warm. Heart pounding in her ears, dread rising up to squeeze her chest, she sensed the approach of something vile. The fire in her hearth flared, the flame turning blue, then white.

Hundreds of miles away, as the household slept, the fire in Lexi Balefire's hearth did the same.

Shyla's wards were grains of sand before a mighty wind when Diana yanked the cabin door off the hinges.

"Little witch, little witch. Let me come in," she mocked in a sing-song voice. "Or I'll huff, and I'll puff... oops, too late."

Staring at a face fined down to a sharp and angular but dark beauty, Shyla quested beneath her pillow for the talisman she'd kept there these past weeks, the one the Balefire witch had told her to use if she ever felt in danger. Her fingers closed around the tiny ring of braided hair.

Help me, she thought. Help me.

Hundreds of miles away, Sylvana thrashed in her sleep.

"This place reeks of Balefire, little witch." Diana's tone glazed half an acre of swamp water with a crust of ice. Her feet seemed not to touch the floor as she moved from doorway to bedside. "But you're not one of them. Why is that?"

"Please!" Shyla begged to no avail. Diana's hand was like a vice at her throat. "I'm no threat to you."

Diana's laugh carried a razor-blade edge and turned Shyla's bones to water.

"Silly child." She shook the witch by the neck. "Now, tell me why you smell like Balefire? I won't ask again."

Seeing her own death reflected back at her from the glittering depths of Diana's eyes, Shyla muttered something too low to hear.

"What?" The pressure eased just enough for Shyla to take a breath.

"I said." Shyla's irises flipped from warm brown to ice blue as she uttered the results of her vision, "Your time to repent has passed. You will die screaming."

"Nice trick with the eyes, but I have to take off points for the trite prediction."

Shyla gasped as the pressure returned, the scream echoing through her head but finding no breath with which to escape her lips.

"I hate witches." Diana squeezed and repeated, shaking Shyla harder as fury took her over. When she came to herself again, the limp witch was beyond answering. "Stupid bitch." Diana tossed Shyla away as if she were made of crumpled paper. "I intended to kill you anyway."

Putting the fit of pique behind her, Diana set about the macabre business she'd come to this out-of-the-way place to do. A callous wave of her hand cleared the spare, wooden table, upon which she laid the branch from the Tree of Life she'd taken from a hidden storehouse in the forest.

The tail hair from the flying horse had been her first choice to bind the shard to the branch. When that hadn't panned out, she'd come up with a new, more grisly plan.

Diana rambled around the area where Shyla made her potions until she found the dead witch's boline. The sound of the blade as she sharpened it against a leather strop would have chilled the devil's bones had he been there to hear it.

As Diana went to work with the knife, Shyla's spirit rose from her body and hovered nearby to observe the indignity of being butchered like an animal. The blade snicked and slithered, parting tendons from bone.

While the silvery sinews were still wet, Diana slit them into strips. Handling it gingerly to keep from activating the lightning shard, she used the tendons to bind it to the shaft of the branch. Hands red with innocent blood, she picked up the branch and thrust the bound into the witch's fire.

Its heat drying and tightening the macabre bindings, the Balefire tasted things it knew. Witch, and blood, and the branch that long ago had ignited its first spark. Mixed among familiar things, the fire also tasted magic seasoned by violence, mythical power, and darkness.

Satisfied with her work, Diana pulled the staff from the flame, tested the weapon by touching the glowing tip to her palm, and shivering with delight at the pain and blackened skin. If the staff could burn one demi-goddess, it could burn two.

Lexi Balefire would die.

Across the world, for a long moment, every fire in every witch's hearth burned black to match.

Dawn broke as Shyla's final scream finally penetrated Sylvana's dreams. She woke crying, bolted from her lonely bed, and took only enough time to drag on pants before running outside. Still running, she magically shifted to the hut on the edge of the wetlands.

Those few moments gave the evil one just enough time to finish her foul deed, and go home to prepare. The echo of Diana's laugh faded into the burgeoning day as Sylvana's bare feet slid in dew-laden grass. Her knees took the brunt of the fall as she slammed her palms down to keep from face planting, felt something soft, and clutched for it.

"Shyla!" Concern cranked up to a fevered pitch, Sylvana scrambled to her feet, pounded up the steps.

Too late, far too late, Sylvana flew through the open door and fell to her knees beside Shyla's body, the oily feather fluttering from her hand to land next to limp fingers.

"No!" Her keening cries cut the night. "Oh, Shyla. No!"

Guilt settled like a thousand-pound weight over Sylvana's soul as she cradled the young witch's body, rocking and muttering soothing words to deaf ears. After a time, Sylvana rose, stripped the bed, used the sheets to wrap the body.

When it was done, the sun rode low in the eastern sky.

Sylvana conjured fire in her palm, its light casting half her face in shadow. "I swear," she said, "upon my namesake and upon my soul that I will avenge this death."

In response, the flame in her palm shot a column of light toward the ceiling.

CHAPTER
TWENTY-FIVE

Angry, bruise-colored clouds scudded across the sun, turning mid-morning to twilight in a matter of seconds. If you've ever been alone in a house and felt like you were being watched, then you know how I felt. The hair on the back of my neck stood up.

"Something's coming," Kin stated the obvious as he bolted out of the lawn chair fast enough to make the thing collapse.

My guts turned to water, then ice, then steel. No matter the evidence to the contrary, I'd been expecting this ever since Diana's card was what shimmered under Mag's spell and not the evil skank herself.

"Go inside. Tell Salem to call the elders and to open the sanctum for you. You'll be safe there." I grabbed Kin's arm, spun him in the direction I wanted him to go. "Then send him to me. I'll need his help."

When he hesitated, I barked. "Now." With him safe, I could focus on the looming threat.

His lips set in a grim line, Kin ran toward the sliding doors while I slid my feet into a pair of flip-flops and yanked a cover-up over my bathing suit. This was not TV or a video game. Going to war in a pink two-piece was not my idea of cool.

Lightning slashed low above the trees, leaving a ghostly, jagged imprint on my vision.

Thinking it better to draw trouble away from the house, I made my way deeper into the backyard. Rising air pressure signaled the coming storm.

Dollars to donuts, this storm had a name, and it was Diana.

Flip-flops were never meant for running. The space between my toes throbbed, but I managed to keep them on while tapping the shell woven into my hair.

"Evian, I need you."

Where were they? I tried to picture the calendar on the kitchen wall listing their party planning schedule. They'd be prepping for either a wedding shower or a sweet sixteen party.

Evian's voice came back in a hollow echo near my right ear. "Where?"

"The house."

A short silence fell, then I heard her say, "Tag Vaeta. Activate the defenses and hold the fort. You need to buy us ten minutes or so."

"Hurry."

My heel came down on a sharp stone, and I yelped.

For the love of tiny pickles, Lexi Balefire. Are you, or are you not a witch?

My inner voice sometimes sounds like Aunt Mag, but it did jar me out of stupid mode.

"Hexicus Prada." Yes, Prada makes a combat boot. They don't necessarily go with a sunbathing outfit, but I didn't really care so long as they weren't tripping me every third step. In retrospect, I probably should have gone with a nice running shoe, but you can't always think of these things in the heat of the moment.

My footwear issue solved, I made it to the stone ring in the center of our backyard without further incident.

To the uninitiated, the pretty little birdbath bordered by hunks of rose quartz looked like nothing special. To those of us in the know, the elements of earth, water, fire, and air worked into the design were obvious signs of magic.

Lightning struck again, somewhere nearby, thunder coming right behind it. The ground rolled under my feet, but the combat boots held. Not such a bad choice after all. I double-tapped the shell in my hair as I stepped inside the stone ring.

"Vaeta," I managed to get out before another boom threatened to drown me out. "Something's coming."

"I can hear that for myself." Her voice sounded faint. Probably because my ears were ringing. "What are we looking at?"

"Diana Diamond," I said, daring her to argue, "is not dead, and she's coming for me."

Figuring I'd said enough, I tapped the shell and turned my attention toward raising our defenses.

In theory, the sequence was simple, but I'd never done this before, and it would be just like the godmothers to set up some sort of failsafe or booby trap in case a non-magical person happened along.

Earth first. I picked up the lone piece of white quartz sitting in the sand and dropped it into the empty space between two of the pink ones making up the outer ring. The stones hummed in bell-like tones when the circle finally closed.

The thick soles of my boots put a damper on the vibration, but it still radiated up through my bones enough to make my skin itch. A trench of earth shot out in both directions forming a circle around part of the backyard and the house. The displaced soil heaped into a furrow at the edge of the trench.

Next, fire.

This one was easy. All I had to do was light the fire in the brazier set into a circle of sand. Balefire flickered to life in my hand and did the job in an instant. A ring of fire raced along the piled-up soil.

For air, I blew on the set of wind chimes suspended from a hook over the birdbath. Their merry tinkle seemed out of place given the gravity of the moment, but they kicked up a breeze that whipped unseen but for the occasional wisp of a cloud and formed a new barrier just inside the ring of fire.

Finally, water.

Lightning flashed like a strobe as I grabbed the delicate white shell resting on the rim of the birdbath and scooped it full of water. I tipped the scant half-cup full into the trench and watched it magically gout like a flooding river in a widening circle.

Vaeta's air separated water from fire, while Terra's earth anchored the other three elements.

It took mere seconds for the arc to complete, and when it did, air, fire, and water shot skyward, arching in to create an elemental dome over the property.

"That ought to hold her." I hoped.

"Excellent shield." Kin, bless him, never batted an eye at the show of magic. His shirt clung to shoulders made broader from working out over the past few months. I didn't hate the results, only that events like this were why he felt the need to buff up.

Seemed like a pattern in my life. The people around me ended up in situations that tested their mettle far too frequently for my taste.

"Didn't I tell you to stay in the house?"

He arched a brow. "Did you really think I would?"

Salem butted his feline head against my calf. He could at least have had the decency to take human form so I could yell at him properly.

"It's not safe out here."

Stepping up beside me, Kin tilted his head to scan the arch of the dome. "It's not safe anywhere. I'd rather be with you than hiding inside alone. Besides, I brought stuff."

He'd assembled himself an armory of sorts: a kitchen knife, a baseball bat, and the fireplace poker.

"Can you see anything?"

"Not really." But I felt her coming on the wings of hate.

Hate was Diana's stock in trade.

If I was a Fate Weaver, she was a Hate Weaver.

And I wanted to be the one to snip her thread. I wanted it with single-minded fury. She'd come after me and mine without provocation for no other reason than that I existed. She'd killed and would not hesitate to kill again. It was up to me to stop her, and she'd caught me with my pants down—literally.

I wasn't ready.

"You okay?" Kin slid a strong arm around my waist, pulled me close to his side.

"Would you think less of me if I tossed my cookies in the bushes?" I stuffed my shaking hand in my pocket and scanned the sky through the haze of the dome.

The whisper of his breath on my ear made me shiver. How is it a person can think of sex at a time like this?

"Never."

Diana's scream cut a hole in the air, turned my insides out. A split second later, the sky above the dome turned to golden fire. I felt the ground shake just before the boom of thunder practically yanked out my eardrums.

Lightning webbed across the surface of the protective dome, the force peeling it away like the cracked eggshell it now resembled.

A flutter of dark wings arrowed closer, promising doom. I shoved Kin behind me, checked that the Bow of Destiny still rested against my spine, and prepared to let my inner goddess take her due if she could get a shot.

Twenty feet from the ground, she began to change. Feathers turned to leather in the form of a long coat that flapped in the wind, and the ugly beak morphed into lips as black as night. She twirled a staff nearly as long as she was tall, a bright object on the end of it making a circular pattern of light.

"What? No minions this time?" Probably not my best attempt at trash talk.

Skin paler than milk shot through with dark veins made Diana looked as if she'd been carved from a block of marble.

"I've got all the help I need right here." She stilled the twirling staff, banged the end against the ground, and sent a ripple of thunder and motion my way. If not for years of practice during faerie game night, she might have knocked me off my feet, but I leaped clear as the ground heaved past me.

"Nice try," I said, turning my attention to her weapon, parts of which looked quite familiar. Where had I seen that branch with the burned ends before?

Throwing her head back, Diana laughed. Equal parts

harsh and shrill, no fully human throat could have made such a sound. It sent a chill into my bones.

The good thing about a deep chill is that it stiffens the spine a bit. As far as I knew, Diana had very little active magic in her own right, only that which she borrowed, stole, or bought. I needed only be wary of the tools she carried. She'd lost her cards, and I almost wished she had them back because at least then, I'd know what to expect. The staff might be more powerful than anything I had at my disposal, and she wasn't above playing dirty.

But then, she'd played her last card with me—see what I did there—and I could go just as low as her if I had to. Could I kill her? Yeah, I thought I could. Could I live with myself afterward? Without losing a single minute of sleep over it.

Probably.

Except all the cards were stacked in her favor. She had a freaking lightning stick, while my main weapon was a bow that shot heart-tipped arrows filled with love. Probably not the way to go in this situation.

I also had magical fire and a few spells I'd read in a book but never tried.

"Who are you supposed to be?" Maybe I could goad her into making a mistake. "The evil baton twirler in the parade from hell?"

"If you like," Diana waggled an eyebrow and smirked.

I also had friends and family on my side. If I could stall her another few minutes, the cavalry would arrive and help balance out my odds of beating her, and the best way to do that was to keep her talking. The bad guys always like to talk, right?

"Whatever. You're going down." Did I mention I suck at trash talk?

If anything, her smirk got smirkier.

There's little doubt I'd have said something even dumber next but was interrupted by the unmistakable hurking noise a cat makes just before he throws up.

Great timing, Salem.

I glanced down just as he deposited a hairball into the top of my left boot. The damp heat of it slid down my bare ankle.

"Eww, Salem!" I shuddered. "That's disgusting."

Diana openly laughed in my face. "Not so formidable without your protectors around, are you? I don't know why I thought this would be difficult." With a flick of the wrist, she threw a small bolt of lightning at me.

I called the balefire, and it answered. Oh, boy, did it ever. Flame erupted over my body, a living shield. Fight fire with fire, right?

Next time, use the mirror charm. Salem's voice echoed in my head.

How are you doing that?

The hairball, you idiot. If you'd done your research properly, you'd have made a talisman from my fur, and I wouldn't have had to resort to undignified behavior.

You could have told me.

What would be the fun in that?

"Where'd you get the weapon?" Evian's ten minutes must be close to past by now. I just needed to distract Diana for a little longer.

"What?" Diana drawled. "This old thing? It was a gift from my grandfather." Holding the staff up in front of her, she surveyed her handiwork. "The best part of it, anyway."

Practically purring, Diana caressed the aged wood but carefully kept her fingertips clear of the business end—a jagged, glowing stone lashed into the cradle formed by a charred fork.

Again, I thought the staff looked familiar. The memory tried to bob to the surface like the prediction die in a Magic 8-Ball, floating and spinning, but refusing to fully come to the surface.

Whatever the source of the lightning she'd been throwing around, if she didn't want to touch it, I definitely needed to stay clear. But maybe I could use whatever it was against her. You know, if I could get it away from her without it killing me first. A big if.

You ever seen anything like that in the texts? I thought at Salem.

"Rowr," He snarled and arched his back. The motion revealed something I hadn't noticed before—my Fate Weaver wand tucked under his collar. If only he could get close enough for me to grab it.

That's not an answer.

Casually, Diana flicked another bolt of lightning in my direction. Trying to remember the mirror charm, I barely dodged in time. The bolt flash-fried a small pine tree behind where I'd been standing.

Diana howled her displeasure at my narrow escape and tried again.

In panic mode, I ran in the wrong direction, nearly slithered to safety, but the searing heat passed close enough to burn a furrow across my left cheek and sizzle away half the hair on that side of my head.

Pain blossomed. She'd nailed me pretty good.

"That's gonna leave a mark," Diana gloated.

"You bitch," I screamed. "You burned my hair." I didn't stop to consider if it was a good idea when I snatched my wand from Salem, called Balefire into my palm, and growled, "Momentum."

A comet of bespelled fire slammed into Diana's weapon, tasted the wooden staff and the binding she'd used to lash the shard in place before winking out like a snuffed candle. The memory niggle grew stronger, but not enough to pull any sort of visual into focus.

Mirror charm, Salem reminded. I waved him away. He'd lose all respect for me if I admitted I couldn't remember it.

Thin tendrils of smoke curled upward, gathered itself with visible purpose. Behind me, Kin let out a gasp of disbelief as he recognized the distinct shape of a human woman forming in the air.

My wand hand went the kind of cold that crept along flesh, leaving numbness in its wake. Time paused. The smoke specter wafted closer, its form sharpening until I could make out the facial features of a young woman.

"Vengeance." From the smoke woman came the sibilant whisper. "Pleasssse."

I hadn't noticed when my heart stopped beating, but I sure noticed when it started up again, pounding in my chest.

Two and two went together pretty quickly when I noticed the way the ghost's smoke stayed tethered to the bindings I'd assumed were made from rawhide.

Goddess save me; she killed that witch to build her weapon. Only Salem needed to hear that particular revelation. Kin wouldn't hesitate to put himself in danger if he'd known.

Do not throw up.

Shut up. I'm fine.

That was a lie.

Keeping my gaze trained on Diana, I gave the ghost a slight nod.

"Thanksss." Taking some of the chill with her, she dissipated, leaving one more black mark in the Diana column. What cold remained came more from my own fury than from the spirit of the dead witch. With the ice came clarity. With clarity came memory.

I knew exactly where I'd seen Diana's staff before.

I didn't need the faeries to come to my rescue. Or anyone else, for that matter.

I was Lexi Balefire. Witch. Goddess. Keeper of the Flame. Fate Weaver. It was time to weave Diana's fate, and this one wouldn't have anything to do with soul mates, true love's kiss, or heart-tipped arrows.

Maybe she noticed the stiffening of my spine or the fire in my eye because Diana's expression turned feral. "Little girl finally ready to play?"

"Bring it," I gritted out from between clenched teeth.

TWENTY-SIX

Keep Kin back. I trusted Salem to do as I asked. *And be ready to back my play. You'll know it when you see it.*

Two minutes into the battle, I realized game nights really had been training me for this moment my entire life. You don't believe me; you try a round of Hungry Hungry Battleship Hippos and see for yourself.

While I dodged lightning strikes and made liberal use of Salem's mirror charm, I worked out a plan. First things first, I couldn't take the chance of Diana dragging the poor, dead witch's spirit down to hell. Whoever she was, she belonged in the Summerlands, and since I was the only witch available, it was up to me to perform the ritual to send her there.

There wouldn't be powders or potions to ease her trip, so I hoped she'd forgive me for the bumpy ride.

Stalling for time, I continued to bob and weave, drawing Diana's ire, keeping myself just out of her reach while I recited the words of the passing ritual.

From the Goddess, we have hailed

And to her breast, we shall return

Once you walked upon the earth, grounded in
*   her stability*
Once you breathed the air and reveled in her
*   freedom*
Once you played with the fire and lost yourself
*   in her passion*
Once you bathed in the water and got lost in
*   her dreams*

Now you dance with the spirit

You have become that which encompasses
*   us all*
You have passed into the lands of Summer

We will meet again someday, sister witch
Blessed be

Trying to remember the exact phrasing, I got distracted twice and paid for my inability to properly multitask with a scorch mark seared across my calf and another blazed along my right biceps.

My breath whistled in and out as I tried to ignore the pain and the blood seeping from the puckered edges of the wounds.

It couldn't just be hey, it's been nice, see you on the

other side. No, the ritual had to be long and hard to remember. Worse, it had to be repeated aloud, so other than lobbing fireballs, I couldn't cast any defensive spells until I completed it.

But I got through the whole thing and even managed to land a solid fireball strike that singed off the stupid skank's eyebrows.

"Your aim is lousy." I taunted while I maneuvered into position. More than just releasing the witch's soul hinged on what happened next. "You think you've got it all figured out, don't you, Diana? Well, you're wrong!"

Diana's laugh ringing in my ears, I ducked under her final volley, rolled, and came up closer than she expected. Close enough to hit the shard bindings with a thin shaft of flame. As I did, the witch gave me the image of Diana's treachery.

White as the driven snow, my balefire-strengthened intention burned the tendon bindings to dust. The lightning shaft wobbled in its unfettered, former cage, forcing Diana to shuffle and juggle to keep her scepter of doom intact.

The very air sighed as the soul of the young witch departed, leaving only Diana to face me alone.

Maybe she could have grabbed the shard and used it against me, but I didn't give her time to try. Digging ruthlessly at the burn on my arm, I reopened the wound, and my hand came away red and wet.

The witch feeds the flame, and the flame feeds the witch.

I called plain old witchfire into my bloodied palm and let balefire kindle in the other. Eyes locked on Diana's face, I brought both hands together, rolling the combined flames into a powerful whole. The flickering ball tasted my blood offering—fed on it to grow and quest for something else it had tasted before.

"But you probably shouldn't have used the branch that lit the Balefire."

Magic flowed around and through me in a heady rush as the ball of flame arced from my palm to the last—so far as I knew—piece of the tree of life burned the forked end of Diana's staff to ash.

The shard wobbled. She made a grab for it.

Behind and to Diana's left, a faint shimmer bent the light flaring off the burning branch. It had to be Evian using her old water and mirror trick to get into flanking position. The faeries had finally arrived.

Emitting little crackles of light, the shard tipped over and began to fall. Diana arched her body to catch it before it hit the ground.

Everything hinged on this moment, and I'd thrown everything I had into my one chance at disabling Diana's weapon. By the time my magic recharged for another blast, it would be too late. The muscles in my legs bunched as I prepared to leap.

I never got the chance.

Kin let out a shout of triumph as he barreled past me, an oak baseball bat held in a two-handed grip. Diana's fingers barely brushed the shard. If he'd been even half a second slower, the outcome might have been very different.

Oak cracked solidly into the short, molten spear, sending it arching like a comet until the light winked out. Home run of the century. Momentum carried Kin well past Diana before he crashed heavily to the ground and didn't move.

Everything in me wanted to run to him, to make sure he was all right. But Diana Diamond stood in my way—both literally and figuratively.

Evian's shimmer split into two, one changing course to follow the shard, the other heading toward Kin. The faeries would take care of him for me while I finished what I had to do. I looked at Diana: he woman—if you could still call her that—who came from a similar background to mine. Who had been born with the power to do great things if she hadn't been so twisted and hellbent.

Diana was a lesson to me. If I hadn't known that before, I did now. Chase power long enough, and for the wrong reasons, and you might just find you're the one being chased.

Didn't matter now. She'd made her choices, and it was time to make mine. If using magic to kill turned me wicked, I'd have to face that obstacle once the deed was done.

I clapped my hands together and then pulled them apart to let a new ball of witchfire grow in the space between. Every ounce of fury, pain, and anger went into the building fire, blackening it with my intent.

It occurred to me that if I could generate black witchfire, I wasn't nearly as different from my mother as I wanted to think. At that moment, I didn't care. I wanted to be her. To know, I could kill if I had to and not count the cost.

That need went into the crackling fire that greedily devoured the daylight. Against its dark glow, I caught the faint reflection of the returning faerie shimmer, heard something drop near my feet, but didn't spare a look.

It was time, and my weapon was strong. I drew back my arm and prepared to throw Diana the killing blow.

"Get ready to—" The words died in my mouth.

"Ligabis, Ostium, Carcere." The whispered spell hit me from behind. An invisible force twined around my arms, binding me in place. My witchfire flickered out. Something wasn't right.

"Die, bitch." Sylvana strode past me, a length of gallows rope sticking out of the back pocket of her black leather pants. She spared me only a glance that showed half of her face. Seeing that much chilled me to the bone.

I knew that face—every expression a mirror of my own. Under the brow furrowed with fierce resolve, her eyes carried sorrow.

With a motion almost casual, my mother flicked an

unspoken spell toward Diana that rocked her back on her feet.

Shock—made even more evident by her lack of eyebrows—rooted Diana to the ground. She made quite a picture as she stood staring at my mother with nothing in her hand but an old stick. A true Kodak moment, but being locked in a binding spell, I couldn't pull out my phone to snap a shot.

Lexi. Lexi. Lexi. How long had Salem been trying to reach me? His thought voice sounded frantic.

I can't move. Can you see Kin? Is he all right?

It's—

Being wicked is a choice. Pure and simple, black and white. I'd based my life around that belief because I'd grown up with the bone-deep knowledge that the wickedness running in my blood needed to end with me. Because I needed to feel like I had some say over how I'd turn out. Because I thought I could redeem the Balefire name.

But nothing is ever that simple. Especially when it comes to my family.

We're messy and loud and don't always get along. We're made up of pieces and parts, bound together by magic and tragedy, but most of all by love.

Recovering from her dismay, Diana lunged forward, whirled the branch, and aimed for my mother's head.

"If Zeus couldn't kill me, what makes you think you can? Don't you know who I am?"

Sylvana danced back, ducked, then moved in to deliver a short-armed punch to Diana's throat.

The fight was on.

Black-clad figures whirled, came together, and parted in a blur of motion. Diana spit blood from her cut lip while Sylvana shook her left arm to regain feeling after taking a heavy blow from the branch. The two women reassessed each other, then went in for round three.

Why didn't she just use witchfire?

"That's for hurting my kid." The satisfaction in Sylvana's tone answered my unspoken question. Her fist slammed into Diana's gut, but she took a heavy blow to the side of her head and went down hard. She must have lost consciousness for a second because her binding spell dropped.

Freed, I took five running steps and launched a roundhouse kick to Diana's head. "That's for hurting my man." Nothing had ever felt so good as the singing pain shooting up my leg.

Behind me, Sylvana dragged herself back to her feet.

"That's for killing Delta," I got in an uppercut that snapped Diana's head back before Sylvana surged past me and headbutted her in the face. Blood fountained.

"That's for Shyla." Reaching down, Sylvana scooped up the shard from where one of the faeries had dropped it.

Darker than night, witchfire coated jagged stone with certain death that slid between Diana's ribs to pierce what was of her evil heart. Diana went down and lay on her side.

"And that's," my mother's voice had gone rough, "just because you're you."

Flipping Diana over with her foot, Sylvana grabbed the branch and used it to pound the weapon home until it pierced Diana's back and beyond.

Newly-grounded, the stone shard blazed to life with the fury of the gods. Or really, just the one who'd sent it in the first place. If Diana hadn't already been dead, the hundred kajillion volts it sent through her would have done the trick.

She went up in a black cloud of foul-smelling smoke, leaving nothing but ash to smear the air.

It was over. I took a deep breath, let it out on a sigh.

And then, my mother turned to face me, her irises gone as dark as the fire she'd used to kill her foe.

It was not over.

Not even close.

Horror turned my guts to water. The space between us opened up as I took two hurried steps back.

"Mom," was all I could force out between fear-clenched teeth. I didn't hear or see Aunt Mag and my grandmother step out of the empty space on either side of me. I only knew they were there when I heard Mag order, "Sleep."

She clapped fingertips to thumb in a closing gesture. Clara rushed forward to catch her daughter before she hit the ground, ended up sitting with Sylvana's head cradled in her lap.

"What did she do?" Aunt Mag took me by the shoulders, shook me a little when I didn't answer quickly enough.

Having taken his human form, Salem put his hand on Mag's arm, gently tugging it to get her attention.

"Lexi needs to see to Kin now. I can tell you everything you need to know." He turned me, gave me a little shove in the direction he wanted me to go.

"How bad is it?" I wasn't just talking about Kin.

"We'll take care of her." My grandmother's face was as grave as I'd ever seen it.

Leaving them to it, I walked away.

TWENTY-SEVEN

Gloating over the demise of Diana Diamond would have to wait.

I turned toward the huddle of faeries surrounding Kin. Dread pooled in my belly, my heart lodged behind my tonsils. All I could see of him was a pair of jean-clad legs sticking out past Terra's bowed back.

It was bad. I didn't need to see the grave concern on Evian's face as she watched Terra work on him to know it was bad.

My feet wanted to drag, and they also wanted to fly.

The godmothers had been speaking in hushed tones, but when they heard me coming, silence fell like a curtain.

"Is he..." I couldn't bring myself to say the word dead.

"No." Evian shook her head; a tear of sorrow glittered on her cheek. "Not yet."

Not yet. The words rang in my head like the tolling of a bell. A death knell.

No. Not my Kin.

Soleil scooted back to make room for me, and I fell to my knees beside his still form. His face, the face I planned to wake up next to for the rest of his life, was nearly the same color as his T-shirt. The gray of old tombstones.

Was this what death looked like? I laid my hand on his cheek. It was still warm.

Hope flared.

"What can we do? There must be something. A spell, a potion."

No answer came.

"Terra, please," I begged. I'd have made a deal with the devil for my soul at that moment and never counted the cost. "Do something."

"I can't. I'm so sorry, but there's nothing I can do. He's beyond my reach."

"What does that even mean?" I demanded as I watched the shallow rise and fall of his chest.

"He's in the gray world. The world between. You know we're not allowed to go there."

Hope flared in me, then died. I'd been to the world between before. With Delta. But she was gone, and I didn't have any idea how to get back there on my own.

"Do you know the way? Tell me! I'll do anything."

I felt Aunt Mag's presence at my back. Turned. "What about you? Aunt Been There, Done That. Got anything in that fanny pack that will help?"

Yelling at my elders probably wasn't the smartest thing to do, but I didn't care. Let her strike me down for it. At least I wouldn't have to live with the pain of losing Kin again, and probably my mother, too. This time forever.

"Lexi! I'm—"

I cut her off. "I don't care if you're sorry. Can you fix this? Fix him?"

The withdrawal of her presence was my answer. I turned back to Terra.

"Help me."

She'd never refused me for anything that mattered in the past, and she didn't disappoint me now, either.

"You'd need someone with ties to Olympus."

Delta was gone, which left me with one option. I needed to find my father.

"How much time do I have?"

"A day." The faeries traded a look. "Maybe two if we—"

"You know we're not supposed to," Soleil offered a token protest, then shut up when Terra burned her with a look. Not an easy feat considering Soleil was the faerie of fire.

I leaned down, kissed Kin's forehead, leaned back, and brushed my tears from his skin. "Take care of him for me. I'm counting on you." I kissed Terra. Let the balm of her calm spirit wash over me for just a moment.

I wanted to tear myself into two pieces so I could help the elder witches with my mother and save Kin at the same time.

After a last, lingering backward look, I walked toward the house to plan my next move. With Kin's life on the line, I needed help, and only one other person besides my mother had ever shown an interest in finding my father. I pulled out my phone and shot Serena a text.

I need Jett. NOW. Life or death.

Her response came back before I swung through the sliding doors.

Three hours. Best he can do. What happened?

Later.

I didn't have time for even the short version.

You okay?

I will be.

I had to believe that, or else I wouldn't be able to move.

I had to move, or I would fall apart.

"Lexi!" Preoccupied with the million things running through my head and the one I refused to even contemplate, I hadn't heard Salem trying to get my attention. "Lexi!" His hand came down on my arm, pulled me to a stop.

"What's the plan? I want to help."

Looking at the sympathy I knew I'd see in his bi-colored eyes might derail me, so I angled my gaze away even as he leaned down to rub his cheek against mine. A cat at heart, he needed the comfort of touch nearly as much as I needed not to give in to the urge to curl up and cry.

Still, there was something he could do.

"Find Flix," I yanked the stone necklace off my neck and held it out. "Show him this, ask him to find out what it is and how to use it. Jett said he got it from one of the fae, and it might help with finding my father."

I dropped one portion of hope into my familiar's hand before heading into my sanctum to work on the next.

If the past year had taught me anything, it was that you always end up having to do all the hard things, so instead of moaning about the situation, just pull up your panties and get on with it. If plan A doesn't work, you'd better have a plan B and a plan C, D, and E to back it up.

Delta might be dead, but she was the only person I knew who had had her feet planted firmly in both the worlds that interested me right now. I needed to talk to her, and I knew just the person to help me get the job done.

TWENTY-EIGHT

With no time to waste, I reviewed my options for getting to Oakville: I could drive or suck it up and travel the witchy way. No, I don't mean by broomstick, though I suppose we could call that option three.

Broomsticks don't come with saddles for comfort, and as much as I hate to admit it, I drive like an old lady. Or maybe I don't. Aunt Mag is the only old lady I've ever ridden with, and she drives like a bat out of hell.

With Kin's time running out, there really only was one option.

So, I hit Google maps and brought up the street view to refresh my visual of Kat Canton's house. Sunny yellow with white trim, a riot of pink, white, and red blooms flanking the steps and running along the picket fence, the place didn't scream, *here's a good place to come talk to the dead.*

I settled the image firmly in my mind and cast a distraction spell on myself to keep the neighbors from noticing me when I appeared on the front porch, and a glamour to hide my disheveled appearance.

What I forgot to do was take a Dramamine.

"Lexi," Kat opened the door as I stood there wondering if skim-sickness was why witches were often portrayed with green faces. "Welcome."

"I'm sorry about the short notice, but this is a bit of an emergency. You're sure I'm not intruding?"

Pretty brown eyes twinkled at me as the psychic medium reached for my hand. "So long as you're comfortable with a few extra participants in the session." She pulled me inside. "Gustavia was here when you called. You sounded so upset, we invited Amethyst in case your aura needed clearing, and Julie was with her, so we're all here."

"As long as we can get this done in a hurry, it's fine by me." Oddly, I felt comforted rather than intimidated by being part of a larger group. The other three women greeted me warmly, and a hug from Gustavia helped settle my jangling nerves.

If she could figure out how to make them a global experience, I'm convinced one of Gustavia's hugs could bring about world peace.

"I'll do the best I can," Kat said. "But the spirits control how long the process takes. I'm only the conduit."

I accepted the offer of iced herbal tea and let a moment or two of bright chatter wind its way around me until my belly felt less jittery. The four women seemed so easy with each other. I didn't have a single woman in my life I could laugh about little things with.

There was Serena, but years of sniping at each other still showed up in our interactions. Then there was Mona. Nice woman, but I had too many secrets from her to totally let my guard down.

Who did that leave? The godmothers? My mother, grandmother, and aunt? Um, no. All wonderful and wise women, but also a lot of work and prone to drama.

Coming to stand behind me, Amethyst ran her hands through the space around my head and shoulders, plucking out bits of tension and smoothing my aura.

"You've really been through the wringer, haven't you?" The sympathy in her voice nearly set me off, but this was not the time to indulge in a crying jag. I didn't have time for that.

When I sighed, Gustavia patted my hand. "Try to relax."

"Can we just get on with it, please? I think I'm as relaxed as I'm going to get."

Kat nodded. "I'm ready. Did you bring an item I can use for channeling?"

"I did, but I'm not sure it's exactly the right thing." I pulled out the compass I'd separated from the Bow of Destiny and laid it in the middle of the table. "This didn't belong to Delta, but she carried it for a while before she gave it to me. It's all I have."

Gently, Kat picked up the compass, cradled it in her hand, and closed her eyes.

"Strong vibe. Very clear. Yes, I think it will do."

Kat's face went slack for a long moment. I sent a questioning glance toward Amethyst. She nodded encouragement, so I waited. Then Kat frowned.

"This is odd," she said. "There's something...I can't quite...I'm not sure she's actually—" Breaking off, Kat frowned again, then her face smoothed out.

"Okay, I see. That's new, but I am getting a strong vibe. Did your friend ride a motorcycle?"

"She did." My chest tightened. We'd ridden that motorcycle to the very place I needed Delta to help me find. It seemed like a good omen for Kat to bring it up now.

Still holding the compass, Kat turned her head sideways as if listening to something only she could hear. I'd expected the process to have a bit more pomp and circumstance. Eyes still closed, she smiled.

"I like her," Kat said. "She's sassy."

She took a breath, and the world stood still, just for a moment.

When it started up again, Kat looked at me with Delta's eyes.

Creeped me right out, I don't mind saying. You'd think it wouldn't, given I'd recently brewed a potion with dragon dung as the main ingredient. After that, most anything pales in comparison.

"Pretty," Amethyst tilted her head sideways as she read Kat's new aura.

"Lexi Balefire." Even Kat's posture had shifted. She

leaned back in her chair, hooked one leg over the wooden arm in a languid pose that still somehow felt powerful. Typical Delta. "How's tricks?"

Her voice raised the hairs on the back of my neck, sent a wave of goose pimples across my arms.

"I...uh." Now that I had her here, I wasn't sure what to say. Worse, unshed tears gathered, prickling at the corners of my eyes. I blamed Amethyst and her magic fingers for that.

"I'm sorry." My throat threatened to close up. "I didn't mean to get you killed."

Kat/Delta waved that away with a flick of the wrist. "There she goes again thinking she's the pivot on which the world turns. Whatever would we do without Lexi Balefire at the center of everything."

The snark in her tone burned off my attack of nerves. "Death doesn't seem to have changed your nature much."

"Why should it? I am who I am, and I am who I ever was."

Under the table, Gustavia's hand landed on my knee, gave it a supportive squeeze. She, Amethyst, and Julie remained silent, watching the exchange like it was a game of tennis.

"What was so important you had to disturb my eternal slumber?" Delta wanted to know.

"Is that what it's like?" I couldn't help asking. "One giant, cosmic nap?"

The response came with a quirked eyebrow over a

pointed stare. "You know I'm not telling you anything about the afterlife. It's supposed to remain a mystery for a reason." Then a conspiratorial grin. "But I can say Diana's experience here hasn't been what she expected. Now, what can I do for you? As if I haven't done enough already."

"When we...uh...my mother took care of Diana, there was an accident." I described what had happened to Kin. "He's stuck in the gray lands. I need you to tell me how to get there before his time runs out."

The sympathy that washed over her face could have been coming from either Delta or Kat. I wasn't sure which.

"I'm sorry, but I can't help you. Even if I could give you a set of directions, you wouldn't be able to get there on your own."

"Why not? What did you have that I don't?" I was desperate.

"Besides style and panache?"

I literally saw red.

"This is a matter of life and death. I really don't have time to trade witty banter."

Delta sent Kat's hands slamming down on the table-top. "Fine."

I jumped half out of my skin. Gustavia's chair scraped against the floor as she shoved it backward. Julie clapped her fist against her chest, and Amethyst swore.

"Sorry," Delta lied.

"Never mind. This was a stupid idea. I'm sorry for

wasting everyone's time." I pushed back my chair, began to rise. "I shouldn't have bothered you, Delta. It won't happen again."

"Sit back down!" Delta roared out the order, then waited for the flurry of response.

I wanted to sink beneath the floorboards, never to be seen again.

"You're not the boss of me," I muttered.

Nothing like being yelled at by the channeled spirit of a supernatural bounty hunter to make one feel like a spoiled child.

I sat and trained my gaze on Kat's collarbone.

"Why haven't you found your father?" was not what I expected to come out of Delta's mouth.

"Excuse me if I've been just a bit too busy dealing with spoiled rejects from Olympus who want to take over the world."

Delta stayed silent so long I chanced a look at Kat's face, saw the raised eyebrow, and took umbrage. "Poor excuse since I know that just happened today," she said.

"Then why did you ask? The afterlife must be pretty boring if you don't have anything better to do than watch the Lexi Balefire show."

Gustavia let out a small laugh. When I looked at her, she'd curled her lips in, biting down on them to keep from doing it again.

Delta shrugged Kat's shoulders, dropped her leg from

the chair arm, and leaned forward. The intensity of her gaze felt like a searchlight in the darkness.

"Do not underestimate the choice your mother faced in ridding the world of Diana Diamond." Given their history, the admiration in Delta's tone took me by surprise. "Or the reason behind it."

My brain struggled to keep up with the conversational version of whack-a-mole. "I don't…what?" I pressed the heel of my hand to my forehead to stave off the pressure settling there. "My mother is a whole other problem." One I wasn't ready to face.

"Come on, Lexi. Think about it a minute."

Every minute I spent here was a minute I wasn't navigating the world between to bring Kin back. "What does this have to do with saving Kin? Can you help me or not?"

"I know who can, but first, answer the question."

With all eyes focused on me, I was beginning to regret having so many witnesses to this debacle. "You didn't ask a question."

"Fine." Delta rolled Kat's eyes. "Do you know why your mother killed Diana Diamond?"

The memory of those moments scrolled through my mind. Sylvana had come out of nowhere at the precise moment I'd disarmed Diana. Just in time to strike the killing blow.

"For the glory and attention?"

"You really are an idiot."

"Then why don't you enlighten me?"

"You know what? I think I'll let you figure it out on your own."

My nostrils flared as I sucked in a breath. "Whatever, Delta. I should have known not to expect any sort of gratitude from Olympus or any sort of help saving Kin, either. If you're still in touch with them, tell your people thanks a lot, but don't expect me or mine to jump in the next time the world needs saving."

I rose to leave. Coming here had been a waste of my time, as had all that time I'd spent mourning Delta. "Have a wonderful afterlife."

A prickle of power ran over my skin, and the way everyone at the table reacted, I wasn't the only one who felt it.

"To get to the gray area," Delta's said, her voice softer than before. I stopped and waited for her to continue. "You need a two-headed silver coin. You'll know it when you see it. There aren't many of them left. Your father had one, and if he still does, he's the only one who can help you now. If you play this right, you might end up saving two loved ones at the same time."

It didn't take a road sign to figure out who she meant. Shame washed over me for being so caught up in worry over Kin, I'd deliberately pushed out of my head the implications of my mother's actions.

"I might be wrong, but I think my mother has to save herself." My voice dropped, "and if I *am* wrong, my father might be the only one who can stop her."

Historically, wicked witches don't last long. They do plenty of damage on their way down, but some hero always comes along and takes them out. If there was a way to save Sylvana, I'd do anything, even confront my daddy issues. If not, I needed someone ruthless enough to do what I couldn't.

Kat's nails ticked against the table while Delta pondered.

"I can't fault your logic."

My blood hummed with validation.

"Good, then tell me how to find him."

"Sure."

I leaned forward, anxious to soak up every little tidbit of bounty hunter information.

"Get out of your own way."

Steam probably didn't come out of my ears. It just felt that way.

"What the hell does that mean?" Did everyone in my father's world find it necessary to speak in riddles?

Delta flicked Kat's fingers in a dismissive gesture.

"It's witchcraft 101. What's the first thing you need to cast a spell."

Too many worries muddled my head. "Magic would be my best guess, but I'm assuming that's wrong." It almost had to be given her expression plainly said I was an idiot. Then it came to me. "You're talking about intent, right? Every spell begins with a clear intention."

If Salem had said that once, he'd said it a hundred times.

Delta nodded. "Give the witch a gold star."

"Bite me."

But the message finally penetrated my brain. If I wanted to find Cupid, I needed to really *want* to find Cupid. And there's a sentence that sounds stupid, but it made perfect sense.

Seeing the light dawn over me, Delta nodded. "My work here is done. Catch you later, Balefire." And she was gone.

Kat blinked her eyes back to their normal hue. "Wow! I feel energized. She's a firecracker, that one. Did it help?"

"So much." The chair nearly flipped over because I rose so quickly. "I know what I need to do now."

I didn't even bother to step outside before I shifted to my office at FootSwept. And I didn't think to pay Kat for her services. I hoped she'd forgive me and made a plan to make it up to her when all of this was over.

Maybe a nice fruit basket.

CHAPTER

TWENTY-NINE

At about the same time Lexi sat down at Kat's table and considered the amount of drama brought about by her closest family, Mag and Clara Balefire stood on opposite ends of the sofa where they'd settled Sylvana and prepared to have it out.

"Whatever it is you're planning, you'd better think again." The fire in Clara's eyes belied her even tone. "Don't you forget for one minute that this is my daughter. She's not some rogue witch going about the countryside withering crops and curdling milk as she passes."

Mag tucked her thumbs under the belt of the fanny pack she wore over a long skirt and rocked back on her heels.

"We didn't exactly give her a chance, but would it make a difference if she were?"

"Not to me." Clara's chin shot up. "She's my daughter, and you will not hurt her."

"I wasn't planning to do anything to hurt her."

Tilting her head, Clara turned a narrow-eyed gaze on her sister and attempted to parse the statement. Having spent her youth quelling rogue magic, Mag could lie with the best of them. She could also put on an innocent act worthy of a grand stage.

Clara could find no evidence in Mag's expression to support her suspicions.

"I'd hate," she warned, "to turn Lexi into an orphan again, but I will if I have to. You mark my words, Margaret Balefire, if you set yourself against Sylvana without giving her a chance to turn from the path of wickedness, you will answer to me."

Mag flinched almost imperceptibly. "I give you my word I will not lift a finger against Sylvana. Anything she does to bring about her downfall will be by her own actions and none of mine."

The air shivered and set all the glass in the house tinkling with the force of the vow.

With that, Clara decided she must be satisfied. Still, she gave her sister one more level look before turning to reach into the fireplace and trigger the door to the sanctum. Hungry for every last glimpse, Mag watched the back of Clara disappear.

"Goodbye, Clarie," she whispered into the sudden silence, laid one hand on Sylvana's arm, concentrating on dropping the sleeping spell, and sent her niece someplace where they would have complete privacy. It was the last place Mag intended to go. Ever.

Following behind, Mag reappeared in the alley behind an all-night diner doing a brisk business during the daylight hours. A pretty tame place to beard a wicked witch in her lair. In Mag's day, villains comported themselves with a bit more flash and flair.

Really, would Aurelia Grimsbane have been caught dead in a place like this?

Not hardly.

Still shaking her head, Mag circled the building and mounted stairs leading to the apartment above. Not bothering to knock, she slammed the door open with a flicker of power.

"Syl-va-na," she singsonged. "Auntie's here."

Tightly closed shades and curtains shrouded the apartment in darkness, casting Mag's body in sharp silhouette against the open door. Instincts honed over years of hunting screamed for her to step inside, take shelter against the predator in the darkness. She ignored them all.

"Come in, Mudwitch. I assume you're the reason I woke up on the floor."

Mag continued to keep her distance until Sylvana stepped into the slice of light angling through the open door. If not for the red of her lips, she could have passed for a black-and-white photograph, so pale was her skin and so dark her hair.

"If you don't mind, we can dispense with the banter." Mag funneled power into her hands, coating them with a thin layer of white fire that dripped and dribbled sparks to the floor. She waited for her niece to follow suit.

Instead, Sylvana barked out a harsh laugh.

"Let's have it, then," Sylvana taunted. "Take a shot at me." She held her arms out wide in a defenseless posture. "We both know you've been waiting my whole life to give me what you think I deserve. Look at all the pretty white magic."

Hands still at her sides, Mag never twitched a muscle. She hadn't been lying when she made the promise to her sister. Killing Sylvana wasn't the plan.

As if reading Mag's mind, Sylvana grated out, "Do it. Kill me. You know you want to."

"Is that what you want?" Something in Sylvana's tone gave Mag pause. "To die by my hand?"

"What if I did? Would you oblige my dark desire? Put me out of my misery?"

"Your mother would never forgive me." It was nothing more than bedrock truth, but what was Sylvana playing at? She'd gone wicked; anyone with eyes could see that much. She should have been flinging black spells by now.

"What's stopping you, then?" Sylvana's eyes glittered darkly, narrowed to slits as she tilted her head to regard her aunt thoroughly. "Oh, I see."

"What do you see?"

"Oh, Auntie. What were you thinking?" Sylvana moved so quickly it seemed as if her feet hovered above the floor as she crossed the room, the movement bringing her uncomfortably close. Head tilted, she reached up to stroke a fingertip from Mag's temple to the corner of her mouth. "Such a pity, what you've come to these days. Mag

Balefire, doer of good deeds, ridding the world of evil one raythe at a time."

"Honest work." Other than a twitch as the fingertip paused at the corner of her mouth, Mag's face remained impassive under the gentle assault. "Good work."

"And just look what it's cost you." Sylvana dropped her hand, walked across the room to flop on a newish-looking leather sofa. "I'm not going to grant your wish and kill two birds...or would that be two witches...with one stone."

A laugh trilled out of Sylvana. "Or one stoning, anyway."

Uncertain, Mag stepped into Sylvana's narrow little one-bedroom apartment and closed the door behind her.

"Did you know," Sylvana propped booted feet on the coffee table, "that I idolized you until I was six or seven? You were everything my mother was not. You were out there using your magic, not sitting at home in front of the fire or listening to idle witches prattling about why their potions came out wrong. I wanted to be you when I grew up."

Despite herself, Mag let out a snort. "You'd have had to develop a moral compass."

"Touché." One eyebrow went up, and Sylvana smirked. "But what makes you think I have no moral compass? Don't you think ridding the world of Diana Diamond was the good deed of a lifetime? The entire world should be thanking me."

Mag shrugged. Sylvana had a point, just not a good one. "You look in a mirror lately? Even good deeds can have bad consequences."

"If that's not a classic case of the pot calling the kettle black, I don't know what is." Sylvana let her gaze roam over Mag from head to toe.

At some point, Mag had let the magic absorb back into her hands. She'd staged this showdown intending to use their history to goad Sylvana into doing something rash. She'd expected to end her day as a pile of ash at the feet of a stone statue. Not to exchange home truths about that history with a wicked witch who seemed to have her temper on a tight leash.

"One of these days, that smart mouth of yours will drag your ass down the path of no return…if it hasn't already." Eyes burning with frustration, Mag decided to test the theory. "Hold still."

Sylvana bristled. "Don't do anything you'll be sorry for later. You have no idea what I'm capable of these days," she warned and began to rise.

Negligently, Mag tossed out a spell that rocked Sylvana back into her former seated position. "Shut up, you ungrateful whelp. Just because you're hellbent on setting a course for destruction doesn't mean my sister deserves her heart broken more than it already is."

"Charming." Despite being essentially frozen in place, Sylvana retained the power of speech. "But my mother is no saint."

"Well, who is?" With that, Mag pulled out a well-worn wand and cast a spell. "Illuminata Reveliate."

Spider web strands of pure magic burst from the wand to form a shimmering golden grid above Sylvana's head.

"Activius," Mag cried out the final word to set the spell in motion. Amber-colored light flooded from the shining grid to slide down, over, and into the captive witch

"What is this?" Sylvana's tone held all the moisture of a bottle of talcum powder. "Witch version of an x-ray?"

Closely watching the play of light, Mag said, "Near enough." When it reached the area of Sylvana's heart, the amber light shot off a very small spark, then continued right down to the tips of her booted toes without further incident.

Given Sylvana's expression mimicked that of a ticked-off honey badger, Mag wisely sidestepped as she let the magic dissipate.

The scent of dark magic rose off Sylvana's body like tainted perfume, wrapped around Mag's, and tweaked her nostrils until they twitched.

"Reel it in, girl."

It wasn't that Mag entirely disapproved of dark magic. Hecate knew she'd been forced to dip into that well a time or two just to save her own bacon. But she knew enough not to get sucked in by the seductive power of the black. She held no illusions about Sylvana's abilities to touch but not take. The woman had never been known for her self-control.

"I'm not a girl," Sylvana bit off the words, moved her boots off the table. Tension pooled in her body, turning it into a coiled spring. "I can handle myself. You do know the distinction between wicked and evil, do you not?"

Mag slammed hands on hips, her elbows jutting out sharply. "Damn few know that lesson better than me."

"Then you know we all carry the seeds of wickedness within our souls. It's the insidious voice in the back of our heads urging us to do something without worrying about the immediate consequences." Sylvana tossed ebony hair back over one shoulder. "Just because I want to hex the man who feels the need to jam his thumb into every peach to find the ripest one doesn't make me wicked so long as I never cast the spell. I haven't always been disposed to darkness. I've merely been annoyed for the better part of my life."

As someone who shared a similar disposition, Mag allowed herself a small grin.

"Now what?" Mag still hadn't taken more than a few steps beyond the door. The quick, clean death she'd come here to find was already ten miles in her rear-view mirror and fading. The whole predicament left her feeling vulnerable and embarrassed.

"Well, I'm not going to kill you," Sylvana's smile left a chill. "At least not today, anyway, so I think we're done here. I'm sure you can find your way out."

In that freaky way of moving again, Sylvana was in front of Mag before she could get to the door.

"And don't even think about—"

"Sleep." Repeating her earlier gesture, Mag caught Sylvana's body before it hit the floor—no small effort for the elder witch—then transported them both back to the Balefire house before Clara could realize they'd gone.

CHAPTER

THIRTY

*S*alem. *Can you hear me?*

The moment when I could get the wet hairball out of my boot could not come too soon. For now, I only hoped the thought connection would work from a distance while I looked at my mother's Cupid-tracking board. Intention aside, I had to start somewhere.

Quit yelling.

Fine. I toned my thoughts down. *Status report.*

Flix says it's an amplification stone that gives the wearer a powerful boost, but it's a one-and-done kind of thing, and you should probably assume there are hidden rules.

This information would have come in handy before.

You know how tricksy the fae can be. Flix had to call in a few favors to get that much information, so use it at your own risk. It's just like them to hand over something useful but hold back on the caveats.

That trait wasn't confined to just the fae. I had a time-traveling ring and a sentient bow to prove it. In this case, I had no choice but to use the stone and hope for the best.

Okay. I looked at my watch. Jett should be along at any

time. His three hours were just about up. *Watch for Jett. When he arrives, give it to him, and send him to FootSwept.*

Will do.

Kin? My mom?

The pause before Salem answered set my heart hammering.

No change. Jett just left. He should be there—

"Hey, sis."

—About now.

"Here's the bauble." Jett held the necklace out to me. "What's with the 9-1-1? Serena didn't say much and cat boy only snarled at me to bring this to you at the office."

"I'm sure he'd rather be known as cat man, but that's whatever. Are you still interested in finding our father?"

Jett's body language changed, took on some tension and some serious lines.

"You know I am. Did something happen?"

I gave him the abbreviated version of events, watched his face when he learned of Diana's very timely end. They had a history

"I need someone with permission to access the gray area in between worlds. I don't know if that's the official name for it, and I don't suppose your Fiach training got you a pass to get there." It was a long shot, but I had to try.

Jett shook his head. "Sorry."

"Well, Cupid does."

Light dawned. "Do you have a lead on our father, then?"

My hand closed over the dangling stone necklace. "So long as this does what I'm hoping it will, I think I do."

After dragging the compass chain over my head, I held it in my right hand, saving the left for the stone I hoped would amplify the weak nature of my intention. That and Jett's intense desire should be enough.

"And what might that be?"

"Hush up, put your hand in mine, and give me a minute to concentrate."

Half-brother and sister we might be, but I never expected to end up holding hands with Jett Striker. Based on his frown, neither did he.

My opinion of my father based on what I'd seen during my travels to the past hadn't predisposed me to think of him as an asset to my life. What I needed was one of those sitcom dads. The kind ready to swoop in and kiss booboos, patch torn kites, or just listen to my tale of woe over some boy who'd broken my heart.

I needed Philip Banks, Jack Geller, Phil Dunphy, and Tim Taylor all rolled into one, and Cupid was not going to be that guy. Still, there had to be one redeeming quality about him. Anything to spark a wisp of desire to find him that didn't have to do with my mother or with Jett. I needed to want to find him for *me*.

Replaying the series of events leading up to his disappearance, I latched onto the one moment of vulnerability, the one right before he walked away. That man might be worth a second chance. Acceptance fed intention, which I channeled into the compass.

A faint tingle.

"Is it working?" Jett couldn't be quiet if his life depended on it, but along with the question came the lilt of excitement. The tingle got stronger.

"A little." I stepped outside, and the sensation ramped up even more.

In retrospect, that should have been enough of a warning, but I slung the chain over my head anyway. Big mistake. Stupid thing buzzed and zapped me right in the heart.

"Ouch." I let go of Jett's hand.

Magic will only mask so much, and me dancing around in the middle of the sidewalk while being shocked half to death went beyond even the bow's scope of power.

"Miss, are you all right?" This from a concerned man in a nice business suit. When he put a hand on my arm, I got another tingle.

Not that kind. Sheesh.

Sometime in the next few weeks, the man with kind eyes and a nice smile would become a target, but that was a problem for another day.

"I...uh...I'm fine. There was a bee." Lying isn't one of my strong suits, but it worked well enough.

Once he was gone, I ducked into an alley between two brick structures for a little privacy. Jett followed behind.

Detached from the bow, the compass worked like any

normal one would, except that instead of always pointing north, the needle swung toward the closest person in need of a love match.

Now, the needle pointed to a flashing heart that appeared in the southeastern quadrant of the face. Cupid's symbol, I assumed, and if the buzzing electricity running through it was any sort of indicator, he wasn't far away.

My fingertips went numb. Maybe it was the shock factor coming off the compass, or just the after-effects of the day, but probably not. It didn't matter if I was ready or not. It was time to meet my father.

He was my only hope for Kin and probably for my mother. She'd gone as wicked as a witch could go. If Diana had carried even a drop of witch in her blood, we'd have had another statue to grace the grounds.

Maybe that would have been for the best, but the girl inside me who had longed for her mother all those years wouldn't let that thought take root. Even if I couldn't save her from herself, I had to hope my father could. He was, after all, a mythical being. The god of love and the mate she'd chosen.

Love conquers all, right?

So, I followed the compass a whole block and a half from the office building where I'd done business for years. With each step, the energetic current running through the compass increased, and so did my anxiety level.

"How much farther?" Two years ago, if you'd have told

me I'd be playing the *are we there yet* game with my half brother, I'd have called you unflattering names, but here we were.

By the time I halted in front of a hole-in-the-wall pub I'd never seen before, my nerves were at a fever pitch. I'd passed this spot a thousand times, and I'd be willing to swear on my own grimoire that bar had not been here before.

I love my city, and I know it like the back of my hand. How could I have missed a bar called Lucky's not more than a block from my office? I couldn't have. It didn't make sense.

Still standing in the middle of the sidewalk, I pictured myself walking down this street on my way to Sinful. Now that I knew to look for it, the fuzzy place in my memory stood out starkly.

Had to be magic. Worse, it had to be hinky magic.

The pub door shut behind us with a hopeless thunk that made me think of coffin lids.

"Cheery place."

I barely heard my half-brother's sarcastic comment over the hammering drumbeat of my heart while I waited for my eyes to adjust to the sudden gloom.

Get hold of yourself, Balefire; he's only your father. How bad could it be?

"Do you see him?" Jett said.

"Too dark to tell."

And I was beginning to feel a little stupid for hanging

out by the door. "Come on. Act casual, but hurry. Kin's running out of time." Angling left, I headed toward the bartender, ignored the sucking sounds my shoes made on the sticky floor.

Bald as a doorknob and built like a moose, the bartender ran a gray rag over scarred wood. "Getcha something?"

Not even if you popped out of a bottle on a cloud of colored smoke and offered to make every last one of my dreams come true.

"Thanks, I'm good," I said out loud.

"I'll take a beer."

"Bottle or draft"

"Bottle." Jett wasted no time thinking that one through.

The barstool wobbled as I spun to survey the room. This was a place where men of a certain age whiled away the time between lunch and happy hour. A man in his prime would stand out here. No one did.

"King me," said one gray-haired gent to another as they concentrated on the game of checkers on the table between them. Neither of them had seen sixty during the last decade. A third of the same vintage watched a ball-game on the TV mounted high on the wall in one corner.

Only one other man occupied a seat. This one sat hunched, his elbows resting on the bar, staring down at a glass containing an inch of amber liquid like it was his only friend. Based on what I could see of his face and the dirty dishwater color of his hair, I judged him on the downward slope of middle-aged. The youngest of the bunch.

"I don't see him. Should we ask someone?" Jett's shoulders sagged.

"You realize everyone in here is from a different world than the one we live in, right?" I hissed to keep the bartender from hearing anything. "You ask if anyone's seen Cupid, and they're going to want to buy you a new jacket. The kind with sleeves that tie around the front."

"You're the one who said we'd find him here. Maybe you should check your little gizmo again."

I might have done just that if the fellow at the end of the bar hadn't chosen that moment to slide off his stool and wobble toward the door, his rotund belly leading the way. I spun my stool sideways, shifted my legs out of his way, and the new angle brought us face to face.

We locked eyes, and the world stood still.

"Sylvana," he whispered and lurched toward me. If there'd been time to evade him, I couldn't have done it because my body had turned to wood as his arms went around me.

My father had let himself go.

Based on the pungent scent of him alone, that was a mild understatement, but at least his funk pulled me out of mine. I tried to push him away, but it was like trying to move a mountain.

"Get off her," Jett came to my defense.

Shocking, right?

He gave Cupid a shove that set him back a foot, then did a double-take as the reality sunk in.

"Dad?" Jett squinted, then his head swiveled toward me, his face a questioning mask.

"Looks like." I nodded as the faint hope I'd harbored turned to dust and ash. "Behold, my great white hope."

Meanwhile, our father swayed and repeated my mother's name in a low tone.

"I'm not Sylvana." I refused to call him by any name. "I'm Lexi."

Under the features softened by drink and despair, I could almost see the handsome face I remembered. Almost.

"Lexi?" Utter bewilderment.

"Lexi. Your daughter. Sylvana's daughter," I confirmed. "And maybe you'd remember Jett? He's your son."

It's funny how quickly annoyance can burn off a good case of nerves. Mine chilled down so fast I thought they might crack. Even the butterflies in my stomach couldn't maintain their movement. They fell like small stones cast in the pit of despair.

I glanced over at my half-brother, and for the first time since I'd met him, felt more than a teaspoon of sympathy. He'd waited years and committed deplorable acts in the hope of experiencing this pivotal moment, and by the mixture of horror and disgust on his face, it didn't seem to be living up to the hype.

Bleary eyes blinked, flicked over toward Jett, then latched back onto my face again. Cupid frowned the confused frown of the totally inebriated, weaved a bit, then leaned back and squinted as if that might bring my face into focus.

"Not Sylvana."

"No, but she needs you."

That got a response, but not the one I expected. Cupid shook his head violently, which threw off his already precarious balance, and he nearly fell.

"No. No. No." With each no, his voice rose until the other patrons began to take notice.

"Come on, you're making a scene." I turned to Jett, who still hadn't managed to wipe the horrified expression off his face. "We need to get him out of here before someone calls the cops or something."

"Yeah," Jett said. "Okay." He tossed a few bills on the bar to cover his beer, then grabbed Cupid by the arm. "Come on, dad. Let's go for a little walk. Let the fresh air clear your head."

I doubted fresh air would be enough, but I held the door and let Jett do the heavy lifting.

"What now?" Jett guided the stumbling god of love down the sidewalk while Cupid rambled a string of incoherent sentences. I didn't catch much more than the gist of it, but it seemed my father's self-esteem was in the toilet. Three flushes down, actually.

We weren't too far from my mother's place, and I knew where she kept a spare key.

"Follow me." I moved on ahead to show the way, and I'm not going to lie, I wanted to get downwind of them long enough to think the situation over. Delta hadn't said I needed Cupid specifically, only the coin. If he hadn't used it to tip the bartender sometime during the last quarter-century, that is.

By the time I hooked a right into the alley beside the diner Sylvana lived above, I had formed the beginning of a plan. It was precarious, and there were at least half a dozen ways it could fall through, but also a slim chance it would succeed.

That had to be enough.

THIRTY-ONE

"I'll be right back," I skirted past Sylvana's car and started up the stairs. "While I'm gone, you need to check his pockets for a silver coin."

"Aren't all coins silver?" Jett shot up an eyebrow, then wrinkled his upper lip in disgust. "You made me drag him all the way over here so you could hit him up for nickels and dimes?"

"Nickels and dimes aren't made of silver, you idiot." My feet banged up two more steps. "And this coin has two heads. Just turn out his pockets. Delta said we'd know it when we saw it, so start looking."

If looks could kill, I'd be on the wrong side of the veil in a hot minute. "You do it." Jett jammed his hands in his pockets and presented me with a stony look.

"Just for once, could you not be such a wimp?"

Not waiting for an answer, I stomped up the rest of the stairs, let myself into Sylvana's apartment, and grabbed her keys from the hook near the door. She probably knew a spell for hot-wiring a car, but I didn't have time to work one out. In her current mood, she wouldn't forgive me if I screwed up the wiring. This wasn't the hill I wanted to die on. Not until I'd saved Kin, at least.

"Did you find it?" I swung down the stairs.

"I think so, but I also think I'm scarred for life. A man doesn't like to root around in another man's pockets."

I huffed and rolled my eyes, bit off a nasty comment, then unlocked the car, and opened the back door.

"Help me get him in here." I leaned down, got a whiff of pungent body odor, and straightened back up. "But first." I pulled out my wand.

"Lavacius Medicamentium Perluo!" For a spell I made up on the spot, it worked pretty well, even if there were some unintended consequences. My father went from dry and smelly to wet and soapy in about half a second. I didn't think to add in a rinse cycle.

"Aqualavo! Siccum Linteus!" I rectified the situation and threw in a drying spell for good measure. The whole business took a minute or two, and he smelled a little bit like a wet dog after, but with the majority of the funk gone, he wouldn't make my eyes water while I was trying to drive.

Score one in the win column.

A couple of minutes later, with Jett riding shotgun and my father sleeping it off in the back, we sat idling Sylvana's '77 El Dorado at the mouth of the alley.

"Let me see the coin." The silver felt inordinately cold when Jett dropped it in my palm.

"How does it work?" He asked.

Whoops. "Delta never said, and I didn't think to ask."

"Way to drop the ball, Sis."

Growing up as an only child, I always wondered what it would be like to share my life with a sister or brother. Half an hour spent in Jett's presence gave me a pretty good idea. Maybe I hadn't had it so bad.

"Excuse me for having a lot on my mind. It can't be that hard to work if Delta managed it driving fifty-five on a Harley. We can probably figure it out."

"If it's even the right one."

"How many two-headed silver coins have you seen besides this one? They're not exactly common, and did you even look at it?" I brandished the coin. "There's a man's head on one side and a skull on the other. It's the right one."

"Whatever you say." If he didn't stop swiveling his head to look at the snoring figure in the backseat, Jett was likely to end up with whiplash.

I hadn't seen Delta do anything special before we flipped from one world to the other, and she definitely hadn't uttered any sort of incantation.

Flipping worlds...flipping coins. No. You can't flip a coin while driving a motorcycle without your passenger noticing. There had to be another way.

On closer inspection, the heads on both sides of the coin seemed worn in spots.

"Is it just me?" I handed the coin over to Jett. "Or does it look like it's been rubbed from side to side a lot?"

He checked both sides several times before passing it back. "Kind of. I guess."

My stomach lurched hard enough to tell me I was onto something. Time to give the theory a test, but not in the middle of the city where a vanishing land yacht of a car would not go unnoticed.

"Hold on." I turned right, drove half a block, and nosed the car down a long and narrow alley that wasn't exactly meant for a vehicle that size. When we got to the end, I shot out onto Fuller Street and gunned it to hang a left just as the light at the end of the block went from yellow to red. One more right-hand turn on Mayfair, and we had a clear run for the suburbs.

After pulling over near where my grandmother used to stand frozen, I snapped my fingers for Jett to hand over the coin and sent up a prayer to Hecate for help.

"Here goes nothing." I brushed my thumb over the skull. Nothing was what I got.

"Didn't work," Jett said. "Let me try." And he did, to the same effect.

"I was so sure that would do it." I wanted to cry as my last hope for Kin began to fade.

Jett reached over, took the coin from my loose grasp, and looked it over. "I've got one other idea." He unbuckled his safety belt, spun awkwardly, and nearly kicked me in the face scrambling over the seat. "What if it's tuned to him?"

He grabbed Cupid's hand and basically wiped the coin

across our father's thumb. Again, nothing happened. "Damn," Jett said. "I thought that would do it."

"Try the other side."

"Oh. Good call."

The world on the other side of the windows turned gray. I hit the gas, and while my vision adjusted to the lack of color, we sailed toward the spot where my house sat in the real world.

"Do you see anything?" Jett shifted to peer out the windows, his voice echoing flatly.

"Not yet." So did mine. Sound didn't carry very well here. "He's probably inside or else still in the backyard." Unless he'd left to scour the grey world for a way back.

Nothing moved as I pulled up to the muted, almost one-dimensional version of my house, not the flutter of a leaf in a breeze, not the twitch of a curtain at the window. The place looked empty and desolate.

I shoved the door open and was halfway out of the car before it rocked to a full stop. "Stay here. Keep an eye on him." I pointed my thumb toward Cupid. "This won't take long." I rushed to the door, my feet making a hollow-sounding thump on the porch floor.

"Kin, are you in there?"

"Lexi?" Even with the weird echo effect, his voice had never sounded better or more welcome. The door opened from the inside, and there he was. Gray and muted as the rest of this place, he still looked amazing to me.

"I knew you'd come." He cupped my face and kissed me until I melted against him.

The muted echo of a car horn broke us apart.

"Come on, let's get you home," I dragged Kin toward the car.

"Who's that with you?" He ducked his head for a better look through the windows.

"About that. Some stuff happened after you left. Jett and I, well, we found our father."

Kin's eyes went wide under brows arched in surprise. "That's epic."

"That's the understatement of the century. Get in. We need to get you back before it's too late."

"Too late for what?"

I couldn't remember how many hours had passed since he'd crossed over and didn't want to tell him his body was dying. He'd already be gone if the faeries weren't doing their best to keep that from happening. "Nothing. Everything is fine. Just get in."

He did, but not before taking a curious look at the man lying halfway across the backseat.

"It's a long story. I'll tell you all about it later. For now," I turned to Jett, "Get us home."

"Happy to."

Jett reversed the process with the coin, but when we shimmered back to the world of color, there were only three of us in the car.

Salem, I called out in my head. *We're back. Kin should be awake. Did it work?*

Sorry, no change.

"What the hell?" My annoyed shout startled Jett in the act of opening the car door.

"We have to go back," I told him. "Do your thing again."

"What's the problem?"

"I'm not sure, but Kin's soul or life force, or whatever it is that's in the gray world, it didn't go back to his body. We have to try again."

We shifted almost before I finished speaking, and this time, Kin stood ready. "What happened?" He slid into the seat.

"I don't know. I was so preoccupied with figuring out how to get here; I just assumed taking you back would be enough."

Kin took my hand, gave it a squeeze. "It's okay, sweetheart. I knew it might come to this when I picked up that bat. There are worse ways to go, and I never felt a thing. At least I'll get a chance to say goodbye and tell you how much I love you."

Grief paralyzed me. I couldn't move. I couldn't speak. I couldn't even cry as Kin cradled me against him, then kissed me, and got out of the car.

I watched him go inside and close the door.

"Lexi."

I'd forgotten all about Jett, so when he said my name, I

jumped. The involuntary reflex pulled me out of my stupor.

"No. This is not how it ends. If Kin's stuck here until the end, so am I. I'm not leaving him again."

"You can't. The faeries will kill me if I go back without you."

I didn't even turn around or say goodbye. "That's a chance you'll have to take." I got out and went inside, where my reception was not all that I had hoped it would be. In retrospect, I probably should have seen the fight coming.

The front door slammed open somewhere around the fifth cycle of *go back,* and *I'm not going back* between Kin and me. I looked over, expecting to see Jett, and barely contained my surprise when my father walked somewhat hesitantly into the room.

A handprint painted his cheek red, but his eyes looked relatively clear compared to their earlier bleariness. Jett wasn't with him. I hoped dire results from the handprint wasn't the reason and gave my brother a mental high-five for having the guts to do whatever it took to sober Cupid up.

Our fight disrupted, I made the introductions between my fiancé and my father. One of the more surreal experiences in my life, and that was saying something.

Whatever father/daughter thing I was supposed to feel for him, I didn't. There was no bone-deep recognition of family there. Not like I'd had with my mother when she first showed up wearing a glamour, but still feeling familiar.

"Pleased to meet you, sir." Kin gave my father a very discreet once-over, then glanced at me. I shrugged. What was I supposed to say? Here's my dad; he's been living at Pity Party Central for the past twenty-five years?

The pleasantries over, I explained Kin's situation, leaving out all the stuff about Sylvana because that can of worms needed to stay shut until this one got sealed back up.

"Now that you're up and around, you're going to help me get Kin back in his body." The *you ditched me and left me for an orphan, so you owe me* was implied.

He looked at me as if I'd sprouted a second head or something.

"Maybe once, but not anymore. Everything I touch, I hurt. You should have left me alone."

"You're a god, for freak's sake, but why wouldn't you decide to indulge in an existential crisis right when I need you most? You walked away from us before. Jett has a similar story, so I guess that's your pattern, and I shouldn't expect anything more from you now."

Cupid barked out a harsh laugh. "You have no idea what happened. I had my reasons." Hunched shoulders, head hanging in shame, he couldn't or wouldn't look me in the eye.

"Excuse me, but that's where you're wrong. I was there." His head came up. "Twice, as a matter of fact, and I have the DVD to prove it. I watched you throw everything away. My mother, me, and even this." I leaned into the fury, and pulled the bow from its hidden resting place, brandished it in his face.

"You take this back," I shouted. "I want no part of it if it comes from you. My life has been a constant battle since the second I learned about you. I wish I'd never laid eyes on this thing."

Okay, the part about the bow was a huge lie. Some good had come from it, after all.

Cupid arched his body away from the bow as if the touch of it might burn. "I can't," he whispered. "I'm not worthy to carry it anymore."

"Now, that's something we can finally agree on." I tossed the bow at my father anyway, ignored the odd clatter when it bounced off his ample belly, and fell to the floor. "But I'm done with it, and if you can't help Kin, I'm done with you. Rub your little coin, take Jett back to the real world with you, and don't let the door hit you in the butt on your way out."

"I think arrogance might be a family trait." Jett had come in so quietly I didn't know he was there until the comment spun me in his direction. "But at least I have my father's eyes." Bitterness twisted his words dark and sarcastic—probably because he'd pinned more hope on finding Cupid than I ever had.

Still in Kin's arms, I felt his intake of breath at the same time the bowstrings chimed a discordant series of notes. Gently, Kin turned me toward my father, released me, and gave me a little push. "Help him," he said.

"I can't," Cupid kicked the weapon across the floor, but I wouldn't pick it up.

"Don't you think you've wallowed long enough? Just man up...or god up...whatever it takes." At least the witch half of my heritage had some fortitude.

"You don't understand, Lexi. When your grandmother used my own arrow against me, it," he paused to find the right phrase. "Showed me things. Things I'd done, matches I made that ruined lives. I bent people to my will without a second thought for theirs or the consequences I left behind while I went my merry way. When I matched Bonnie and Clyde, I knew exactly what they'd become. I saw every misdeed in their future, and I did it anyway."

"Bonnie and Clyde murdered children because I saw they were a good match, and I made it so." For the first time all day, he looked at me with clear eyes. "Clara awakened something in me that I didn't have before. A conscience. Regret is the best teacher, and what I've learned is that I don't deserve to have power over others."

If he was looking for sympathy, he'd come to the wrong daughter.

"And instead of making amends, your response was to drink yourself stupid and stay that way for years. Real mature."

Cupid's mouth snapped shut, and Kin gave me a little shake. In his present state, I didn't think I was in any danger from an emotionally crippled god, but being snippy to someone in obvious pain wasn't like me.

"Look, Kin's time is running out, and while I'd normally be sympathetic and helpful, I'm not feeling that way at the moment. I won't let you waste the last moments I will have with my soul mate, so I'm going to give it to you straight."

Moving close, I drilled my finger into my father's chest.

"Regret is fine to a point. It means you're less likely to treat people like pawns on a chessboard in the future."

Jett snorted and earned himself a quelling look.

"But if you let regret be the boss of you, then it just means you wasted the life lesson your own arrow tried to give you. The only thing stopping you from being worthy of that bow is you. And you know what's worse? You're immortal, so you can afford to walk away right now and take a thousand years to figure all this out for yourself. But Kin isn't, and he's everything to me. If you finally ever do get over yourself, remember you once had a daughter that needed you,"

Magic sang in my blood, but vengeance played the tune.

I only had to look at the door for it to fly open.

"And instead of being there for her, you chose to be a self-indulgent weenie. Now, get out."

When the flat echo of my voice died away, utter silence fell until I broke it with a sob. I will never know if it was the shock of being told off or my tears that shredded my father's bout of self-pity. It's a subject we never talk about, and it doesn't matter to me anyway.

What does matter is that instead of slinking away to drown himself in cheap booze and pity, he set his jaw, leaned down, and picked up the Bow of Destiny.

Music crashed to ear-jarring life, and the bow shot out a beam of light so bright I saw bows etched on my eyelids every time I closed them for an hour.

When the light show died down, Cupid stood before me in all his former glory.

"Go ahead and smite me," I lifted my chin and waited to die. "I deserve it."

Instead, he closed the distance between us and pulled me into his arms. "Ah, my darling girl. I'm a lover, not a smiter. And I owe you a great debt."

After a moment, he pulled back, and I got a better look at his face. Gone was the arrogance that had marked his features as he gazed at me warmly. Jett, receiving the same fierce embrace, clapped his father on the back, then cleared his throat gruffly and turned away.

"There's only one thing I want." Tears muffled my voice. "Please. Tell me how to save Kin."

"Do you want to go back, son?" My dad went over to Kin, rested a hand on his shoulder, and watched his face for the truth. "Or do you want to move on from here? It has to be your decision and yours alone."

"But," I began.

"No," Cupid cut me off. "This is the lesson I've learned at great cost. We shouldn't interfere with free will, not even for the sake of true love. If he wants to move on, you will let him go."

"I do not, sir." Kin broke in before I could argue the point. "What I want is to go back and marry your daughter."

"Are you asking my permission?"

"If you don't mind me saying so, Lexi's future with me is not up to you, so no, I am not asking your permission."

Cupid threw his head back and laughed. "Good man. Takes a bit of spine to keep up with a Balefire witch."

"If you're done with this minor male bonding ritual, could we please get on with things before it's too late? There's still my mom to deal with, and I doubt she's getting any less wicked as time goes on."

Plus, I figured the mention of Sylvana might light a fire under Cupid's butt, and it worked like a charm.

"My coin?"

Jett handed it over. He hadn't said much since the great Cupid metamorphosis, and I made a mental note to make sure father and son had a minute alone together once we dealt with whatever waited for us on the other side.

To get Kin back where he belonged meant figuring exactly where his body was in the regular world.

"It's best if we keep you out of sight until we have Kin sorted. I have no idea what kind of reaction you'll get from the elder Balefires, but I suspect it won't be good. They're really not fans."

To achieve that goal, only Cupid and I went back.

Salem, did the faeries move Kin's body at all?

No.

Okay. Bringing him back, let Gran and Aunt Mag know.

We flipped back, raced into the house, and got Kin into place as quickly as possible. Cupid leaned down to whisper something in his ear, made sure we were all in physical contact, and rubbed the coin.

I felt the change in my soul this time and knew Kin had come through even before he sat up, and chaos erupted.

THIRTY-TWO

"You," Sylvana screamed. A seething spell ball whizzed past me to slam into Cupid's chest. "What are you doing here?"

I grabbed Jett by the shirt, dove for the ground dragging him with me, and used my body to flatten Kin as well. Cupid could stand on his own

Taking her cue, Terra slapped a hand on my back, and ported us all into the kitchen where the rest of the faeries followed.

Even with events unfolding outside, I stopped to give each godmother a hug for all they'd done to keep Kin alive. I saved Terra for last, and as we pulled apart, realized she not only looked exhausted, but there was a thread of aged silver running through her hair.

Gray hair on a faerie was as rare as a tie-dyed unicorn.

"Are you okay?"

The fae cannot lie.

"Well enough. We'll talk about it later." When Terra sets her mouth in a thin line, I know better than to argue. Not even when the godmothers exchanged a look, and I probably should have. Not that it would have made any difference at the time. The choices had already been made.

Instead, I broke out a bottle of Terra's special tonic from under the sink, and made them all take a healthy dose. Kin, too.

"What are we going to do about that?" Jett asked.

Through the relative safety of the sliding glass doors, we watched Sylvana toss dark spells at the man she'd professed to love. What no one said, but we were all thinking was that he deserved whatever he got.

After a minute or two, I noticed some family members missing from our little group and went looking for my aunt and grandmother. I found them sitting on opposite sides of the sanctum, backs to each other, both looking a bit worse for the wear. Gran had several deep scratches on her arms, and Mag looked like a giant had mistaken her hair for the dandelion clock it resembled and given it a blow.

Aunt Mag shot me a look over one shoulder then went back to poring through some of the oldest spell compendiums. The ones from the high shelves that I'd been told were off limits.

The ice between the sisters put a chill in the atmosphere.

"What happened while I was gone?"

"Is Kin okay?"

Clara and I spoke at the same time.

"He's back, safe and sound. I'll tell you the whole story

later, but here's the short version. A medium put me in touch with Delta. She told me how to get into the gray world, but I had to find my father because he had the only key. Jett helped me find him, and now he's outside getting a butt whooping from Mom."

Mag processed the story first, turned back to me, and cocked an eyebrow. "Well, now. That changes everything."

"How so?" I chanced a look at Clara and was glad the sour expression on her face wasn't directed at me. Or maybe it was. A little.

"Well," Mag slammed shut the book she'd been leafing through. "He has access to the portal prison, doesn't he? Best place for her, you ask me."

My grandmother's glare dropped the room temperature another few degrees. "Good thing nobody asked you, then. Isn't it, Margaret?"

Uh oh.

"You saw what she did to me." Mag rolled a shoulder, winced as if it caused her pain, and explained for my benefit. "She knocked me on my keester."

Gran muttered something about Auntie wearing her keester on her shoulders, and I nearly choked on an ill-timed laugh until the seriousness of the situation hit me.

"How bad is it?"

I could probably answer my own question given the way Sylvana dispatched Diana Diamond, but wasn't that ultimately a good deed? Did she deserve to be branded with a big W for wicked over it?

"Your aunt," Gran glared at her sister, "only ever looks at the worst-case scenario, and then jumps to the scorched earth conclusion."

"The hell I do."

And they started up again.

"Really? What do you call attempting to goad my girl into murdering you, then? Honestly, Margaret. Did you stop to think how I would feel to lose two of my closest family in one fell swoop?"

Mag had the grace to look chagrined. "She didn't do it, though, did she?"

"Exactly my point," Clara wagged a finger. "She. Didn't. Do. It."

This looked like it could go on a while, so I left them to it. Outside the sanctum, I took a moment alone to work through what I'd just heard and reconcile it with what I knew of my mother.

Sylvana was single-minded. Willing to get her hands dirty if she needed to. Loyal, and protective. She could also be spoiled, willful, and prone to wicked deeds if she thought they needed doing, but everyone has their faults.

Most of all, no matter what else, she was my mother.

I walked back into the kitchen. Kin, Jett, and the faeries stood watching the battle as it raged outside the sliding doors. Impatient, I pushed my way through.

"You're not going out there." Terra didn't ask exactly,

but I didn't listen, and stepped out onto the patio anyway. When Kin would have followed, I shook my head, and shut the door in his face. This was a family moment, and despite what it looked like, I knew I was in no danger.

Too busy watching the action, none of them had taken time to look closely at my mother's face. Or if they had, they didn't recognize her expression for what it was.

Since hers was the face I saw in the mirror every day, I knew it as well as my own.

Under the anger, under the rage and fury, I saw so much more. Pain, betrayal, despair, and worse, acceptance. Fear washed over me as my heart broke for her. And for me, because if I couldn't reach her, she might do something stupid, and I'd lose her forever.

I dropped my wand on the patio table, kicked off the Prada boots, and walked forward into the fray, my hands held out to the sides to show I was unarmed and vulnerable.

Black hair, black eyes, black intent, Sylvana threw spell after spell at Cupid with the fury of a woman scorned. At some point, he'd slung the Bow of Destiny over his shoulder, and now faced her with nothing other a fleetness of foot that kept him out of the line of fire.

From the kitchen, you couldn't tell, but he was begging her to stop, to listen, apologizing. She wasn't having any of it. In what felt like slow motion, I moved toward him, got close enough to put my hand on his arm.

When I did, the bow broke into a stirring rendition of All You Need is Love by the Beatles.

I couldn't think of a more appropriate tune.

"Mom." I stepped in front of him to catch her night-dark gaze. It should have creeped me out. It didn't. She was my mom, and I loved her no matter what.

"Go back to the faeries, Lexi. There's nothing for you here." But I noticed she didn't toss any spells in my direction. It boded well for me.

"You're here for me, and I know I haven't said it enough, but I need you."

Her harsh laugh hurt my ears, but not as much it hurt my soul.

"Are you sure about that? Look at me. Could you love me like this? Because this is who I am. You're looking at the real Sylvana, and I can tell that all you want to do is change me. What if I'm happier like this? Did you ever think of that?"

What a steaming load of BS. Happy people don't carry sorrow in their eyes.

My father's breath felt warm on my ear when he leaned in. "It's too late. Even your own kind won't suffer a dark witch to live. I can put her somewhere where she'll be protected."

Over my dead body.

One day, not long after she'd come back into my life, my mother showed me her softer side with a positively magical display in front of a waterfall. I'd managed to convince myself that moment was an aberration, because I'd needed to stay mad at her, and it was easier to do when I chose to look at the worst pieces of her.

I'd been wrong.

My mother had shown me her truest self that day. Now, it was my turn to give her back her light.

I had no idea how to weave sunlight into rainbows, but there were plenty of other symbols and elements in my life that could work the same.

"Leave us." I stepped in front of my father so there would be nothing and no one between me and my mother. "Go. This is for me to do, and I don't need you."

Reluctantly, he did, and once I felt his presence gone from behind me, I closed my eyes, reached deep down inside to touch the purest source of my power.

A glittering heart-shape wrote itself into the air between us, and hovered there. A good start, but I had more. So much more. A child of Cupid, witch, keeper of the flame. More than one type of magic ran in my blood, and I planned to use them all.

As my mother had the day she'd charmed me, I used my hands as if directing an orchestra and called forth balefire in every color it could command. I wove the rainbow flames into a ribbon, threaded it through the heart, tied it in a bow.

I wept silent tears for the woman who'd wanted nothing more than to be welcomed home with open arms, but instead found fear and resentment.

Being wicked is a choice, Sylvana had made it hers, but only to protect me. Could I do less than love her for it?

"You're amazing, Mom. Strong and brave and selfless. I see that, and I see you. All of you. I love you, and I want you to choose the light, but if you don't, I'll love you anyway. Always."

She heard me. I knew she did. Her irises flickered green for an instant, then back to black.

"Lexi." She said only my name, but she took a step forward.

"I love you, Sylvana Balefire."

Another step.

"Please. Mommy, come out of the dark."

"I can't," Anguish roughened her tone.

I held out my hand. "You can. Wickedness is a choice. Choose light."

Another step took her right to the edge of the fiery heart—the best representation of my own I could produce.

"Mom."

"Lexi. My Lexi."

Her emerald gaze locked onto mine as she made her final choice, walked through my balefire heart, and let the symbol of my love wash the blackness away.

Dressed in flowing, moonbeam pale silk that matched her hair and her soul, Sylvana Balefire, the white witch ran toward me, her daughter. Being in her arms felt like cinnamon, and puppy kisses, and comfy socks.

Finally, I pulled back, brushed the tears away from her cheeks as she did the same for me, then arm in arm, we walked toward the house.

Looking both handsome and hesitant, my father met us halfway. A glance at the faces nearly pressed against the sliding door glass proved he hadn't been the only one watching the show.

When she saw him, I felt the yearning go through her, but she stayed with me.

"Go to him. I think you've waited long enough." My suggestion released her, and I got to watch one of those movie moments where the couple finally runs to each other, and they embrace. Sylvana fairly flew across the grass, and leaped into Cupid's arms. He spun her around, then kissed her soundly.

Maybe he did love her after all. For her sake, I hoped so.

The atmosphere inside the house could only be described as joyful, and for good reason. I spent the next five minutes being passed from person to person, kissed and hugged by everyone including—total shocker—Jett.

What's more, he had big news for me. "I'm giving up my Fiach training because Dad gave me this." He held up the Bow of Destiny. "Is that okay?"

I only had to think about it for half a second. "It's perfect. I've been missing that personal touch, and you're not confined to the general area, so you really are the more logical choice. Just leave Port Harbor to me, though. Okay?"

"But I can call you if I need help? I mean, Dad said he'd be there, but you and me, we're still family, right?"

Rocky though our road had been, family is family, and he *was* trying. "We are. You've only to call if you need me."

We exchanged an awkward hug, and he headed for the door. "Time to try this bad boy out."

"It—" I started to tell him the bow had a mind of its own, but then decided to let him figure that out through experience. I almost wished I could be there to see how it all worked out.

Once he'd gone, Terra collared me, and I realized the other godmothers had left while Jett and I chatted. "I need a minute. Bring Kin."

"Okay." We followed her to the empty wing of the house where she'd lived with her sisters. Without all their stuff, the walls echoed our footsteps. I found it unnerving, but not nearly so much as seeing age lines on her face. "What's up?"

"I'm not sure how to say this."

She looked so grave all my happy vibes slithered away. "What? Are you okay? Tell me."

Terra glanced at Kin, bit her lip. I'd never seen her unsure before. "You know we can't heal the gravely injured, but in Kin's case there was a little wiggle room, because he wasn't exactly injured so much as absent from his body, so we used drastic measures."

It all came out in a rush.

"Drastic, how?"

"Well, he was dying, you see, so I...shared myself with him."

Kin frowned, and so did I. "I'm not sure what that means." It sounded slightly dirty, and put a mental image in my head that I really didn't want to see. "You'd better spell it out for me."

"I only meant to give him enough to live a few extra days, but I overshot the mark and fed him more immortality than I planned."

Ignoring the mechanics, I went straight for the key word in the explanation. "You made Kin immortal?"

But Terra shook her head. "No. Not immortal. Just enough to live a thousand years." She made it sound like a bad thing.

"What's the downside?" Kin wanted to know. He'd followed the dots well enough and picked up on the most positive outcome. "The way I see it, it's more time with Lexi and there's nothing wrong with that."

"What about you?" I remembered one of the faeries saying something about going against the rules just as I'd left to talk to Kat. "Will there be repercussions for you over this?"

Terra finally smiled as some of the tension left her. "Nothing I can't handle." I wondered if that were true, but she excused herself before I could pursue the issue. "Go back to your family, dear ones. We'll have plenty of time to talk about this later."

"You're family, Terra. You will always be family to me."

"I know." She kissed me on the forehead, and then she was gone.

Clara found us there, still staring at each other as we realized 'til death do you part had just taken on a whole new context. "Lexi, I've been looking for you."

"You found me."

Tears in her eyes, she hugged the stuffing out of me. "You're a wonder to me, did you know that?"

"I love you, too, Gran."

Bedtime found me curled up on the sofa with Kin while we watched the balefire flicker through a rainbow of colors for our amusement. When my phone signaled a text, rather than leave my comfy spot, I did something I rarely do and called the phone to me with magic.

"It's not work, I hope," Kin said.

"It's not. It's mom." I thumbed open the screen and saw a single sentence.

Hey Lexi—where's my car?

THIRTY-THREE

I could have glamoured myself to spell and back and looked positively perfect for Flix and Carl's wedding, but it would have felt wrong so I decided, again, to do things the old-fashioned way. After two hours the path between the vanity in my bedroom and the adjoining bathroom looked like the floor of a Sephora after a flash sale.

On the plus side, I'd managed a set of finger curls Clara Bow would have been proud of.

A flick of my finger and a tendril of intention ensured the room would be clean by the time I returned from the party but I'd already decided throughout the course of the morning that a bit of remodeling was in order.

If Kin and I were to live here, he'd need a studio and we'd need a bigger bedroom and en suite. The faeries old wing, already having been appropriately soundproofed, was a good solution for the first problem, but the second would require more thought. Gran had already moved her things out of her old bedroom and we were sitting on more space that we'd probably ever need.

I vowed to start discussing plans with Kin just as soon as the wedding was over and reached for my shawl, in the process knocking over the bag from Athena's Attic and spilling its contents onto the floor. I didn't remember asking for the raspberry-fennel tea; it must have been part of the sampler pack Athena had added to my order. Making a mental note to brew a cup later I tossed everything back in the bag and clicked down the stairs in my kitten heels.

The ceremony turned out—in an anti-climax because we all knew the faeries gave the best parties—positively perfect in every way. My idea for a change in theme had gone swimmingly, and while not exactly understated at least we'd avoided Disney princess territory.

Why Carl's obsession with the 1920s hadn't been considered in the initial planning process, I couldn't tell you, but I'd discovered a gorgeous, out-of-the-way venue near the seaside town of Camden and it hadn't taken much of a push from there. Not when Carl had been informed of the clincher fact: well-known poet Edna St. Vincent Millay had grown up in the area and had frequented the Whitehall Inn throughout the roaring 20s.

He had, thank the goddess, latched onto the theme with even more gusto than the golden carriage, and that was all the faeries had needed to hear.

Now, the ceremony over and dinner having long ago been cleared, I found myself at our table surrounded by the rag-tag assortment of people I considered family.

Kin's hand had remained glued to my leg beneath the table for the last hour. If my thigh was coated in a layer of sweat, I'd go to the grave keeping that fact to myself. I suspected we'd cling to one another until our latest scare was a distant memory. Luckily, I thought with a sigh, we'd have plenty of time to forget about it—thanks to my godmothers, who I now owed even more than I could have ever imagined.

Serena sat on my left, Mona and her husband, Mark, opposite, with Gran, Aunt Mag, and my parents making up the rest of the group. *My parents.* I still couldn't get used to the concept.

"Seriously, your aunts should be planning events in Hollywood; they'd make a killing," Mark gushed. As a DJ who did a lot of weddings, he ought to know. Today, he'd gotten off easy since he was an official guest and the guys had decided to go with a band instead—more elegant, Carl had insisted.

By now, even my godmothers had decided to let the staff handle serving the cake—one of Mona's more gorgeous creations in classic white fondant with sugared roses—and were each perched on a chair opposite Kin and me.

"Stop that waiter," I said, pointing and beginning to stand. "I haven't even had a glass of champagne yet. I think the servers are avoiding me."

Mona gazed longingly at the bubbly liquid and patted her swollen belly while Vaeta made a noise that sounded somewhere between a snort and a giggle. She received sharp elbow jabs from both sides courtesy of Evian and Soleil, who flanked her.

"What?" I asked when Terra refused to meet my gaze.

"What's going on?" my mother echoed the sentiment, but Cupid kept his mouth set in a straight line, a twinkle in his eye.

"Lexi, dear," Terra said as though I were a two-year-old, and flicked her gaze between Mona and me. Or, more accurately, between me and Mona's baby bump.

My mouth dropped open and Kin's hand clenched around my thigh. "Oh. My. Goddess."

"Oh my goddess is right," Terra replied, sitting back in her seat and breathing a sigh of relief. "Sorry to have sprung it on you like this in front of everyone but we've been holding onto this secret for weeks."

Vaeta winked at me and said, "We're going to have to swap your Twinkleberry wine collection back out for the real thing now. What's there is the magical equivalent of O'Doul's." That explained why my plan to get my mother drunk the night of the hot tub party hadn't gone exactly swimmingly. "Not that you can have any for another few months anyway; it's all raspberry and fennel tea for you now."

For crying out sideways; even Athena had been able to tell I was going to have a baby, and I'd been oblivious. The phrase rolled over in my mind again. I was going to *have a baby*.

When Kin took me in his arms and kissed me, I thought I might swoon. It wasn't fair for two people to be so happy—but then I decided we'd had a bumpy enough road as it was and that I should just enjoy the feeling.

I also made a vow, then and there, to put some serious effort into my studies. Our child deserved a mother who knew enough to recognize pregnancy tea when she saw it, and I also suspected I'd need all the knowledge I could get to raise a Balefire witch. The next generation keeper, no less.

A Balefire witch and a fate weaver besides. The thought rolled around in my head for the rest of the evening. By the time morning arrived I'd come to a conclusion; one that needed confirming and so after attending to some preparation in the sanctum, I placed a phone call and got dressed.

Leaving Kin alone in bed wasn't easy but it had to be done. I'd wake him up with his favorite blueberry coffee from The Grindhouse, and he'd never even notice I was gone.

When I crept into the sanctum this time, Salem following behind, it didn't need to rearrange itself. This house—the Balefire family home for over two centuries; the one with the screened-in porch and the chimney that spit rainbow-colored sparks into the air; the one that sat across from that statue of the wicked witch that simply disappeared one day—was mine now and mine alone. Well, mine and Kin's and our future child's.

Salem watched in approval while I worked a simple spell, sticking to his cat form, and then, purring, twined through my legs while I exited back through the fireplace.

Fifteen minutes later, I picked up a bleary-eyed Serena and climbed into my shiny SUV. Soon, I'd probably be trading it in for a minivan but decided to put a pin in that thought for the time being.

Hot pink and sea green balloons tacked to a folding sign marked the intersection where we were meant to turn, and when we approached the three-story beachside mansion, it was to find Nadia tying a second bunch to the mailbox.

I pulled over to the other side of the road and put the gear shift into Park, grateful my windows were heavily tinted, reaching over to stop Serena from opening her door. "Wait. We're just going to watch."

A few moments later, another vehicle pulled up behind us and out stepped a man I'd never met or even seen before but recognized immediately: Dean James.

"That's the guy; the jerk Nadia's in love with," I explained, expecting Serena to either tell me I was an idiot or slap me upside the head. Instead, she tilted her head and peered at the couple contemplatively.

"You think there's more to them, don't you?" She asked without judgment.

She was right on the money. "I do. I think there's more to all of it; I think this baby will be an even bigger handful than Kaine; and I think I'm going to need some help. I might just have a job for you, Snodgrass."

"And I might just let you help me find my soul mate, Balefire."

EPILOGUE

TWO YEARS LATER

Chubby fists twined in my hair, pulled my face close. I inhaled the glorious scent of my daughter's head, kissed her rosy cheeks, and tucked her pink-and-white blanket a little tighter.

"Don't be scared, little one," I whispered, knowing it was a waste of breath. If there a happier baby had ever been born in the world, it would have to be this one's older brother.

"Just do it already," Aunt Mag propped her feet on the edge of the coffee table and flipped a lock of blond hair behind her ear. "I heard someone say there was cake."

"Of course, there's cake," Soleil said. "You didn't think I'd let my goddaughter's dedication go by without an epic party, did you?"

Judging by the size of the party tent that had appeared in my backyard overnight, I hoped epic wasn't a euphemism for anything that would land us on the evening news.

"Is there chocolate?" Aunt Mag grumbled. "There had better be chocolate."

Being magically restored to her natural age hadn't affected her demeanor—or her sense of style. According to my grandmother, Mag still looked like a reject from the seventies. I couldn't disagree, and it was way too warm for that suede jacket with all the fringe.

Grimmie, as my grandmother insisted we call her whenever my children were around, elbowed her sister in the ribs, then rose to take the baby away from me. "Shut up, Maggie."

"Don't call me Maggie."

Busy making cooing sounds, Clara ignored the smart remark.

Behind me, Kin chuckled, and when I caught my mother's eye across my baby's head, her wink carried a warm twinkle. With my son sleeping in her lap, seated on an ottoman in front of his chair and cuddled back against my father, she radiated happiness, and so did he.

With them living in Kin's old place and the faeries across the street, I had more help with the kids than I needed. Surprisingly, my dad turned out to be amazingly patient with little Kenneth—we'd named him for my great grandfather—, and gentle with the baby. But then, it wasn't difficult to take one look into those emerald eyes and become besotted.

"We're just waiting on Serena," I said. "She's meeting with a new client at FootSwept, and messaged me that it's running long."

Taking Serena into the business had been one of the

best decisions I'd made in years. Since giving birth to a grandson of Cupid, she'd developed an affinity for the work. "I promised we'd wait, and I'll never hear the end of it if we start without her."

Besides, I had news I'd been saving for a family get-together, and dedicating my daughter to her namesake certainly qualified.

"That reminds me." Terra, seated on my left, turned and said to Kin, "You're all ready for the Myerson-Jenkins wedding tomorrow?"

"Sure am."

"And you know you're supposed to—"

"Stay away from any areas where the bride might see me because I'm a surprise." Kin's face went pale pink. You just have to love a man who blushes.

"She's a fan." I grinned at him. "Who could blame her? You're hot."

He blushed harder. The man was just too easy.

During the fifteen or so minutes before Serena finally arrived, I sat back quietly, watched my family, and counted my blessings. Maybe we'd started out a patchwork of people, and things hadn't always been easy, but I wouldn't change a thing. My heart was full. My life was good.

"Sorry," Kaine blew into the room, followed by a harried-looking Serena. "I told him not to run ahead, but he only has two speeds. Off and on."

"Auntie," he landed in my lap. "Look what I can do."

He cupped his tiny hands together, blew into them, then, with a flourish, opened them to reveal a live butterfly.

Beaming, Evian said, "Isn't he just the most adorable thing?" As his faerie godmother, she'd probably spoiled him a little. "And so talented."

"He gets a little older, you can hire him for your parties," Aunt Mag observed in her customary dry tone.

Was she trying to start a faerie fight? I shut her down. "Let's get started."

"Good idea." Clara gave the baby a kiss on the cheek, passed her over to my mom, and began the chant.

Fire to keep the keeper
Flame to heal the healer

A tear glinted in Sylvana's eye as she repeated the kiss, handed my child to me, and took up the refrain.

"Zenicia Balefire-Clark," I kissed my daughter and lowered her into flames as white as my mother's hair. "Blessed be."

The questing balefire tasted the new generation, flared up in approval. Zen's giggle rose over the chant as magic and light tickled across her skin.

There was hardly a dry eye in the room when the balefire went back to its normal color, and the baby dropped off into a contented sleep.

"That was fun," Kaine bounced in his mother's lap. "Can we do it again?"

He gave me the perfect cue for my big news.

"As long as you don't mind waiting a few months." I couldn't contain my smile.

Mom clued in first. "Are you?"

I nodded and braced myself as she launched across the room to hug me.

Life was good and getting better every day.

Thank you so much for reading Lexi's story all the way to the end! You're our favorite kind of fan!

Don't be sad, there's more of Lexi in the Balefire Novella Collection and a spinoff series with Mag & Clara.

QUICK AUTHOR'S NOTE

If you weren't already aware, ReGina and Erin are a mother/daughter writing team, and yes, that means we mix family and work—with all the ups and downs you might expect. But since we're best friends, too, we let that stuff roll right off our backs.

When we set out to write Heaven or Spell, we knew it wasn't just a turning point for Lexi Balefire—it was the culmination of her incredible journey. With everything she's learned, endured, and fought for, this final chapter gave us the chance to bring Lexi's story full circle. From the climactic confrontation with Diana Diamond to the long-awaited revelations about her family's legacy, this book has been both a labor of love and a bittersweet farewell to a character who has grown so much.

It was thrilling to craft moments that tested Lexi's limits, challenged her heart, and celebrated her triumphs. We especially loved revisiting Shadow Hold and exploring the deep, tangled roots of the Balefire family tree. Writing this finale allowed us to highlight how the past, present, and future intertwine in Lexi's world and to give her the send-off she truly deserves.

Though it's always hard to say goodbye, we hope you found this final installment as rewarding and magical to read as it was for us to write. Lexi's journey has been one of love, resilience, and self-discovery—and we are so grateful to have shared it with you.

With Mag and Clara stepping into their own spotlight, we've expanded the Balefire universe to include their unique stories in the Mag & Clara Balefire Mysteries. These books are brimming with their signature wit, charm, and knack for uncovering trouble. If you love the Balefire family's blend of magic and mayhem, you'll adore this spin-off series.

If you've come this far with us and not decided we're complete and total whackadoodles...and especially if you have, we're offering a chance to sign up for our newsletters— the best place to get new release updates, sales notifications, and other fun content.

You can sign up for ReGina's newsletter and/or Erin's newsletter, and as a thank-you gift for hanging out with us, you'll also get a FREE novella that isn't available anywhere else. And of course, we promise not to SPAM your inbox!

Love, hugs, and happy reading,
ReGina & Erin

P.S. If you enjoyed this book, it would be great if you could leave a review or recommendation at your favorite store, GoodReads, or BookBub.

Your reviews help indie authors sell more books!

OTHER BOOKS

If you'd like to meet more people who live rent-free in our heads, here's a list of other series we've written. Our books are all set in fictional towns in Maine, and some characters like to flit back and forth between series. The cast of Psychic Seasons hangs out with Everly and also with Lexi Balefire from the Fate Weaver series. Mag and Clara Balefire are Lexi's grandmother and aunt!

The Psychic Seasons Series
Four women, four love stories, and a whole lot of supernatural surprises. In the quaint town of Oakville, Maine, psychic visions, ghostly whispers, and fate itself conspire to change lives—and hearts—forever

The Haunted Everly After Mysteries
Everly Dupree came home for a fresh start—not a full-time gig solving ghostly murders. But when the dearly departed start demanding justice, what's a reluctant medium to do?

The Ponderosa Pines Mysteries
Nothing bad ever happens in the weird little town of Ponderosa Pines…until someone dies. Now it's up to best friends Chloe and EV to solve the mystery—before the town's secrets bury them too.

The Mag and Clara Balefire Mysteries
Sister witches Mag and Clara Balefire move to a sleepy Maine town for a fresh start—only to find themselves conjuring up trouble, solving murders, and keeping their magic under wraps in this charmingly witchy cozy mystery series

Laurel Haven Witches
Four witches, destined by blood and magic, must embrace their power, battle a dark legacy, and surrender to the love that could break the curse—or bind them to it forever.

Nell Page: Accidental Investigator
Nell Page owns a bookstore, drinks too much coffee, and has a habit of noticing things she probably shouldn't. With warmth, wit, and an accidental talent for investigating, Nell tackles mysteries that don't always involve murder—but always matter.

9 781953 044068